I0598594

The Covington Heights Crew

HACK

DEANA BIRCH

Hack
ISBN # 978-1-83943-948-3
©Copyright Deana Birch 2021
Cover Art by Louisa Maggio ©Copyright February 2021
Interior text design by Claire Siemaszkiewicz
Totally Bound Publishing

HACK

Dedication

For A, my constant bright light.

Chapter One

Rafa

They gym we shared on the third floor in Covington Heights was haunted by the spirit of our former crew member Leo. I was sure of it. As I circled around the blue sparring mat trying to find my next move, I could almost hear him whisper in my ear.

Where's the weakness?

The problem was that the man opposite me didn't have very many soft spots and his steel-blue eyes were like the tip of his sword. They pierced before anything else. As he narrowed his gaze ever so slightly, he would land his next punch. His brick fist slammed into the cheekbone just below my left eye. Pain slapped the side of my face, but I wouldn't let it spread to my ego. It wasn't personal, that I knew. Anton was pissed and working out his frustrations. Hell, we all were.

"Ooo…" He jogged backward. "You okay there, Goldie Locks?" His fake sympathy was followed by a proud smile but he wouldn't get any complaints or signs of weakness from me.

"You know I like it rough." I winked and walked over to the small fridge at the back of the gym where my boy Jackson and I had started keeping ice packs. Shit happened. Anton wasn't as good a teacher as Leo, but practicing was the only way to get better, stronger.

Since Leo's abrupt departure, Anton had been a miserable prick. He'd turned into the crankiest bitch I'd ever seen. And he had a serious alpha complex. His physical dominance wasn't only a reminder that he was a better fighter. It was the exclamation point that our asses belonged to him...or else.

Leo had gotten away with too much, and those who were still around were paying the price. I shot a knowing glance to Jackson, who looked away and continued to do his bicep curls on a bench near the door.

Anton wrapped a towel around his bare shoulders and said, "Jackson, meet me in fifteen at my place. Scooter's bringing the numbers from Bradford South."

I dug out the frozen bag of blue gel then sat on the side of the treadmill as I pressed it into my cheek — bitter cold relief for a festering wound of the bossman's frustration. No one could spar like Leo. *Message received*. No one was going to be allowed to get away with the same disrespect. *Got it*. But penance for other people's sins was getting old quick. Unfortunately, all was fair in crime and crews. Did I like taking a blow from time to time? Honestly? Yeah, I did. I wanted to be better, wanted to learn. I craved more respect and was plotting ways to get it.

Anton tipped up his chin and winked at me. It was his way of checking in. That was also part of his management technique or whatever-the-fuck way he kept us down but happy. Show the power first, then a hint of giving a shit. I'd seen it before. I actually didn't mind it. The familiarity was somehow comforting.

"Let's make some fucking money today." Anton looked us over one last time before leaving, his glare emphasizing that it was a command, not a request.

I walked over to Jackson, my former roommate and literal partner in crime. We'd bonded over not having fucked-up families, just fucked-up circumstances, Xbox and both refusing to become adult enough to drink coffee. Plus, we liked the idea of belonging somewhere. And the money… We liked the money.

Jackson set the weights down on the gray concrete floor. "He needs to get laid."

More like *I* needed to get laid. I'd given up on banging girls from our neighborhood. There was nothing interesting about being worshiped. Besides, they only did it in hopes of making their lives better. None of them really ever bothered to get to know me, not to mention that half of them were customers. That was more trouble than it was worth.

I shook my head. Anton had no problem there. "He needs to make more money." It was true that since we'd knocked off Mac, who had been a regular patron at our backdoor gambling racket, attendance had gone down to zero. No one liked the idea of tempting Anton's quick fuse and ending up in the river — not that we'd thrown Mac in the river, of course.

Lucky for us, the police had written off the Bradford murders as a drug deal gone wrong and hadn't cared to search much further. Our sources at the precinct said there had been mild rumblings of it seeming like a professional hit because of the precision, but, in the end, it was a criminal-on-criminal crime and they tended not to waste too many resources on shit like that.

Jackson stood and put his hands on his hips. "What are you up to later? I'm moving my stuff to Lisa's and could use a hand."

"Aww. You all lonely and shit since I moved out?"

Jackson rolled his dark brown eyes. "Nah. I'm all horny and shit since she finally let me tap that ass. Besides, I like showing Junior what a stable woman looks like." He held my gaze for a brief second.

There was no need to explain. I'd seen Jackson's baby-mama Bridget at our bench in the courtyard too many times in the last month. Selling drugs was a lot less fun when it was to the mother of one of your favorite kids, which brought me full circle to the money problem. We were a small operation. Sure, we had gained territory since the Bradford Towers crew had taken the hit. But with the game numbers down, I was pretty sure that the money decline was tainting Anton's mood more than the loss of his previous sidekick. The bossman wasn't exactly sentimental.

I pressed the cool into my cheek. It had thawed a little and was losing its original stiffness. "I'm working on something…a new business venture. Just waiting on a contact."

Jackson rubbed his jaw. Maybe he'd taken a couple of hits I hadn't seen. "Well, get fuckin' crackin'." He gave me a little salute and was gone.

I reached for a hand towel and wiped the residual sweat off my arms and chest. I hadn't always wanted to be a law-breaking shit who sold people poison. It was just that I'd been bored — bored in school, bored in life, bored everywhere except in my own head. There, everything spun. It was like other people's brains were funnels catching raindrops and all the information came to one eventual stream of thought. Mine? A constant downpour where I wanted to see every single bead of water and analyze it. That was what my high school computer teacher had said, anyway. He'd also said that was why I would be great in IT. Yeah, that 'career path' had taken an odd but predictable turn.

Breaking into people's computers calmed me — and had earned me my first trip to juvey. When I'd gotten out and met Anton... Well, it all just seemed like destiny. But Anton was hard, from his jawline to his inability to show compassion. I didn't have that darkness inside. Not that it mattered... I'd made my choices. A life in a suit and a picket fence with a puppy wasn't going to happen for me.

I left the gym and went across the hall to the apartment I'd shared with Anton since Leo had moved out. The spray of his shower echoed down the hall that led to his room. I headed in the opposite direction, crashed on my bed with a thud and reached for my laptop.

I logged in to my favorite online chat for hackers and it only took a second for my idol to send me a direct message. *Bingo.*

Majel213: Going live in five. Glad you finally decided to show up, Goldie.

As if I would miss it. Majel213 was my Internet spirit animal. I typed my response.

GoldieLocks: Highlight of my day. You know I've been itching to see what you've been scheming.

I always tried to up my nerd and downplay my street vibe whenever she and I chatted. The tech geek in me wanted her to respect my brains, as fucking stupid as that was. Online, I could be anybody. The idea of someone liking me for my intelligence was an out-of-body experience. In the six months since I'd found Majel213 and her wicked tutorials, we'd somehow become friends. Well, maybe not friends — but more than online strangers. It was just that we'd never actually seen each other. I'd never offered a profile pic in our chats and she did all her videos without showing her face.

I was sure that if she knew I was just some street criminal who'd never really carried out an impressive hack, I would lose the connection we'd built. And I needed her. Getting my hands on her malware was a way to keep my Midas touch.

The nickname 'Goldie Locks' had evolved over the years from 'Golden Boy', neither of which had anything to do with my hair. That was pitch black. It was because I was a good earner and I'd gotten the light-eye gene from my Brazilian heritage. The fact that the name had turned into a fairy-tale character didn't bother me. In fact, when I'd first starting using it online, I'd catfished quite a few idiots.

Five minutes later, I clicked over to the 677CrackChat and logged in. Holy hell. Majel213's raspy voice played over my thin speaker and she was transmitting dual screens.

"Meet Nathanial E. Tomjak. He lives in North Dakota, loves to fish and hunt. He's new to all this because, quote, 'my daughter finally convinced me to join the social media thingy.' No one suspects he's not a real person because his picture, which I photoshopped to change eye color, hair color, skin tone and age, is right here for all to see."

She clicked on the picture and enlarged it to fit the screen. If she hadn't said it was altered, I would have never guessed. Nathanial E. Tomjak was the epitome of a Midwestern retired grandpa, complete with triple chin, racing T-shirt and warm smile.

"So, Nate — I call him Nate — Nate was a creation of a profile after I had already found" — she clicked a couple of times and brought up a picture of Caroline Claussen — "this sweet, cat-loving mama."

The kind face of an older woman replaced the screen. "Caroline works for the sheriff of Zapata Falls and is my number one target for malware."

There was a slight East Coast accent in Majel213's voice. Her pronunciation of 'number' sounded a little like a 'numba' and I let myself believe that one day I might meet my nerd crush face-to-face and she would be hot, which was stupid. Finding the sexy librarian type in real life who could live up to my fantasies was proving to be difficult. Also, the whole selling drugs to pay the rent never went over well with the smart girls I liked.

But Majel213? She was my perfect blend of intelligence *and* criminal. By her screen name, she was in camp *Star Trek* over *Star Wars*. Her clever and deviant behavior inspired my own. We were soulmates, I was sure — me and the other four hundred sixty-three dorks watching her show us the latest and sneakiest ways to crack, hack and hide.

I propped up the pillows behind me, workout stank be damned, laid a towel on my chest under my laptop and settled in. I was ready to learn everything she had to teach me.

And listen to her. Fuck, I loved the sound of her voice. It was low and seductive, but she was also funny. At the end of all her tutorials, she would say, "And change your fucking passwords, Geeks!" That usually led me to go around the apartment and do just that. My phone, Anton's phone, Jackson's phone when I'd lived with him, then all sites, all applications... I could spend half my day just doing what Majel213 told me.

And more than once, my own passwords had been changed to her fucking screen name. How I'd become a lovesick dork slash criminal was beyond my comprehension.

That sultry tone went on to describe how she'd found her target and worked backward. How creating a fake person was easy. Once she had the profile pic, the rest of what 'he' posted was either shares from propaganda that aligned with Caroline's beliefs or pictures that he wasn't in. 'Nate' had become friends with one of Caroline's relatives through people who were more interested in having followers and like than caring if they actually knew the person.

Then it had just been as simple as engaging on the same post by the mutual friend and boom! There was a direct line to her target. It required maintenance, but according to Majel213, that was part of the fun. The hard part, she said in the voice that had me wondering how 'Rafael' would sound if she whispered it all quiet and sultry next to my ear, was waiting for the day that Caroline would open her social media on her work computer. But, Majel213 wasn't worried. Caroline had said that she hated texting on her phone and was much faster on a keyboard, so it was just a matter of finding a topic that would inspire Caroline to need to converse faster — like making Nate's tabby cat ill.

Majel213 had a beautifully perverse brain.

She explained that once the application was opened in the office of the sheriff of Zapata Falls, because Majel213 had programmed a sneaky virus that shadowed the direct messenger, the malware would be on Caroline's hard drive in thirty seconds. And that would translate to the entire town being held hostage by Majel213 until they paid their ransom in untraceable cryptocurrency.

And pay they would, she assured, because the counties, cities or whatever were insured…and the FBI would tell them to. Otherwise, all their systems stayed frozen and spun around in the never-ending computer circle of death.

And the real beauty? While they tried to figure out *how* to pay, she just kept stealing all their information. It was pretty customary malware shiftiness. She could get tax returns, social security numbers, backgrounds, criminal records and birth certificates then sell that to criminals like me. Majel213 just made it sound so much sexier than it probably was.

Internal man-dork sigh.

She also sold her out-of-date malware to us nerds who didn't know how to code it as well as she did. The clever thief was always three steps ahead, and the improved versions of her viruses and programs were for her use only.

So it was *that* version—the latest and most dangerous—that I was sure I needed to make bank for the crew, not a malware program an average bad actor could use. Somehow, I was going to convince the normally selfish Majel213 to share her updated goods, and we would go from street criminals to an organized threat to society. I tingled all over just thinking about it.

Her scratchy voice rang out and woke me from my dream of living the calm, boring life of a closet criminal. "Change your fucking passwords, Geeks! Oh, and I'm taking questions for the next five minutes on message chat. Dick picks will result in a virus that sends it to your grandma, assholes."

I shot up and clicked on our message window. Time to make a deal.

GoldieLocks: Brilliant as usual. How do I get my hands on your latest version?
Majel213: Thanks for watching. It's always nice to have you there. The links are up.

I didn't want those old, used-up links. I wanted the version she was hoarding for herself.

GoldieLocks: No, I mean the *real* latest version.
Majel213: Not for sale, sweetie. Sorry. You know that.

My internal ego liked the term of endearment so much that he convinced my brain it was for him. But I wasn't giving up that easy.

GoldieLocks: Everything has a price.

It was a bold promise, considering we didn't have a savings account with money piled up.

The ellipsis next to her name stayed for a minute like she was writing some long explanation. My heart raced and I drummed my fingers lightly over the keys without hitting hard enough to type.
Name your price, baby girl.
Oh, the money I could make for Anton. And I wouldn't have to sit out on that fucking bench and watched addicts wither away with each sale I made. I could perch myself on the couch, post to social media then just wait to pounce. And getting the latest version

of the malware would ensure it wasn't tracible. It would be new and never have been used.

Majel213: Indeed it does. My apologies.

She added a winky face emoji and left the chat. *Shit.* I should have brought up cash. She was always talking about cryptocurrency, but cash was still king for criminals. I should have started with that. *Next time.* Next time I would lead with, "How much cash would it take?"

Fuck. Didn't she know I needed that shit like…yesterday?

I closed my laptop and tossed it to the end of the bed. After a quick shower, I found Anton in a hovered meeting with Scooter at the island in the kitchen. The sour frown on his pale face was enough to know he didn't like what he and Jackson had heard earlier. We needed money. I was the Golden Boy and he was relying on me to make good on my previous abilities to earn.

Working on it, boss.

"I'm headed down to the bench then I have to help with a thing. Later."

I jogged down the stairs and out to the courtyard that connected the three buildings of Covington Heights. A small gathering of black jeans parted and Jackson stood, towering over us all. We man-hugged, the official sign that he was off duty and I was on.

His spot on the bench was still warm, and I draped my arms out, taking as much space as I could.

A new member of the crew caught my eye on the edge of the circle. He was a bit scrawny and had probably come from Bradford. More and more defectors were crossing into our territory. That particular one looked hungry as hell. Sometimes I wondered if the new recruits weren't double agents. I reminded myself to keep my guard up at all times.

Maybe I would do a password sweep after dinner. Although, the skinny kids from the projects weren't much of a threat to the technology that I used. Hell, they wouldn't even know how to put a virus onto a computer.

Like Majel213... Using direct messaging to shadow...

Fucking fuck, fuck.

Mother of all fucks.

My pulse raced and I closed my eyes in horrid understanding. She'd broken into my fucking computer.

Chapter Two

Marigold

Covington Heights?

Never fucking heard of it. But thanks to a quick search and locator of the laptop I'd just hacked, I found out it was just a river crossing and train ride away. And 'GoldieLocks' was the farthest thing from a blonde bombshell or a little girl stealing porridge, not that I'd thought he was. Interesting screen name, 'Rafael Santos'.

I clicked open his messages with one of my other followers. *Oh. My. God.* I snickered at my desk. Rafael had a crush on me. *Hilarious.* His video files proved he was a fellow Trekkie. Okay, that made him moderately cool in my book. But it also made him a dork like me. Pity there were no pictures on his laptop of his probably nerdy face.

There was a password-protected ledger that only took me three minutes to crack and, my, my, my, Rafael aka GoldieLocks was a naughty boy — illegal gambling that hadn't turned a recent profit and revenue that was most likely drug deals. He was like a bookkeeper for a mini-mob — probably a number nerd who'd convinced the thick muscle heads not to beat him up by organizing their money. I could practically see his scrawny ass and pimpled face. *Poor baby.*

I swiveled in my chair with a little smile on my face. The thrill of a hack — no matter how trivial — always made be buzz. GoldieLocks and I had teetered on flirting and, from some of our chats, I knew he wasn't a total idiot. But I hadn't expected him to be a part of a gang.

My pit bull, Spock, barked from upstairs, which meant that he either needed to pee or a squirrel had run up the lone tree in the backyard of our quaint brick Bay Ridge house. There was a sliding glass door that led to a small patio and Spock loved to sit next to it and police his territory.

I stood — my black gamer chair rolling to the wall behind me — locked all my screens with a mandala design that moved like an animated kaleidoscope and stretched. I'd been sitting for over an hour. Fresh air would be welcomed. My basement hideaway was dark and comfy, but also tended to be dank and chilly — and lonely, very lonely. Online 'friends' were nice, but I craved the real deal.

Upstairs, my mom was cutting apples into small cubes to dry in her dehydrator. It had been my gift to her on her fiftieth birthday two years prior, and she'd used the shit out of that thing. The fruit in front of her was no doubt intended for her homemade granola, which would not contain any other form of sugar. I'd eaten it since I had been able to chew, and while it was healthy and I appreciated my parents giving me a start in life without chemicals and preservatives, I was unequivocally over it — and them. Especially her.

My hippie parents hadn't stopped at controlling my diet. I'd been homeschooled, never had an antibiotic and pretty sure the vaccines I'd gotten behind their backs when I was eighteen were the first actual medicine to ever enter my body. It was hard to know who wondered more where the other came from — my parents or me.

My dad was a good guy, but my mom ruled the roost. Over the years I'd learned his sympathetic eyes were the closest thing I'd get to having him on my side of an argument. It disappointed me, but it had also kept me at home, afraid that if I didn't rebel, no one would.

My mom glanced over her shoulder at me in the doorway of the basement. "I hope that's organic charcoal around your eyes. The name-brand crap is not just harmful to you. It's tested on innocent bunnies."

Here we go.

"Mom, we've been through this. My body, my choice." Throwing her feminist talking points in her face was my favorite way of talking back to her.

"My house, my rules."

Jesus, I need to move out. And financially, I could. The problem was, renting required a proof of employment that I didn't have. There had been too many scams of people creating fake jobs, so landlords were able to crosscheck a paystub with the government — and the officials required phone numbers and addresses. I'd tried to find a few places that would rent or sell to me on the down-low but after one glance of my combat boots and colored hair, the answer had been a resounding 'no' each time. But I was a hacker. I would find a way.

Deana Birch

Until then, I still needed to get out of the damn house, and a walk around the block would never be long enough. After a frown, my mom turned back to her apples. I rolled my eyes and asked my giant dog, "Wanna go for a walk?"

His gray-blue ass wiggled, and his tail beat against the wooden floor of our small kitchen. He followed me to the front of the house, where I plucked my backpack from a hook and threaded my arms through it. Next, I grabbed the short leash I kept Spock on, keys, phone and the big blue bag that had four holes for Spock's legs.

"Come on, big boy. Let's go."

My dog happily trotted to the door where I reached down and clipped his lead to his thick, black collar. Only a second later my mom was wiping her hands on her long, flowy beige skirt and leaning a shoulder into the arch that connected the hall to the kitchen. Had the woman not heard of dish towels?

"You going into the city?" She jutted her chin to what I was holding. Dogs were allowed on the train as long as they were in a bag. Spock was huge, and probably not the kind of dog the city had meant when it had made the ordinance, but he'd be following the rules, so technically was not breaking the law—just bending it, which made me smile.

"Yeah. Don't count on me for dinner." I prayed that vague would be enough.

My mom frowned. "Where are you going?"

To none-of-your-fucking-business land.

"I'm going to see a friend." *Oh shit.* An incredibly stupid plan formed in my head the second the words were out of my mouth. But it would just be to get a glimpse of him, give me something to do—like a detective or a spy.

"What friend? You shouldn't trust those people who you chat with online, Marigold. They're never who they say they are."

No shit, Sherlock.

She stalked slowly toward me and the dog, who couldn't figure out what the hold-up was. "You're being stupid and irresponsible again, I see."

The insult slid under my skin and sliced a vein. It made me want to bleed out then and there in the hall. First of all, I was the farthest thing from stupid. And secondly, it was such typical shit from her. She wanted to keep me inside. The veil of it being for my protection had grown thin.

My mother didn't work. And, while ten years prior I had loved the attention she'd given me, it had flipped into an obsession. She wanted to know where I was at all times, how much I'd slept. Hell, I was even suspicious that she was tracking my bowel movements. I was the only thing she thought about. It was unhealthy and creepy.

After a challenging tilt of her chin, she asked, "What friend?"

I held her stare with my heart racing. "Bye." I turned and walked out of the door with the dog. I headed down the street and toward the train station that led into the more populated city.

At the deli on the corner, I ordered a coffee, loaded it with artificial creamer and two packets of sugar then paid with the crumpled-up bill from the pocket of my cut-offs.

Every time I went to buy something, it was the same problem. I had a secret account online with thousands and thousands of dollars in currency. But one transfer to my actual account and the questions would start flying. I had enough money to buy a house and vacation on white-sand beaches. But sharing that I was an online extortionist with my parents wasn't exactly something I looked forward to confessing over green tea at the kitchen table.

In their hearts, they were good people—Earth-caring, tree-hugging, sweet angels who loved me more than anything. How was I going to explain that being an only child who had zero friends had spawned an interest in computers? And that it turned out I was pretty fucking good with them? The homeschool education of building curiosity and being autonomous had worked well. *Too well.*

Spock and I walked to the train station and I downed the rest of my caffeinated, overly sweet hot drink. I tossed the paper cup in the wire trash at the top of the stairs and shook out Spock's travel bag.

If dogs could give side-eye and frown, I'd been served. But he lifted a front paw and climbed in anyway. He was right, the poor beast. The crinkling of the plastic as he walked down the steps was humiliating, and his ears laid back as far as they would go. Once on the train it was better, because fellow passengers would fawn over him and he'd smile and wag his tail.

It wasn't that I had *intended* to ride the train below the more interesting neighborhoods of Downtown or the touristy part of Midtown. It was the stupid curiosity inside me that led me to get off way Uptown in a neighborhood I'd only recently heard about.

GoldieLocks hadn't been the first person to ask for the latest version of my malware. He'd just been the only real criminal to do so. The rest had been nerds like me who wanted to start making a little money on the side and see what they could get away with—all-the-while bringing some much-needed excitement to their otherwise-uneventful lives.

We exited the train, and at the top of the stairs — and in a completely different world — I took Spock out of his bag and stored it in my backpack. As my dog sniffed an orange grease-stained wrapper caught between the railings of the stairs, I pulled out my phone and clicked on the email I'd sent myself with the coordinates.

I tugged at the leash and Spock and I walked two blocks over to Covington Heights. Tall, weather-stained and dreary buildings flanked us until we were across the street from a barren courtyard. Directly in front of it was a sad excuse for a park with a street gang in all black huddled together.

It probably didn't help that I hadn't thought about a plan. Maybe I didn't even need one. I'd really just wanted to see what GoldieLocks and his illegal ledgers of money had been about. And from the looks of it, they were drug dealers like I'd thought. *Big whoop.*

Now that I was there, though, I was even more curious. I needed to think. There was a run-down diner a block lower that wouldn't give me a visual on the courtyard but would at least allow me to come up with something before just hopping back on the train to eat tofu nuggets and return to my solitary life.

Spock and I walked down the street, and when we entered the diner, the metal on the bottom of the door scraped against the tiled floor and created a horrible shrill. An older lady with droopy skin and a jaw that circled with every chew of her gum looked up at me.

"Hi." My voice was as sweet as I could get it. "Do you mind if I come in with my dog?"

Her dull eyes raked over me once and she answered with a scoff, "He probably smells a lot better than most of my customers. Sure, doll. Thanks for asking."

I found a circular booth in the corner and tucked Spock under the table. He rounded into the base and was completely hidden from view. With his head at a small angle and on his front legs, he closed his eyes.

Without a computer, I wouldn't be able to break into any legal records or police reports to find out what Covington was all about, and my impulse move to discover it seemed stupid in retrospect. I could have stayed home and learned more than I would in the beat-up diner.

The waitress came over. She had on an old-fashioned uniform and a stained white apron. Her laced-up comfortable shoes must have been white at some point, but they were scuffed and yellowish. An obvious bunion protruded below her big toe on the right foot.

"You lost?" She smacked her gum and tossed a laminated menu on the sparkly Formica table.

"No...I was supposed to meet a friend. He must have gotten hung up."

She narrowed her eyes, probably detecting the lie. "Coffee?"

"Sure." Anything to escape her scrutiny.

I checked my phone for messages and sent a few back to my online buddies. I liked the virtual world where I could be anyone and everyone, but it lacked honestly and true connections — something that I'd already missed out on for twenty years with the small exception of my family.

The need for some actual friends who would see more than just the side I was trying to show them had been eating at me for a couple of years. Yes, I had followers and maybe even some fans. But as flattering as that all was, it drove a bigger wedge between me and something real. And since I'd started posting tutorials a year prior, some of that online community had put me on a very unwelcomed pedestal.

I wanted to fit in, not stand out. But then again, I did have multicolored hair, so being different was in my DNA.

The waitress was back, holding a pot of coffee, and she flipped the cup on the saucer in front of me.

"Can I interest you in a piece of pie? Maybe a sandwich?"

I grinned. Pie was one of those desserts that my mom had ruined with odd fruit on a gluten-free crust that tasted like bad jam on cardboard. But real-world pie? *Yes, please.*

My reaction brought a flicker to her eyes. "I make them myself."

In my limited exposure to the public, I understood one thing for sure. If you could find something that someone was proud of, you could use it for your advantage.

"I would love to try your pie. Surprise me with your favorite."

"You got it, honey." There was a little pep in her step as she returned behind the counter and replaced the coffee pot on its burner. She even hummed as she cut me a slice and grabbed a fork from a metal bin, rattling the others left behind.

Within two minutes she was back, holding a small plate above the table.

"It's a classic, but it's my most popular. Cherry," she said as she slid the dish in front of me then placed a napkin and fork next to it.

My mouth watered. It didn't look like anything special, but then again, it didn't have to. The bright, unnatural red seeping out from under the beige flakey crust spoke to my junk-food-junkie self.

I tugged the small plate closer and picked up the fork. My mother would have asked for a knife. She hated when people changed the duties of utensils, but I cut into the sinful triangle and brought a bite to my mouth.

Yep. No organic fruit to be found. Only canned deliciousness.

"Perfection," I said after I swallowed.

She slid into the bench opposite me with a warm smile. "I'm glad you like it."

I took a few more bites and a sip of my coffee. "What's your name?"

"Jessie."

After a wipe of my hand with the paper napkin, I held it out. "I'm M. Nice to meet you. Your pie is five-star."

Jessie sucked in air through gritted teeth. "You don't really have a friend, do you?"

"That obvious?" I cringed a little.

"I've lived here all my life, sweetheart. An outsider sticks out as much as your rainbow hair."

I frowned. "Sorry."

"I get it. No one walks in the door and says, 'Hey, Jess, tell me everything you know about Anton Myers and his boys.' People think subtle will work."

Anton Myers must have been the A in all Rafael's ledgers. Jessie had given me some new information. She didn't know I was working with a geek's laptop and nothing else.

She tapped the table twice with her dark-pink fingernail. "Listen. I get it. Bad boys are fun to think about. And these guys? Well, you know after what happened with Bradford, they're confusing. They don't seem all bad. But trust me, honey. They are not waiting to shine into saints. Go back to wherever it is you came from and forget about Covington Heights."

I stroked Spock's back under the table. "Right." There was no need to argue. She'd seen through me the second I'd walked in. A tough girl from the streets wouldn't have asked for permission to bring in her dog.

Commotion at the door drew both of our attention and Jessie turned and looked over her shoulder.

Under her breath but loud enough for me to understand, she said, "Speak of the devil." She pushed into the table, took a deep breath and set her shoulders before walking over to greet the group of young men in black jeans and black tanks.

They were an odd bunch...a mix of everything. All races and all sizes, the only thing uniting them was their clothes. It was almost endearing...or welcoming somehow. But there was most definitely one who stood out.

His build was thicker, and all eyes followed him...even Jessie's. He wasn't the tallest, but he was in charge. The group separated while he walked to the opposite end of the diner, then followed after he sat down.

I couldn't hear what they ordered, but Jessie nodded and took notes from a small pad she'd pulled out of a pocket. On her way back to the kitchen, she shot me a glance of warning above a tight frown.

I tried to busy myself with my phone, but a stare from across the room was burning a hole in my head. Jessie was right. I didn't belong in Covington Heights. Hacking and cracking were one thing. Putting my crime out in the open would require an amount of courage I didn't think I had.

The laser energy on me grew and I continued to tap into my phone. Shit, I'd been spotted and was in way over my head. The ability to swallow was somehow forgotten. Boots scuffed on the tiled floor closer and closer to my table. It was possible my hands might have been trembling, so I dropped my phone and sat on them. A drip of cool sweat ran down my hot spine.

Yeah. In the flesh, bad guys were way more intimidating than online nerds who thought my voice was sexy. I wasn't just in a different ballpark. I wasn't even playing the right sport. I wrapped a leg around Spock and willed it to stop bobbing up and down.

"You don't look familiar. I think I would have remembered your hair." He glanced under the table. "And dog."

He was the boss. There was no mistaking it. The rest of his crew smirked from afar, waiting for him to flex his muscles against a helpless girl like myself. My heart thudded between my ears and my brain turned to fuzz. I didn't know how long I stared back at him, his light blue eyes both haunting and mesmerizing.

He sat in the booth opposite me and crossed his arms. Holy hell, criminal muscles covered in tattoos were bigger in real life than in the movies. He had the intimidation game on point.

The way I saw it, I had two choices — own up to why I was there or cower away and continue living a massive lie in my parents' basement. My chance had presented itself. *I might as well roll the dice.*

Somehow, I puffed out my chest and hoped the gesture would lead to a smidgen of confidence. "Are you Anton?" By the grace of a god, my voice didn't shake.

He smiled. It wasn't warm or friendly. No, it was delightfully devious. I admired it.

"Sorry. You're not really my type."

"I can assure you the feeling is one-hundred-percent mutual." Apparently, my poise had convinced my nerves to take a backseat. I wiped my bangs from my forehead. "I have a business proposition for you." *I what?*

He chuckled. "Oh, yeah, Rainbow Brite? What's that?"

"It would be much easier to show you. Do you have a computer around?"

Anton studied me as he sat back in the booth with one arm extended and the opposite hand running up and down the inked muscles of his forearm.

"Who are you, exactly?"

I swallowed down the sour saliva from the acid brewing in my stomach. "You can just call me M."

"You a cop?"

"Nope."

A heavy silence fell between us as he evaluated my answer.

"I gotta admit, it takes some balls to proposition me. My curiosity has been sparked." He looked over his shoulder and jutted his chin in some kind of language only his crew was privy to.

"Okay. I'll bite. But my security guy has to check you for listening devices and all that shit." His cracked his neck like a dare.

There was no going back, and the previously wonderful pie flipped like a brick in my stomach.

"Not a problem," I faked. *What the fuck is wrong with me? And who the fuck is the confident chick at the table across from a hardened criminal? Jesus, I could get raped, or killed or...*

Finally, some street sense kicked in. "I just need a laptop. I can show you from here."

Anton dipped his chin. "That's the smartest thing you've said so far." Over his shoulder he yelled, "Scooter. Call Rafa and tell him to come down with a laptop."

I hid my grin. I'd stay safe and in public, although Jessie was probably the kind of witness to crime who was conveniently in the back when anything bad happened. But also, 'Rafa' was very obviously Rafael Santos aka GoldieLocks. I'd get to see his dorky face fall when I took over his spot as resident money-making nerd.

Because even though my proposition was only being formulated as I sat in front of Anton, I knew what my stipulations would be. Most importantly? Inclusion.

I wanted be part of something. Make friends, even. Hell, that Anton wall of angry muscle seemed okay. I mean, there weren't a lot of females around. *Wait!* There weren't *any* females around.

Jessie brought a veal chop over to Anton and my mother would have wept for the dead baby cow. With every bite he took, I grew less and less sure of myself. Every instinct I had to fidget was being held down by a very fake sense of bravado I didn't know I'd had. But faking it would be the only way out of the door I couldn't stop eying every ten seconds. Best case, Anton could say no, I'd have had a little adventure then I could go back to my safe basement and overly interested parents.

Worst case? I couldn't go there.

The moment Anton crumpled up his napkin and tossed it onto his blood-stained plate, the door open and another bulk of a man came in carrying a black laptop. He looked to the crew huddled on the opposite end of the diner first, then over to Anton and me with a bewildered scrunch on his face.

"Hey, Goldie. Over here." Anton snapped and pointed to our table. My heart stopped, *That* was GoldieLocks? *No fucking way.* The massive man strode over, sizing me up with every step.

Little did he know that I was doing the same thing. *And boy, oh fucking boy*, had I been wrong about him. If he was a geek, I was a supermodel. His olive skin was flawless and he wore a perfectly tattered baseball cap, which did nothing to hide his beautiful amber eyes. His hair was coal black, and while he was trimmer than his boss, he was layer upon layer of muscle. Instead of a black tank, he wore a black T-shirt, and it looked as though it might rip at the shoulders because it was stretched so tight.

In essence, he was the opposite of what I'd imagined for a hacker...and everything I'd fantasized about in hot men, men who I would never approach in a zillion years. I let out a labored breath, one I'd been holding since he'd started looking at me.

"Who's this?" he asked Anton. Rafael stole a glance at my off the shoulder T-shirt and narrowed his eyes. Yeah, Trekkie alert.

Anton shrugged. "Says her name is M, and she has a business proposition."

I held out my hand. "Nice to meet you, Goldie." My smirk widened as his face fell.

Chapter Three

Rafa

Blood drained from my head and weighted down my chest. I knew that rasp. I'd dreamt about it. But the little multicolor-haired girl sitting across from Anton had warped a previously beautiful tone into a screeching nightmare. She'd fucking beat me at my own game. In what? Three hours? I *knew* her accent was too much like my own. To think, she was in the same city as me all that time. *Sneaky bitch.*

If maximum hatred hadn't been pumping through my veins for Majel213, I would have noticed that she was pretty. I would have found her deep blue eyes that shimmered in the center of the black makeup enticing, maybe even remarked she had one of noses that was long and straight, yet managed to button at the end, making it perfect, and would have liked that her high cheekbones were shadowed by a pink blush that brought a shine to her lovely tan skin.

The list would have continued to the short pink and purple locks on her head. Her gray *Star Trek* T-shirt fell off one shoulder and a bright pink bra strap poked out, completely out of place yet perfectly matched to the rest of her. The entire look, nerd-sexy, was wrapped into a perfect bow. Even with my arm twisted behind my back, I would never have admitted that she was hotter than I could have imagined — because she was so much fucking worse.

Not in a million light years would I have thought she'd have the balls to just walk into Covington Heights and get a face-to-face with Anton. How *had* she managed that? Did she not do any fucking research before coming here? We were drug dealers, killers, thieves and overall assholes.

Sure, hackers and crackers had skill, but we were the street. The realization that she might just be in over her head spread a slow grin over my face.

I turned to Anton. "You check her for bugs? Take her phone?"

"I thought I'd let you do the honors." Anton lifted his eyebrows once in evil encouragement and I could have kissed him. It wasn't just a lesson for Majel213. It was a show for the boys on the other side of the diner. That was probably how it had started, the bossman wanting to flex his territorial muscle to an outsider. Because, holy fucking shit, she was the epitome of a sore thumb.

I placed the laptop on the table in front of the bossman and opened a palm to the tricky bitch to my left. "Phone."

"What? No." She snarled, and I loved it. Yeah, we didn't play nice. "You know I'm not a cop."

I scoffed. If she wanted to play ball, I had the home-field advantage. "I don't know a damn thing about you, baby girl. Phone." I waved my fingers in a 'give me' motion.

"I'm not your *baby girl*."

The dirty look she tried to send me only fueled my petulant fire. I may have been a little late to her party, but this boy knew how to dance. She turned to Anton and her bitch face morphed to a gentle smile.

In a soft tone she said, "I really don't see the need to take my phone."

Anton stared back at her with pouted lips. After a slow exhale, he turned to me. "This is a waste of time." He started to stand when Majel213 stopped him.

"Okay. Okay." She dug into her backpack and I noticed a leash under the table.

I bent to get a better look and found a huge blue pit bull looking up with sweet, light eyes. She'd seriously picked the wrong canine if she was hoping for protection. The adorably dumb expression on his face exposed him for a giant teddy bear whose only assault would be licking a face. For someone who had her virtual shit together, Majel213's real-life schemes needed some serious rethinking.

She handed me the phone and I called over my shoulder. "Scoot!" Scooter came jogging up and I tossed him her device. "Burn that." I winked. Scooter knew I would never trash an electronic device without scouring through it.

"Hey!" she objected, but it was too late. Scooter was already on his way out of the door, followed by the two minions he was training.

"Stand up." I crossed my arms and waited.

It must have hit her a little harder, the brutal reality of the position she'd put herself in. We had her phone. She was on our turf. If she'd thought anyone in the diner was on her side other than her harmless dog, the anticipatory glare from Anton informed her that she'd been dead wrong.

The air thickened with her understanding. After glances to the bossman and back to me, she slid out of the booth and stood next to me.

I wished she didn't smell like she did—like candy and sugar and delicious sin. It would have made it easier to kick open her legs and enjoy the little stumble when I did. I checked the soles of her combat boots then ran my hands up her fishnet stockings. Her legs were thin and firm. *Probably a runner.* When I got to her little cut-offs, I dug extra deep into her pockets and emptied her measly amount of money out onto the table.

Anton and I exchanged a grimace at the crumpled bills. We both liked to steal, but her ten bucks wasn't worth the effort.

Her breath caught as I palmed her flat stomach. She leaned into me and for a millisecond it registered that she was the perfect fit. The short hairs at the base of her neck tickled my chin as I took one more whiff of her syrupy perfume.

For my ears only she said, "Don't forget how I found you, asshole." The words broke her spell and I nudged her forward then demanded her bag.

Her lip trembled and betrayed her feigned confidence. The gravity of the situation was weighing on her. *Good.* Let her shoulders droop a bit, keep that frown on her face.

I didn't find anything interesting in her bag and tossed it back to her. I checked the dog and its collar last, rewarded with a sloppy kiss on my cheek that confirmed he was not much help to her.

Anton had been busy on his phone while I'd gone through the security measures and only looked up when I said, "She's good."

He asked in a bored tone, "So what's this proposition?"

Majel213 gave him a tight smile and reached for my laptop. She opened it and stopped herself from typing. A knowing grin spread across her face. *Shit.* She knew my passwords. Heat flushed my cheeks. She *was* my password.

But for whatever reason, she slid the computer back to me and scooted deeper into the booth. I sat next to her, typed in her stupid fucking name and slid it back, playing along. I couldn't help myself from reaching down and scratching the dog's head. I was a sucker for animals and kids. It ruined the entire 'tough guy' image I was going for but I was already exposed as a fellow geek. I might as well double down on sharing secrets.

Majel213 walked Anton through basically the same presentation she'd shown her followers that morning. His eyes would occasionally find mine and I would nod in a sign that she was legit.

At the end, Anton leaned back into the booth and asked, "So what the fuck do you need us for?"

It was the same question that had been burning a hole in my brain since I'd came to the horrible conclusion about her identity.

"I need cash. If I transfer too much money from the crypto, questions start to come up."

"Why wouldn't I have the same problem?"

Her nose did an odd little wiggle and, had we been friends, I would have called her out on the quirk, but we weren't. She'd hijacked my entire business plan and made it her own.

She forced out a breath. "You will...for now. But I am working on something to eliminate that barrier."

Anton scoffed. "You want me to pay you for money that you can't even get a hold of? Do you think I'm a fucking idiot?"

But what the bossman didn't realize was that she would get the money. She could get the money. Cracking code was in that girl's blood. Everyone online knew it. She was offering us fucking gold. The only question remained why.

"What else?" I asked.

"A place to live and a cover for a job." Below the table, Majel213's leg bounced, rubbing against mine. She was going all in. *Respect.*

Anton laughed. "Is that all? I don't know what you think we do here, but running an employment agency isn't on the list." He turned to me. "What do you think?"

I'd weighed the position I'd take throughout her spiel. The end goal was more money and a bigger operation. She was a risk worth taking, and since Anton had trust issues — among many, many, others — I would no doubt be put in charge. Majel213 might have thought that she'd one-upped me by going directly to the boss, but she didn't understand how it would play out in real time. However she *had* calculated that she needed me. That was why she had yet to sell me out as getting hacked.

"What's the cut?" I leaned back and crossed my arms.

"Fifty-fifty."

"Nope." Anton popped the P. Negotiations were his favorite part of the game.

"Try again." I licked my lips. I loved the taste of money.

Majel213's eyes fell to my mouth and I must have been high at the idea of making bank because I was sure she'd swallowed hard as she tracked my movement. For the first time since I'd been in the diner, it occurred to me that she might just like what she saw. *Holy Shit.*

She shivered, straightened and said, "Fine. Seventy-five, twenty-five."

"You're heading in the right directions, Rainbow Brite." Anton smirked.

"Eighty-twenty." Her nostrils flared. *Fuck.* She was one of those girls who were hotter when they were pissed off. That was kryptonite for my Brazilian blood.

"I'll think about it." Anton stood and the minions at the end of the diner did the same. They'd been watching his every fucking move. "Wrap this up and meet me at our place in fifteen."

I nodded and we waited for him to leave before I turned to her and scowled. "You are fucking lucky, little girl."

"I want my phone back, asshole."

God, her flushed cheeks were gorgeous.

I grinned. "That thing is long gone by now. A boy can never be too careful, so I've recently learned."

She snarled then shook her head. "You really should be ashamed of yourself. I basically told you I hacked through messaging, then you direct messaged me." She tapped her forehead with her index finger. "Hello."

Okay, fine. That had been stupid. What could I say? I'd been excited.

"Me? What about you? You walked into one of the most dangerous neighborhoods in the city with…what? Hopes that your dog's slobber would make a criminal slip and fall like a banana peel in a cartoon?"

She gasped. "Spock would protect me if push came to shove."

I exaggerated my laugh to annoy her even more. I dropped my head into my hands then turned. "Spock? You have to be kidding."

"It's clever." Majel213 smacked my shoulder. "Spot...Spock?"

The dog must have understood we were talking about him and he nuzzled between our thighs. I grabbed his huge head and scratched behind the ears. "I'm sorry, buddy. Your owner is one of those rare breeds—half genius, half idiot."

"Fuck you."

I licked my lips, all slow like, then clicked my tongue. "Is that what you been thinking about, baby girl?"

"Eww. Gross."

"I'm a lot of things. Gross ain't one of them."

Majel213 stared out of the window then fluttered her lashes back to me. "I've heard of insta-love. But I gotta admit, insta-hate is brand new for me."

"Uh, huh. Rii-ight. More like insta-lust. You're still trying to understand how I'm not some fucking skinny geek like all the rest of your followers." How I'd kept myself from saying 'fan' instead of 'follower' was a miracle. God bless my ego.

"Do you have to pay for friends? Is that why you need money?"

"I have plenty of friends. Oh my God." A wicked grin spread on my face as a bell sounded in my head. "You don't." I dropped my head back and faked my laugh harder. "You're lonely and you need a crew, so you decided to step all up in mine. That's adorable...and fucking sad."

"You need me, asshole." Her disgusted look practically gave me a hard-on. I was fucked. History proved that I was immediately attracted to any girl who hated me. I'd never tried to figure out the reason. I'd always just gone with it because it made for hot sex.

"You keep calling me 'asshole'. It makes me think you like it in the back door, like some kind of code or Freudian slip."

Her eyes widened. "You are the most disgusting human I've ever met."

I shrugged. "I'm a criminal, baby girl. So are you, by the way. Our ability to decipher right and wrong is fucked up." I winked and she frowned like she'd eaten a shit sandwich. As I stood, I said, "I'll be in touch."

I was pretty sure she flipped me off with both hands as I walked out of the door. And while I jaywalked over to the courtyard, I knew I would do whatever it took to convince Anton to take her up on her offer.

Fucking with Majel213 while I made money? I had a new lease on life.

Chapter Four

Marigold

I helped Spock step out of his bag as the train whooshed past and sent a gust of polluted wind up my T-shirt. Once free, we exited the station and climbed the grimy steps.

There was *nothing* to like about Rafael Santos. *Dick fucking squat.* He defined the word 'cocky' and while some girls might fall for a prick like that, I would not be one of them. *Nope.* I was pretty sure I loathed every fiber of his being, right down to those beautiful hazel eyes that had tiny specks flickering with mystery and sin.

Okay, fine. He was hot. Anton's crew looked like they spent as much time in the gym as they did breaking the law. But that didn't mean I actually liked him. He was crude and gross. Hell, he'd probably been one of the assholes who'd sent me dick pics early on. *Foul fucks.*

And he was way, way off base to think that I had any sort of real attraction to him. *Yeah, fine.* I'd expected a typical computer nerd to show up and not a muscle-head model. He'd been right about that. He'd also nailed the whole 'I'm a criminal' bit—and didn't have friends. God, that overly confident asshat had been on point with almost everything he'd said. Maybe street smarts counted for more than I'd given it credit for.

Spock and I headed down my tree-lined block. He stopped to sniff his favorite hydrant and lifted a leg. It wasn't that I didn't like my home in Bay Ridge. It was the desire to experience something else, along with my deviant ways that I could no longer keep secret in the basement. I had goals. Building my online reputation as one of the top malware providers was just that.

And I couldn't look my father in the face anymore while I was doing it. Rafael had been right about something deeper. My moral compass had gone wonky somewhere along the way. I didn't just want to make money. I liked the chaos I caused and the panic that ensued once I'd gotten a victim where I wanted them.

It was perverse, wrong and thrilling. And sitting alone and having no one to chat about it with was borderline depressing. So while I was pretty sure I'd get the call—or message, since those Neanderthals had stolen my phone—to say that we would move forward, I was still nervous that they wouldn't.

And to be honest, pretty damn proud of myself that I'd gotten out unscathed.

I unclipped Spock's leash from his collar and unlocked the front door. He barreled between my legs, eager to see if my mom had left any scraps for him in his bowl. The clanking of metal on the tile floor proved his instincts correct.

My parents sat in the study, both reading in their chairs. My dad's feet were propped up on the end of the recliner and his slippers dangled from his toes.

"What didya do in the city?" he asked as he stuck a bookmark in between pages and closed his book. Part of me wondered if my mother had told him to ask me.

"I met up with my friend Rafael. He might have a job for me."

That got my mom's attention and curious eyes.

"Huh," she said, with her specific and tiring air of judgment. "If it doesn't work out, I saw a sign in the window at PBJ's. They're hiring."

PBJ's stood for Plant Based Jim's. It was a clothing store for vegans. I referred to it as Plant Based Junk, because Jim's idea of style was sad and depressing. Once I'd seen an actual potato sack for a dress for fifty bucks. I was working on the evolving thesis that Jim had smoked too many plants over the years. My mom suggesting that I'd like to work there was further proof that my parents did not understand me.

"Oh, I dropped my phone down a gutter. So if you tried to call and I didn't answer, that was why."

"What?" My dad sat up. "That doesn't sound like you."

No. No it didn't. But me throwing my parents under the bus for a mistake was something they could relate to. "I was fumbling with the newspaper to pick up Spock's poop." Plastic bags had long been outlawed in our house. They would be happier I'd used paper than upset I'd lost a phone. It made no sense, but so it was.

"Maybe you don't need to get a new one." My mom's eyes lit up. "I barely use that old one I have. You can have it."

That would be depressing. I shuddered at the thought of one of my followers seeing me with a flip-top portable.

"I'll be downstairs if you need me."

My dad smiled and I was sure both sets of eyes followed me to the door leading to the basement. Spock stayed with them—he liked being spoiled with tummy rubs and fruit—and I closed the door behind me. On the wall, I flipped on the light and headed down to my desk in the corner.

I probably should have done some research before going to Covington, but I'd found out more there than I would have online anyway. A quick search didn't show any rap sheet for Anton. That made no sense. Someone must have buried it deep in the police basement. The juvenile record was trickier to get, but not impossible, once I'd found his social security number. Robbery, assault and possession of a controlled substance at the age of twelve. He'd been busy.

Next up was fuck-face Rafael, and his story was a little less typical. He'd gone to a private Catholic school until he'd gotten arrested. After serving several months for attempted extortion, his address had officially changed to Covington Heights.

What had the other thing been that Jessie had mentioned? I zoomed out of the map of Covington and was reminded. *Bradford Towers.*

I hacked into the police database and searched for mentions in the previous six months. When the word 'homicide' popped onto my screen, I gulped. *Yeah, okay.* Anton and Rafael were an entirely different breed of criminal than I was. I was officially in over my head.

I lugged up the stairs, unsure of what I'd gotten myself into and half-hoping I'd never hear from them again. But the other half? The evil twin inside me? She had her bags packed and was already decorating a make-believe apartment on the other side of the river.

She rubbed her hands together in greed and delight at the idea of a *more* criminal future.

"Night," I called to my parents and went up to my bedroom. Under my pink fuzzy blanket, I wondered how I'd managed to put my destiny in the hands of a hottie wanna-be hacker and his boss.

* * * *

The next morning, my dad had already gone to work, and my mom had left a bowl of her granola on the table for me with a note to say that Spock had been fed and walked. Bowl in hand, I descended to my workspace, Spock following me. He hopped up onto the tattered couch opposite my computer screens and I logged on to social media as Nate to give a few updates about his sick cat. Then I read through old posts from Caroline Claussen to try to figure out how her cat had died three years prior.

I was in the middle of reading her recipe for fried chicken—the woman used frosted cereal and I *may* have been drooling—when my messenger dinged.

GoldieLocks: You dream about me?

Majel213: There's another word for that. It's a nightmare.

GoldieLocks: Both usually result in screaming. Good point.

Majel213: Or maniacal laughter.

GoldieLocks: Are you self-projecting again?

How had he become more pompous than he'd been the day before? *Gross.* GoldieLocks was fucking gross and arrogant and…the key to my future.

Majel213: Are you sure it's not you? You probably jacked off to feeling me up all night.

GoldieLocks: The only thing true in that statement is the part of it where I last all night.

Majel213: Your wrist must me sore then. Get to the point.

GoldieLocks: Email a list of what you need to Rafa@CriminalsRUs.com

Majel213: Really? That's your fucking email? Why aren't you still in jail?

GoldieLocks: Awww... Rainbow Brite finally did her homework. I'm flattered. And no, that's not my email. Get your ass over here before A changes his mind. And your split is the same as the rest of us. 90-10.

My heart rate sped up. I'd been hired. I had a place to call my own and a built-in crew of accomplices. The split sucked, but it was a way out. Besides, it wouldn't be forever. *Bye-bye, lonely basement.* I clapped my hands and woke up Spock, who thought it was meant for him.

I popped up from my chair and powered down all my computers. I skipped up the stairs and a curious Spock trailed behind. In the shower, I shaved my legs and bubbled up in my favorite soap twice. With my hair dry and styled, I applied my mom-illegal makeup nice and thick.

My outfit was intentional—a tight black shirt with short black shorts, black tights and my boots. I could *kinda* fit the part. I decided to leave Spock at home. I wasn't sure how long I would be gone and my parents might think it was suspicious that I took him with me to my 'new job'.

I grabbed a coffee from the deli on my way down to the train and sipped it all the way to Covington Heights. It was weird not having a phone to hide behind, and the lack of security brought everyone else's screen addiction into a giant exclamation point of anti-social behavior. How odd that the bulk of their social interactions happened through a filter. Then again, I was no better. In fact, my failed attempts at friendship were what had driven me to be a hacker. I hated norms, nice girls who were actually mean as fuck and rules.

A tweaked-out hippie. Maybe I wasn't so far off from my parents after all. I was just born in a different era. They solved their problems by living a clean life and I solved mine by giving society a general 'fuck you'.

The wind whipped between the tall buildings surrounding Covington Heights. A storm was moving in from the ocean. I could smell the salt in the otherwise-exhaust-ridden air.

I crossed the street and entered the cement-cracked courtyard. A group of black-jean-clad men huddled around a bench. In the park, a rusty swing rocked by itself in the wind, creating a high-pitched *squeak* that swirled with children's laughter and made for an eerie soundtrack. The sea of criminals parted and a huge black dude sat, legs wide, on the bench. My throat tightened as if someone had a hold of it, and heat spread like wildfire over my body.

"Hi. I'm looking for Rafael." *Oh, for fuck's sake.* My voice had cracked and I had no idea where to put my hands. Crossing my arms or fiddling with my fingers didn't seem right. The reality of my surroundings hit me hard, like it had the day before in the booth, but to my surprise, again, I found my stability. I shoved my hands in my back pockets and rocked on my heels.

Come on, confidence. You must be somewhere.

"*You're* looking for Rafa?" The black dude chuckled. Whatever was funny had gone over my head. But it struck me again that Anton, Rafael and the guy in front of me... They were all dangerously handsome...and built like brick houses. *Damn.*

I set my shoulders. "Is he here?"

"You." The guy snapped his fingers in the face of a younger member. The kid blinked a few times then stood straighter. "Walk her up to the boss's place. And don't talk to her."

I wasn't sure why the minion couldn't speak to me. Maybe it was just a test. A 'thank you' brewed in the back of my mouth, but I remembered that I wasn't in polite society. I nodded instead and followed the kid. His black jeans were baggy, and his arms were noticeably skinnier than the rest of the guys.

Inside the center building, the lobby was in a sad state. Banged-up metal mailboxes lined one wall and an old elevator creaked after Skinny Boy called it. Inside, he pressed the round button for three and it lit up with a dull glow.

When the doors closed in front of us, I wondered if I was a spider or if I was the fly in its web.

After two dings, we arrived. The third floor was nothing like the lobby. In fact, it was the opposite. The sealed concrete floor shined below my black boots and dark wood doors lined the hallway. The kid walked me all the way down the hall to the left and knocked three times on the last door.

After thirty seconds, no one had answered and my palms had started to sweat. What if it was just payback for me trying to take advantage of him? What if Silent Teenage Bob understood that 'don't talk to her' was code for 'throw the bitch in a dumpster'?

He knocked again, louder. Muffled stumbling came from the other side of the door and it eventually flew open. When it did, my escort scurried away and left me alone with Rafael.

There was a joke somewhere about the fact that he was foaming at the mouth. But it was stifled by my eyes, which may have been bugging out. GoldieLocks was shirtless and his hairless ripped chest taunted me like my favorite bag of sour gummi bears.

Somehow—I really didn't know how—I managed not to reach out and touch the ripples in his stomach or reach for a coin in my pocket and see if it would bounce off his fucking pectorals. *Jesus*. His tattoos were colorful and vibrant. A Brazilian flag was over his heart. Aww, he was sentimental…but still an asshole.

Rafael opened to door wider and motioned for me to enter. Once I managed to yank my eyes off his bare torso and thank Jesus that he at least had jeans on, the state-of-the-art everything dazzled around me.

The open kitchen had an island with a granite countertop and barstools on one side. The giant leather sectional on the opposite side of the room faced the biggest flat-screen television I'd ever seen.

As the door shut behind me, Rafael brushed his teeth all the way to the kitchen sink. He spat, rinsed his brush, then wiped his mouth with the back of his forearm.

"That was quick. Couldn't stay away?"

"Ha. Hardly. I'm ambitious. I want to get started." I crossed my arms and let out a little huff.

He grinned. Did he like pissing me off?

It was like my eyes had a mind of their own — with an overactive imagination to boot. I checked out his rippled abs and noticed he had one of those damn V things at his hips.

"Like what you see?"

Who wouldn't? But I couldn't let him have the upper hand so easily.

"Go put some clothes on."

"Sheesh." He lifted a shoulder. "So demanding. And we haven't even kissed."

I fake-laughed. "That will never happen. I don't date caveman assholes."

"Lemme guess. The last guy you had sex with was at a *Harry Potter* convention and was dressed like Malfoy."

That was entirely too close to the truth. It had been a *Game of Thrones* convention and a Jamie Lannister lookalike.

"Get dressed, shit-stain."

Chapter Five

Rafa

Had I purposely answered the door to show off my body? *Yes*. Had it worked like a fucking charm? *Absolutely*. It was probably petty and beneath me to be so obvious, but I had to destabilize her somehow. Hell, her all-black outfit and pastel hair was fucking hot, especially since she smelled like candy again. And I didn't waste my chance to take one more whiff of her as I passed by to finish getting dressed.

It hadn't been easy convincing Anton to welcome a woman into our crew. He was skeptical as fuck, and I thought it probably had more to do with not knowing how to keep a girl in line than anything else. After all, what was he going to do to show he was alpha male to M? Hit her? That wasn't how we rolled.

So I'd had to take responsibility for everything, remind him that I was the Golden Child and illegal money came to me like moths to a flame. In the end, he'd liked the idea of overreaching from our territory. He wanted to expand, and it was a good experiment to do so. Plus, there wasn't a ton of risk. M had more to prove than we had to lose.

With my black T-shirt on, I grabbed my phone then headed to the living room.

M leaned against the couch, her legs crossed at the ankles of her thick black boots.

"What's the M stand for anyway?" I asked when I caught her gaze.

"Mind your own fucking business." Her little snarl held more information that her sassy tone. She didn't like her name, whatever it was. And I would find out. It would be one more way of me getting the upper hand.

"Have it your way, Rainbow Brite." I opened the door and ushered her across the hall to my old apartment. The furniture wasn't as luxurious as in Anton's, but it was still a far cry from the other residents in Covington Heights.

I cleared my throat. "You got lucky. We just so happened to have an open apartment in our management division. We can use one bedroom for the computers, and you can take the other. M snooped around the corners then came back to stand in front of me in the kitchen.

"I'll take it."

I rolled my eyes. She really didn't understand the real world of criminals. "There are some other things you need to know about being a part of this crew."

"Like what? I have to get a matching tattoo or pledge allegiance to black jeans?"

I cut through her mocking tone with a sharp frown. I was serious. "No drugs. We sell them, but we never use them."

"Smart business." M continued her exploration as if my guidelines were boring. She opened the fridge, found a bottle of water and took it. Then she walked over to the other side of the big couch, plopped down and crossed her legs. "What else?"

"You're on the third floor. That gives you a certain level of respect, but it doesn't keep you safe."

"That sounds like your boss isn't able to control his crew." She lifted her thin eyebrows.

I supposed she had a point, but her over-confidence was stupid. We broke the law for a living. Although we had a general rule about girls, it wasn't like a crew member was going to be reported to the police for sexual assault.

I cleared my throat and continued, "Obviously no narcing. What happens between us stays between us."

"Duh. Is there more? Do I have to sign a non-disclosure or something?"

That made me laugh, because on the street a piece of paper meant nothing. Our words were our bond. And since she was utterly clueless about us, I decided to fuck with her.

"Yeah, the last thing. You have to work out with us every morning. It's when we discuss the day...like a meeting. Hope you like kick boxing."

She sat up slowly. "You're joking."

"Nope. You want to be one of us then you have to live like one of us." My tone was flat. There was no way she could detect the lie. "Deal breaker?"

She narrowed her eyes. *Damn, they were pretty.* "Oh, you'd like that, wouldn't you?"

No. No, I wouldn't. I shook my head and opened the drawer where we kept the stash of burner phones. I grabbed one and tossed it in her direction.

"Try not to lose this one."

M fumbled with the phone and her bottle of water spilled on the couch. "You stole the last one. I didn't lose it."

"Was it yours?"

She squinted and shrugged. "Yes."

"Do you still have it?"

"You *took* it."

"What did you think would happen to something that could be used as a recording device when you popped into a diner to talk to criminals?"

She frowned. It was sexy as fuck. "You could have given it back."

I still could. It was in my bedroom and I was trying to unlock it, but the normal password-cracking program wasn't working.

M stood and wiped her bottom lip. It was the perfect color of pink and just plump enough to suck. She really was far, far prettier than I'd imagined.

"You ready to go get our supplies?" I asked as I closed the drawer.

Her eyes lit up. "Oh! Yes. Shopping. Do you think we could stop at a home furnishing shop? I want to get one of those soft throw blankets."

I tucked my chin and stared at her, flaring my nostrils in utter disbelief. Yeah, she was confused about how I obtained my computers and phones. "You'll have to do that in your own time, baby girl. You're officially on the Covington clock." I walked over to the door and held it open for her.

She side-eyed me on the way out. I bet she thought that had some kind of effect on me, like she was sending me a warning signal to not mess with her. But I'd figured out years prior that fear was bullshit. Fear only existed in your head if you let it in. And I hadn't let fear come into my thoughts since. Plus, she was like a gnat…annoying but zero threat.

What I didn't expect was how penetrating her gaze was. It was unnerving and sexy wrapped in one. I lifted my eyebrows, daring her to discover my real thoughts.

"Eww. Don't fucking look at me like that." M smacked my shoulder and the sweet smell of her wrist made me wonder how she liked to be kissed. There was an underlying innocence about her. Maybe gentle was her cup of tea. Then again, she'd sought danger and it had landed right in her lap.

I watched her little ass all the way down the hall to the elevator then pressed the call button. "You ever physically steal anything before?"

"No." Her tone was flat, cautious—as if I would consider it a bad thing or be judgmental.

"Then better leave today to me." The doors opened and we boarded.

On the way down, M twisted her hands until she shoved them into her back pockets. She followed me to the bench where I greeted Jackson with a man hug and fist bump. To the crew I said, "This is M. She's with us now." The snarl I added meant she was also *with me* and they'd better get a fucking clue. I mean, I wasn't going to date her or any shit like that. But if there was going to be any fucking in the future, it would be with me.

Multiple head nods and chin juts followed with a whispered chorus of, "What's up?"

Jackson shot me a questioning glance until his eyes rolled with total understanding. He knew my type. M's gaze raced over the gang of misfits and a bit of color left her face. Her forced smile told me she might have finally begun to understand what she'd gotten herself into. She swallowed hard. Yeah, it would have been better to have just sold me the malware.

I led her to the train station and swiped her through. When we found a seat, she crossed her arms and slumped. It was about as spot-on for 'grouchy tantrum' as one could get.

It was also hot as hell.

I opened my arms in a surrender. "What's done is done, baby girl. Ain't no goin' back."

She frowned deeper. "Stop calling me 'baby girl'. It's fucking annoying."

"You like it." I tilted my head and smirked.

"I most certainly do not. Jesus… If I'd known you were going to be a Neanderthal, muscle-headed misogynist, I would have never come here."

I laughed but then turned serious. "Let me tell you something you haven't seemed to figure out yet. Your opportunity here? It's not because you decided. It's because Anton did…after I vouched for you. After I took sole responsibility for you and this fucking project. Me giving the boys an introduction? That was to protect your boney ass. But that doesn't make you invincible. You've been looking at us the wrong way. We're not good guys. Any one of those low-rung fuckers would use you to get closer to the bossman. I did you a fucking favor…again."

Her scowl softened. I let her stew until we got to Midtown.

"This is our stop." I stood and stretched with a smile. Fuck, I loved ripping people off. The nerves of anticipation and getting caught transformed into an intense satisfaction of walking away with a prize. It was an addicting high.

We climbed the crowded steps to the busy streets of tourist central.

"Come on." I headed over to a massive hotel, and as I passed the entrance, I grabbed the computer backpack hidden from street view by suitcases and I turned the first corner. It was almost over too fast. But that was the key to stealing. Spot the object, take it and leave. Zero hesitation. Unattended bags were as easy to pluck as low-hanging fruit. The hard part? Being casual when your blood was pumping with the rush and keeping a cool head while the tingling hum flooded your brain.

"Holy shit," M said under her breath. "That didn't even take you a minute."

"I may have done it before once or twice." *Or hundreds, maybe thousands of times*.

I kept a casual pace toward the park. We walked until we found an empty bench under a huge maple tree. Pigeons bobbed their heads as they searched for crumbs left behind by the city's outdoor diners.

"Let's see what we've got." I sat down, positioned the gray bag between us and unzipped the back pouch. A brand-new laptop shimmered with the reflection of the sun as I pulled it out.

"Score." M's blue eyes lit up.

I hadn't been sure how she would react when shit got real—as in 'I really stole that bag and she was really an accomplice'. I dug through the rest of the guy's shit and found a roll of cash in a sock. My luck was ridiculous. I pocketed the wad and M slid the laptop back into place. With the pack secured on my back, I led M out of the park on the opposite side.

"Let's head back to Covington. We can get a car and use the money to buy a tower and screen."

"We're gonna keep the laptop, too, right? I have a password cracker that works like magic." M followed me like a little puppy.

It was probably fucked up that I was already plotting to use her own program on the phone I'd taken from her the day before. But after all, she'd started it by hacking into my computer and pitching her scam to my boss before I could. Technically, I owed her a little payback.

"Yeah. We're going to keep it. You can even have it."

We stood at a crosswalk and waited for the traffic to stop. M pushed me on the shoulder. "Aw…a souvenir from my first physical theft. You're actually sweet under all those thick muscles that make you stupid."

I grinned, but not because she'd given me a backhanded compliment but because the dumber she thought I was, the more she would underestimate me.

The signal flipped and we dashed across the street and down to the train station. I swiped her through again then followed.

It wasn't until we were seated in the empty mid-day train that she spoke.

"I know I didn't do anything, but I still felt the thrill. It's the same one I get when my marks pay me and the bank balance grows." She swiveled to me. "The way it feels so good to be so bad."

I knew exactly what she meant and I'd stopped trying to figure out why I took so much pleasure in an illegal lifestyle. I'd also stopped trying to imagine that I'd felt guilty about it. I didn't. I was happy. Sure, it was fucked up on a societal level, but so was plenty of other shit that was actually legal.

I gave M a soft smile. "You want to go out later and celebrate?"

"Like on a date? No. Your little demonstration hasn't made you any more appealing. You're still an immature idiot with too many muscles."

"Not a date...like work friends who blow off steam. I know this amazing club downtown."

"I didn't bring a change of clothes." M tugged at her black shirt. "This is all I have."

"That's perfect. You in or not?"

A small plump came to her lips and she looked from the speckled floor of the train and back to me. It was impossible to know what her deliberation process was, but damn if she wasn't just as cute and sexy when she did it as when her hot temper flared. Yeah, there was definitely a softer side to her that was a mystery.

Where did she come from? What motivated her to steal people's information and money? How had she started down the dark path?

"I don't have my ID and I realize I look like a teenager." The rasp in her voice reminded me of why I liked her.

But I shook my head. Why would she think that would stop us from getting into a club?

"The owner is my cousin. Well, my cousin's cousin. You're good."

"You're not going to slip a mickey and do all those things you've been dreaming about, are you?" She scowled.

"Not my style. I like a little more fight. Sorry to disappoint you."

Her face fell and she chewed on her bottom lip. Eventually she said, "I realize I'm in over my head here and that I shouldn't have ever stepped a foot in your neighborhood. But I really, really don't want to get raped."

I had to give her a little credit for wising up and being honest with me. But keeping her scared worked better for me and fucking with her kept me amused. "But it's okay for us to kill you? Jesus, M, you really have no fucking clue."

She blinked several times and her nose went red. *Oh fuck. No, not tears.* She needed to harden the fuck up. But that didn't stop me from feeling just a little bad for her. She was fucked no matter how she tried to play it.

The train stopped at a busy platform and an elderly woman with a cane sat next to me. I leaned into M's ear and whispered, "I don't rape. I hate-fuck. It's completely consensual. Nothing hotter."

M's eyes widened. "Oh my God. You are fucking sick in the head."

"Language, young lady!" the old woman to my right scolded before doing a double-take of M. "And your hair is atrocious, darling."

M lifted a finger and sent me a warning glare. "Don't say another word."

I shrugged a shoulder and turned to the woman. "I like her hair."

"That doesn't speak well for you either, son."

She exited the train two stops later and I finally let out my laugh. The buzz of the afternoon floated between us and M actually smiled as well.

When we got to the top of the stairs that would lead us to Covington Heights, M said, "Fine. I'll come tonight."

As if she was ever not going to. And maybe she'd realized one thing. Keeping me close was the best thing she could do for herself.

Chapter Six

Marigold

In front of my new apartment, Rafael punched in a
security code and the door popped open.

"Fifty-one, fifty," he said then narrowed his light
eyes. "Sorry. You can't change it. And please don't take
that as a challenge."

Rafa's strong arm held the door open for me and it
hit me how confusing everything was. Yes, we'd just
stolen a bag and someone's money. But then he would
be a gentleman and had manners. *Conscientious
criminals?* It had to be a joke.

I didn't know how to make sense of it, so I just said,
"You're weird," and went inside.

He followed and swung the backpack onto the
couch. "Wanna grab a bite before we get the tower? I
need to eat soon."

"Aren't we taking a car? We can just drive-thru
somewhere." If I told him that I'd never been to a drive-

thru fast food place, he would have probably laughed at me. Also, it would have been entirely too much information and a glimpse into my actual life. Hell, I could count the number of times I'd been in a car with my fingers and toes. My parents were all about public transportation. We'd never owned a car. As a matter of fact, our neighbors rented our driveway to park their minivan. Everybody won. They avoided tickets on their second car and we looked like normal people who were home.

"I don't eat fast food." Rafael shot me a look like I was an idiot. Maybe I was. I'd seen his body.

But I decided to push. "Ever? Is that against Anton's rules for upper management?"

"There's no rule. You know what they put in that shit? Some of it isn't even meat."

Oh no. No, no, no, no. It was as if my mother were standing in front of me. Getting away from a clean, sheltered life was the entire point. How could that guy be more worried about fake food than the chemicals he sold to junkies? Again, confusing.

I dropped my head back. "If you want this arrangement to move forward, you will have to promise me one thing."

Rafa squinted. "I doubt that's gonna happen."

"You don't get to lecture me or judge my food choices. It will make me hate you more than I already do."

His eyes lit up and he grinned from ear to ear. *Oh, Christ.* I'd given him ammunition. He *wanted* me to hate him. He thought it was hot. He was into *hate fucking.*

"You're sick in the head," I said, adding a disgusted frown for good measure. "But yeah, let's get some food. You're buying."

Back down the elevator we went, and in the lobby we ran into Anton, who was flanked by three of the crew. The bald one's dark eyes ran the length of me and he licked his lips. A cold shiver shot up my spine. I would be toast if it weren't for Rafa.

"Rainbow Brite and Goldie Locks. You make me any money yet today?" Anton clicked his tongue.

I hadn't even been there three hours. How was I supposed to have made him money?

"As a matter of fact, we have." Rafael dug the wad of cash we'd found — well, he'd found — out of his pocket. "The backpack I stole had this." He tossed Anton the money with a bemused smile.

"See?" Anton turned to the guys behind him. "This? This is what I'm talking about. Goldie delivers. What have you three done today?" Then to Rafa he asked, "Where you going?"

"Gotta get another computer. You need anything?"

The crew's dynamic fell into place. I understood the reason Rafael lived with Anton. Not only could he provide, but he took care of the bossman. If I hadn't witnessed Rafa finding the money with my own eyes, I would have thought the exchange between them had been rehearsed. There was an obvious lesson for the rest of the crew. *Shit.* That included me, too. I eyed the money in the Anton's thick, scarred hands. Was I imagining that it was thinner than what I'd seen at the park?

"Jimmy…" Anton tapped the back of the youngest of the three. "You have double bench duty today. Let's see if you can make more money than Goldie." They disappeared behind the elevator doors and we exited the building.

"Come on." Rafa lead me to a black SUV and the lights flashed as he pressed on the key fob. I hopped into the passenger's side like it was no big deal to be in a car. We drove south along the river and I wondered about what I'd gotten myself into. What would happen to Jimmy if, and probably when, he didn't make as much money as Rafael? And what would happen to me if I didn't make Anton money? It remained essential that I keep my life a secret. I didn't want anyone showing up on my parents' doorstep if I decided that the crew wasn't for me. My entrance strategy had been a joke. The exit would need to be considered carefully.

Rafa turned into Midtown and found an outdoor lot for the SUV. "There's a salad place on the next block," he said once he'd handed over the key to the attendant.

"I don't want to eat a salad."

"It's your lucky day. They have sandwiches, too." Rafa faked surprise or disdain, I couldn't tell which, but I followed him anyway.

Inside the shop, we waited in line, and when I heard the guy in front of me order a BLT with mayo, I nearly kissed him for his sandwich inspiration. I asked for it on white bread, just to make sure to really disgust Mister 'I don't eat fast food' Rafa, and laughed while he ordered a salad, without dressing, and three chicken breasts on top. Minus the meat, my mama would have been proud of his food choices. The reasons to despise him just kept rolling in.

Rafael stayed to collect our order and I found a high table next to the window. I opened my bottle of soda and took a swig. I liked being in the city and having a small purpose. While I wasn't going to make friends with the crowds of strangers around me, it was still more lively and reassuring than my basement.

I'd need to go back and copy some of my work onto a hard drive so we could officially set up in Covington. And what would I do with Spock? Maybe he would be better off with my parents. But then, how would I sleep?

"One fat sandwich with a side of artery clog." Rafael slid a red plastic basket toward me. My mouth watered and I wiggled my fingers in delight. He could take his bland salad and suck it. I was eating bacon, lettuce and tomato. My ratio for bad-to-good was better than normal.

I tore off a bite and smiled my way through the chewing.

"So how long do you think before we get paid?" Rafa stabbed leafy spinach with his plastic fork and popped it into his mouth.

"It depends. We need to find a target, then a person, then create a fake friend. Probably six months."

Rafa choked then coughed. "But you already have the Zapata Falls connection. That could be a matter of days."

Instead of taking the bite I'd intended, I froze and glared at Rafa. The sandwich was inches from my mouth and mayonnaise mixed with tomato seeds to create a pink stream down my wrist.

"Zapata Falls is mine."

After a slow swallow, Rafa brushed his tongue over his teeth with his mouth closed. "You showed the bossman Zapata Falls. That's what he thinks he's getting."

"In no uncertain terms did we agree to that." Heat crept up my neck and I licked the drippings from my wrist before chucking the sandwich into the basket. I'd lost my appetite.

"You belong to Covington now. What's yours is ours and vice versa, baby girl."

Ugh. He was *not* serious. And he'd called me 'baby girl' again. *Asshole.* I shook my head. No way they were getting my Nate loot.

Rafa tilted his head, his eyes were almost forgiving and pretty. "M, you made a grave error in coming to us. You should have sold me the malware and counted your money in your unicorn-themed bedroom. Now that Anton knows what you can do, he wants you to prove your worth."

"And if I don't?"

"Then I follow you home, discover what or who you're running from and find a way to motivate you to come back." He softened and his pity stabbed me in the chest. "This isn't a game."

My heart stopped and my mouth went dry. He was serious. "I thought you were nice."

His warm eyes flashed a sad apology. "Are you who you say you are online?" He held my gaze until he looked down and pronged more salad like it was no big deal what he'd just said. Like I wasn't essentially being held captive.

How had I been such an idiot? Right, the entire zero social skills and street smarts.

I witnessed the rest of the outing like an out-of-body experience. We bought a monitor and a tower—Rafa hadn't given all the money to Anton—then we carried them back to the car.

When we got to Covington, the first drops of rain started to fall and the wind picked up. The storm I'd sensed earlier in the day was coming in. Random litter swirled in the courtyard and my short hair flipped.

"There go our plans for tonight," Rafa said once we'd entered the building. "Can't go to an outdoor bar in a rainstorm."

"I should go before it gets too bad." I set the monitor at his feet. "I'll see you tomorrow."

Rafa puckered his lips and closed an eye. "But you live here now, baby girl. Remember, you said, 'I'll take it.'" His thick eyebrows jumped once.

My heart dropped into my stomach. I probably should have fucking run but I didn't. Instead, I did the same thing I'd been doing the whole damn day. I followed him like a lost sheep. I even punched in the code to my new apartment and opened the door while he carried the heavy computer tower into the bedroom to the left.

Time and a clear head — that was what I needed. I would make good on my promises then get out. Hell, maybe I could give them Nate and Zapata Falls then be on my merry way. But one thing was becoming more and more evident. I'd bitten off way more than I could chew.

Computers and the virtual world were effective for hiding. Real life? Well, it was…real.

Rafa came back to the common area of the apartment. "Don't worry," he said with a sarcastic smile. "I'll get the screen."

I rolled my eyes. "I need to make a private phone call." After one more sour glance in his direction, I headed to the bedroom I'd claimed as my own. Not only did I close the door, I went into the bathroom, shut that one too, and flipped on the sink and shower. I dialed my mom's number and she picked up after three rings.

"Hello?" The confusion in her voice probably meant that the number on her screen was blocked.

"Hey, Mom." I cleared my throat and hoped it wiped away the hint of emotion. "I'm going to stay with my friend in the city tonight. You know I hate to walk home in a storm."

"I know you hate storms in general. That's why you spend most of your time in the basement. But do you really think it's a good idea to stay with him? I know you're twenty, but, Marigold, I hadn't even heard of this person until yesterday. Now you're spending the night?" The judgment in her voice reminded me why I'd fled in the first place.

But the more details I could feed her without being precise, the more at ease she would be and it would be one less worry. "Yeah. I'm helping him with a project, so it will be a great distraction from the storm. I'll be home tomorrow."

"Well, I don't like this spur-of-the-moment business. I want to meet this Rafael if you are ever planning on staying there again. Find out his intentions."

"Eww. Ma. We're friends...and I'm an adult." An adult with horrible judgment and spontaneous tendencies that would lead to who knew what. Also, I was a criminal and perpetual liar, perhaps an overall bad person.

Before she could object further, I said, "I gotta run. I'll see you tomorrow."

I shut off the faucets and exited the bathroom. The bed, with crisp, folded-back sheets looked clean and tempting. I sat down on the edge and unlaced my combat boots. There was a hole in my tights at the left big toe and my bright pink polish stared back at me.

Maybe if I curled up, I would eventually wake up and it would be a bad dream. I crawled to the head of the bed and under the covers. I closed my eyes and begged the clock to turn back. It had been beyond stupid to come to Covington without checking them out. I nuzzled into the soft pillow and let out a small whimper.

The only problem with my self-pity was that I knew damn well that I would have gotten on that train and taken the ride uptown either way. I'd seen a real criminal organization interested in my talents and conveniently located in my backyard as a sign that I was ready to play with the rough and tumble.

Cocky. That was what hiding behind my screen for three years had gotten me, an inflated sense of self-worth that didn't translate in person. I was very much an imposter.

And people like Rafa? Half computer geek, half muscle head? Either a genetic miracle or a straight-out abomination.

The door slammed and I jolted. He was gone, had left me alone, and there was a fucking storm outside. *Great.* There were probably cameras all over the building. If I tried to leave, I was sure to be caught. Also, I wouldn't go out in the storm. Its potential destruction was more threatening than the crew. The known fear trumped the unknown.

I bundled myself up in the massive duvet — the king-sized bed was far too big for me — and headed out to the living area. I found the remote to the flat-screen and flipped through the channels.

The rain pelted the window to the side of the screen and I hugged my blanket even tighter. I couldn't risk tears. If Rafa or any of them came in, I would be more toast than I already was.

The six episodes of *I've Never Seen My Fiancé* I binged on weren't doing enough to distract me. I got up and made myself a cup of tea — a funny thing to have in the cupboards for thick and violent criminals — and sipped it as I tried to come up with a plan.

How difficult would a double-hack be? More importantly, how dangerous? *No.* That would be even more stupid and risky than what I was already facing. I walked to the bedroom where Rafael had taken the computers and set my mug on the long dresser opposite the bed. In the bathroom, I found a nail clipper, and with the tiny blade meant for cleaning, I sliced open the tape on the two big boxes.

A gust of wind whipped more rain at the window over the bed. I would never be able to focus with the storm reminding me of its presence. I headed back to the living room, flipped the channel to a vintage punk music station and cranked the music my dad had introduced me to from his days prior to tree hugging. Maybe the anarchist didn't fall so far from the tree after all.

Music blaring, I regained some sense of self and confidence. Hooking up a computer was not a daunting task, but it was a methodical one. It kept me busy and passed the time. I didn't even text Rafa for the Wi-Fi password. I hacked into the system for fun and did an old-school password finder that took me an hour to break. I bet he didn't even realize.

Then I accessed my remote server and grabbed a few of my favorite programs. As the download icon filled, I tapped the metal frame of the laptop. If I just made money, all would be well. And if I could keep Rafa close, maybe my safety would be assured.

Still, I was sure I'd made a horrible mistake.

Chapter Seven

Rafa

As I walked out of my bedroom, the bass booming from the hallway of the third floor grew more annoying, and Anton shot me a snarl from the couch.

"That's on you." He toggled his finger to the door and turned up the volume of the basketball game he was watching with Scooter.

I twisted my baseball cap from back to front and shaped the bill. Yeah, that was on me. Why in the nine circles of hell had M agreed to come back that morning? She'd had a good look at us. She could have just sold us her program. And once she started earning Anton real money? She'd be like the rest of us—here for good. I still wasn't sure how Leo had gotten a pass.

As I reached for my phone, it flashed with a text from Jackson that he was making chili and that I should swing by. With the storm brewing outside, no one was on the bench. Shitty weather was bad for business.

"I'll catch you later," I said and exchanged a nod to the boss. Scooter offered the peace sign as his goodbye. I was glad he was there to hang with Anton. It made me leaving easier.

I got closer to her door and wondered if I hadn't exchanged buddy duty for babysitting. M was a classic nerd and an introvert with no street smarts. But she was pretty...and sexy. Did she even get how hot she was?

I didn't bother knocking. There was no way she'd hear, so I punched in the code and the door clicked open. The music was louder inside and the wall of sound slammed into me and stung my ears. The assaulting source was the TV, and I jogged over to the couch and thankfully spotted the remote. I clicked the power button and I was sure the entire third floor let out a sigh and a thank you.

"Hey!" M came down the hall with her arms crossed. She wasn't wearing her boots, which made her even smaller than she already was—like a little mouse—and there was a hole in her tights where her big toe stuck out.

"You working?" I asked and gestured to the back bedroom. The thought of her punching code just down the hall from me was a bizarre turn-on. That...and her glare. The disdain barreling into me from her blue eyes might have made my dick twitch just a little.

M grimaced. Shit, I was busted again for dirty thoughts. But did I honestly care?

I licked my lips.

"Eww." M shuddered but it was fake as hell. "Come on. You can help me think of things for Nate to say. I'm about ready to kill his cat."

I followed her to the bedroom with the computers and smiled at the wiggle of her thin hips. When I

75

managed to take my eyes off her, I found that baby girl had been busy since I'd left her.

"Do you have a notebook or something? As you well know, I change my passwords all the time and I keep track of them manually." M sat on the floor with her back against the side of Jackson's old bed and picked up the laptop next to her.

"Yeah, sure." I didn't tell her I did the same thing and that I had small notebooks everywhere. I walked back to the kitchen, found one in a drawer, grabbed a pen and went back.

"Here." I tossed them to her.

"Thanks." M's docile smile sparked my curiosity. What had changed from lunch where her face had fallen and the reality of her biting off way fucking more than she could chew had finally settle in? Best to play my cards carefully. She might not have understood the dynamics of a crew and street crime, but being behind a computer was her strong suit.

"I downloaded some of my tools. I have a password breaker that's fucking genius, if I do say so myself." M pivoted the laptop so I could see a program running and code flashing, then set it down to her left. She picked up the notebook and with loopy handwriting began putting some words down.

It was odd, the twinge of guilt pestering my gut. When had I ever beat myself up about being a bad boy? But that tiny sentiment was easily lost in the massive hunger to get my hands on that cracker. I could break into her phone, find out her name, everything, using her own tools against her. It was wicked. I couldn't wait.

"Do you think we could get a couple of desks and chairs? Sitting on the floor like this is not great." M stuck the pen in the spiral of the small notebook and tossed it to the side.

"I'll get them tomorrow. No sweat." I dropped my eyes to the crook in her neck, wondering if she tasted as sweet as she smelled.

"Stop fucking looking at me like you're going to eat me." Her glare was back and I was pretty sure I was falling in lust with it. "Jesus, Rafael. Get a fucking grip. Also, when the storm is over, I need to go fetch a hard drive and some clothes. Probably Spock."

"Yeah, sure," I said with a smile. If I hadn't cracked her phone by then, I'd tail her or just insist on going with her. There was no way I would let her slip through my fingers.

I wondered if her frown meant my agreement was too easy, so I changed the subject.

"My friend Jackson makes a mean chili and is just down the hall." I thumbed over my shoulder. "There's no point in going out. You want to join? Otherwise, I'm not sure what else there is to eat in here. I'll have someone get your groceries once it stops raining." I pointed to the notebook. "Make a list."

M glanced at the window then back to me with an uneasy look on her face. "Actually, that would be nice. Both things." She pushed to her feet. "Just let me get my shoes."

It was a perfect example of how her instincts were off. I was being nice. That should have waved a flag of bullshit and danger. Once she left the room, I set the alarm on my phone for an hour later then slipped it back into my pocket. She really was making it all too easy.

We knocked on Lisa's door five minutes later and Jackson answered with a dishtowel over his shoulder.

Cumin, peppers and tomatoes filled the air and my mouth watered. I loved Jackson's sweet potato chicken chili.

"Jackson, this is M. M, this is Jackson."

"We met before." M held out her hand but was met with a quirked eyebrow. We didn't exactly shake hello in Covington Heights.

Jackson held the door open wider and we entered. Lisa came over with J.J. on her hip. "Hi, I'm Lisa and this handsome boy is Jackson Junior."

J.J. waved before he slid down the side of Lisa's body and toddled over to a kid's table in the corner. A puzzle sat in disarray and he picked up a piece and examined it. Lisa offered a warm smile to M and said, "So you're the new girl. Nice to meet you. Want a beer?"

M's eyes lit up and she grinned. It may have been the first genuine emotion she'd shown all day. "I'd love one." M and Lisa went to the kitchen, Lisa saying how she loved M's hair but would never be brave enough to do that to hers.

Jackson and I man-hugged. "How was the bench before the storm?"

He shrugged. "Slow. And I can't get anyone to come to the dice game. There are still rumors about us taking out our clients."

"Yeah," I said with a sigh. "I mean, I know he had his reasons, but other than a couple of streets north, we didn't gain much. Plus, where the fuck did Leo go?"

Jackson rubbed his bald head and gave me a pained look. "This stays between us. You got it?" His voice was low and more serious than I'd heard in months.

I nodded. Secrets were power.

"Fiona reached out to Lisa."

"Oh damn." That was some serious information.

"Yeah. Damn. Now she's got in her head that there is some sort of 'happily ever after' for us, too." He'd dismissed the idea, but I understood my best friend. He wanted more for his son, for his life. There was a sliver of hope buried under his brush-off.

We glanced over to Lisa and M, who were still talking about beauty products.

Jackson lifted the lid off his big pot and stirred the orange stew. "Anyway, keep that shit to yourself."

I walked over to the corner where J.J. sat at his plastic table and bent down. I made a fist for him to bump and he did without moving his eyes from the puzzle. "What's up, little man?"

"Doing this." J.J. secured the last piece of the border then banged it in with his flat, chubby palm.

I sat and draped an arm over my bent right leg, the left one straight. "You want some help?"

He shook his head. "Nope. I like to do it by myself."

"I get that."

His little tongue poked out of the side of his mouth and he held up a plain blue piece that was the same shade as the sky for his puzzle. It was the exact face Jackson made when he counted money. I wondered how much of the emulation was nature and how much was a desire to be like his daddy.

"Let's eat." Jackson set the pot in the middle of their table.

I scooped up J.J. and began our game of hand monster. I couldn't remember when it had started but it always went down with a fit of giggles. With my fingers held high like a crippled claw, I gave J.J. my serious fake face.

"The hand monster has missed your belly, young Jackson," I said in a slow, deep voice.

J.J. clenched his teeth tight and growled. He made two claws with his own hands. "My monsters have magic powers. They will control your brain." He reached up and planted them on my cheeks.

"Ah!" I slumped, making my movement as dramatic as my cry. "No, young Jackson, please. Not my brain waves." I shook, taking him along for the ride, then dropped to my knees. A little giggle bubbled out of him, and with him still in my arms, I fell back onto the hardwood floor in front of the couch. For the final touch, I closed my eyes and opened my mouth. I made a few choking sounds before I was stiff as a board below the laughing son of my best friend.

"Nice show. Come on. Time to eat." Apparently, J.J.'s dad was less impressed with my acting than his son.

I opened an eye in time to see Jackson roll his. Lisa grinned from ear to ear next to him, probably planning to hit me up to babysit again. M, on the other hand, had eyes the size of saucers and mouthed, "So weird," before she looked away and sat down.

"The hand monster will have his revenge," I whispered.

"Not without a brain." J.J. tapped his forehead.

We stood and I dusted off my jeans. I grabbed my water bottle and we headed to the table where Jackson was already serving us.

To M, I asked, "This going to be okay for you? I can get some mayo or find some butter for you to mix in."

Her reply was a beautiful snarl and I pulled out the chair next to her and sat. She thanked Jackson for her bowl and waited for the rest of us to start eating before she did. *Manners*. A possible sign of a wholesome upbringing—not unlike myself.

After a round of praises for his chili, Jackson cleared his throat. "So, I want to hear more about what you're doing for us, M."

J.J. perked up and studied their new guest while she searched for her answer.

"How come your name is a letter? L, M, N, O, P. It's a letter. Right, Lisa?"

Lisa answered, "I don't know, sweet boy. Maybe it's short for something, like Emma or Emily. We shouldn't presume." She gave him a small smile and a quick glance for approval from Jackson. She didn't want to overstep. To M, she said, "I'm teaching him the alphabet. He likes that part."

"L, M, N, O, P!" J.J. offered up on cue then took a happy bite.

M scooped a bite of her chili, ate it with a smile, then wiped her face with the napkin she'd placed on her lap. Yeah, manners all right.

"I don't want to bore you with the details," she said and did a little wiggle, "but basically it's online theft—not from individuals, more like…organizations. I'm working on something right now that would lift money off of nonprofits. You know, someone gives an online donation, and I just take a little of that for myself, masked as a handling fee."

Lisa and Jackson exchanged glances. Yeah, I'd found someone who liked to steal as much as I did. So what?

On cue, the alert on my phone went off and I stood before digging it out of my pocket. No reason anyone had to know that it wasn't a text message.

"Shit." I swiped a few times all dramatic-like. "I gotta go handle something for the boss. It should only take me thirty minutes. M, why don't you stay? I'll be back in a flash."

She searched around the room, maybe reading the temperature. Lisa popped up and said, "You should totally stay. Have another beer with me. My days of girl talk are too few and far between."

"Do you need any help?" Jackson asked. If I'd fooled him, I was set.

"Nah." I tucked my phone back in my pocket. "Shouldn't be long."

M barely acknowledged that I left, either because she was just trying to be cool or maybe she and Lisa had really hit it off. I jogged down the hall and passed Scooter on the way into my place.

"He's got company." Scooter's jutted chin said it all, but I only needed to be in and out.

In my closet, in the safe where I kept some cash, cards and occasionally a gun or two, I found M's original phone and slipped it into my back pocket. Giggles trailed behind me from Anton's room as the door closed.

I typed in M's code and was on the floor in the same spot she'd sat a little over an hour prior. With her loopy passwords from the notebook, I found everything I needed and I had cracked her phone with her own program within five minutes.

It was too easy. It almost took the fun out of it. *Almost.*

Back at my place, the giggles had switched to moans. Before popping the phone back in the safe, I copied its contents onto my laptop. I'd learned long ago that in theft, curiosity was your enemy and patience was an ushered success. I was dying to know M's name, home, favorite color, everything. But if I started reading, I wouldn't stop, and I had a tight schedule. Besides, my headphones and favorite music would be a much more welcome soundtrack to finding out about M than the current one coming from the bossman and his lady friend.

As I walked down the hall back to Jackson and Lisa's, a strange emotion pestered my gut. I'd stolen so much shit over the years and never looked back. I muttered a little "What the fuck?" then pushed down the twinge.

Chapter Eight

Marigold

Rain pelted against the window and I shivered. Rafael had been gone about a half an hour and Jackson was reading to J.J. in a bedroom. Lisa handed me another beer then joined me on the couch. I liked her. She had a soft kindness that stood out like a vivid flower in a field of weeds. Her smile was gentle, her voice calming.

"Don't like the storm, huh?" she asked just above a whisper, as if it would stay our secret.

"No. That obvious?"

She shrugged then took a drink.

I didn't know why I trusted her, and maybe I shouldn't have—my friend experience was limited at best—but I did.

I cradled my beer and let out a long breath. "I got caught in one when I was little. I was walking home from school and the wind was so strong that I was afraid to keep going. I hid in a doorway and cried until my mother finally found me."

She frowned. "I'm sorry. How awful. Those things mark us, don't they?" She glanced to the bedroom where J.J. and Jackson were, then back to me. "My mom was a junkie. She would have never come looking for me if I got caught in a storm."

Growing up, it was true that I'd been lucky in the parent department. But the day after that storm was when my life had changed. I'd become fearful of everything. I'd refused to go to school. It had taken me months just to go outside again. Forget friends... Little-girl-me had only focused on survival, and that began the smothering from my mother. At first, I'd welcomed it. But after years and years of it, I couldn't take it anymore. I'd changed, but she couldn't see that.

"Can I ask you a question?" I set the beer on the low table in front of us.

"Sure."

I leaned in, the small distance between us suddenly somehow became sacred. "Does it bother you? I mean, you're living with a criminal."

"Ahh...the morals." Lisa let out a little laugh. "Like I said, my mom wasn't great. I'm just happy having someone who loves me and thinks I'm more important than getting high. Sounds stupid and easy, but it's true."

It wasn't stupid — certainly if she'd grown up never feeling loved. What was my problem then?

Lisa went on with a smile, "I had a huge crush on Jackson for years. I practically jumped at the chance to take care of J.J. When he showed some interest in me, I thought I was imagining it or that he just wanted to get in my pants or something. But he loves me. The rest? The rest doesn't matter…not to me."

A light knock came from the door and Lisa went to answer. Rafa's golden eyes shimmered. Whatever his errand had required, it had been a success.

"Thanks for not banging. Jackson's putting him to bed."

Rafa winked at Lisa and a tiny bit of jealousy perked up. *What? No. Ugh.* His demonstration of being normal at family night had dropped my guard. And him stealing? That hadn't been hot…just dangerous and thrilling.

Then again, why not admit I was attracted to him? He checked me out every chance he got. Hell, he'd had a crush on me before he'd even laid eyes on me. Why limit my criminal experience? I could go all in.

I stood and thanked Lisa for a lovely night and she told me her door was always open. Jesus, I might have made my first girlfriend in ages — and in the flesh.

At my place, I punched in the code and the door clicked. "You want to come in for a bit?"

Rafa narrowed his light eyes. The black stubble of his beard shaded his face, and damn it if the heat radiating from his chest didn't hit me in a wave of lust. If he had leaned in, I would have kissed him. He wanted me. What was the point of me denying wanting him?

He dipped a shoulder and pushed by. A dim light from under the cabinets in the kitchen barely lit the open space. I hadn't remembered leaving it on, but then again maybe people came in and out of the apartments. *Shit.* I would need to lock my bedroom door.

Rafa walked over to the couch and sat. He dropped his head back and rubbed his neck. For the first time, I allowed myself to admit how gorgeous he really was. His tanned skin, dark hair and light eyes were exceptional. And his body? Insane. The guys I'd been with in the past were mostly nerdy like me. I'd never explored the possibility of being with a man so fit, so rough. Rafa removed his hat and tossed it on the floor next to him then raked his hands through his hair. It was short, but long enough where subtle curls kissed the ends and the shine made it look soft.

"How many people have the code to this door?" I went over to the couch and unlaced my boots.

"Just the main guys. Why?" He stretched and yawned.

"Someone could just walk in here and—I don't know—rape or kill me."

He laughed. "Not if I'm here."

"Because big bad Rafa can protect me?" I kicked off my boots and the cool air relieved my feet. It had been a big day of walking for someone who normally did a couple of trips around the block and sat in her basement.

"Exactly."

A crack of thunder made me jump.

Rafa peered at me with one eye closed. "You afraid of the storm?"

"No. Don't be ridiculous." I crossed my arms and sat down then pulled a blanket around me.

He studied me. "Did you ask me in not to be alone or because you want something else?"

Both. It was very much both. I brought my fist to my mouth while I contemplated sharing the truth. But there was no need.

A dangerous understanding twinkled in his eyes and a smug grin formed on his otherwise-flawless face.

He crawled over to me until we were nose to nose. I blinked several times. It was a fruitless attempt to deny the pull he had on me. His confidence, his danger, his body... It was all overwhelming. So what if I'd just met him? He'd already discovered more truthful things about me than any other guy I'd ever kissed. And that was basically nothing. Besides, those lonely nights in the basement of my parents' house had left me hungry for attention. I *should have* yanked the emergency brake, but I was already spinning out of control.

His warm breath tickled my neck, and, in my ear, he whispered, "Do you know the best cure for fear?"

I closed my eyes, already surrendering to him. One day? I'd lasted one stupid day. Pathetic.

He trailed a gentle path up my arm and neck with his fingers. He tucked a strand of hair behind my ear and his way-too-soft lips brush against my jaw. I shook my head.

"No, you don't know? Or no, you want me to stop?" Rafa cupped my neck and I shuddered. I had a spot just below my hairline that was a direct line to my arousal and that gorgeous shit had brushed it with his thumb. It would have been impossible for him to know about it. He really was a lucky bastard. With his other hand, Rafa drew me closer to him.

I dropped my head back, giving him more access to my neck. Need pooled inside me as the energy around us swirled and created our own perfect storm.

"No. I don't know." My words were more of a moan. The trance he'd put me in so quickly with just a breath and a touch was alarming, risky and enslaving. He'd reeled me in masterfully and I didn't care.

I allowed him to push me to my back and I searched his eyes before they closed and he went back to my neck. I would have given all the money in my bank account for him to have kissed me right then.

"You have to forget fear, M. I can help you. I can make you forget."

It was already working. And why the hell not? In fact, it was a fantastic idea. It wasn't like it would mean anything. He wasn't exactly the caring type—neither was I, for that matter. Yeah. A little hook-up to pass the time and take my mind off of the pouring rain and whipping winds outside. *Sign me right up, GoldieLocks.*

If I didn't know better, I would have called him a genius.

Rafa kissed around my jaw and my breath became heavy in my chest. He hovered his lips over mine for far too long without connecting.

"Is that what you want?" he whispered. "Do you want me to make you forget?"

My body screamed for his touch and I nodded.

"You gotta say it, baby girl. Say yes." His voice, calm and quiet, still held so much command. I didn't know what his plan for me was, only that he had one. And his tone made it deliciously, sinfully inviting.

"Yes." There was something wrong with my submission, a faint voice in the back of my head cried foul. But it was muted the second our lips met and his slow hypnotic kiss lulled me farther into the spell he'd already cast.

His deliberate movements ran opposite my longing, and when I tried to kiss deeper, go faster, he hindered my advances by pulling away. It didn't take me long to understand that he was completely in charge of me, both mind and body.

He must have spent an hour just unbuttoning my shirt. The curiosity of his next move dug its greedy claws into me while the paralyzing grind of his hips was both agonizingly blissful and splendidly punishing.

And his kiss? It was by far the best sin I'd ever committed. Unhurried twirls of our tongues were perfectly shared with light pecks sweeter than any sugar I'd ever tasted. I was lost and I never wanted to be found. It was almost as if he was the truest form of himself, thoughtful yet sublimely deviant.

Rafa cupped my breast under my bra and let out his own deep-throated moan. At least he'd let me know he was enjoying it as much as I was, which seemed impossible. I'd never kissed anyone so purposefully before. The tiny twist of my nipple shot a deeper need between my legs and I was sure that if he kept rubbing his erection against me, I would explode.

As if reading my mind, he let up and kissed down my neck until his warm tongue landed on *the* spot. I could have screamed, begged him to fuck me, pleaded with him to go faster. But silence was the cloak of our desire, and his drawn-out euphoric torture the chain holding me down, keeping me quiet—making me his.

He was in charge and there was nothing I could do about it—nothing I wanted to do about it. I was confused, and yet everything was crystal clear.

Behind his gentle ways was an underlying roughness, present in his coarse fingertips, the scratchy stubble on his cheeks, the occasional nip that replaced a kiss. It was equally heady as the hesitant game he was playing with my body.

Every inch of my torso had been touched, kissed, licked or nipped before he unbuttoned my shorts. The zipper tick, tick, ticked down, only amplifying my need. By the time he slipped a finger between my folds, I was a puddle.

His sleepy tease hushed all my doubts about what we were doing, what I was doing. I'd never know anyone to be as meticulous and patient. All my other hook-ups acted like they better get the show on the road before I would change my mind.

Rafa? Either he didn't care if I did or was convinced I wouldn't.

When a part of his hand brushed over my clit, I had never been more ready to be undone. The slower he went, the more I spun. He literally had me wrapped around his finger. The path he drew widened just when I thought he would tighten it, which only made me pray harder that he would give me the release I craved.

Rafa paused to pull off my shorts and tights then yank off his own shirt. I allowed myself a glorious glance at him, the beautiful bad boy savoring me. I wondered if I hadn't fallen asleep and it was all a dream. That seemed more likely than the raw truth.

I threaded my fingers through his dark hair as he trailed down my stomach. His tongue replaced the tease of his fingers, its track equally calculated. When a digit slipped inside and taunted a drawn-out come-hither movement and he sucked my clit, the waves of ecstasy that were begging to be released followed obediently.

The crash hit me hard at the base of my spine and warped upward. I shook until I trembled, the pent-up release leaving a buzzing between my ears and flipping my skin from hot to cold in an enraptured second.

Rafa wiped his mouth with the back of his forearm and stood. He tossed the duvet over me and swiped his T-shirt from the ground. Around the couch he walked before grabbing a bottle of water from the fridge. I was sure he would leave, but he went back to the bedroom where we had the computers and closed the door instead.

Right. We weren't the cuddling type. But damn, I guess I'd won the sex lottery because he also wasn't asking for anything in return. I laid there, stunned and confused, until I realized that the rain had stopped and the wind had died down.

The storm outside was over. Without him near me, hushing the voices in my head with his sinful mouth, they chanted a warning of a new storm—one I'd brewed myself. They scolded me for my continuously hurtful and selfish behavior. They begged me to get out and never come back to Covington Heights. They pleaded with me to not act on my destructive instincts.

They were the same voices that had kept me inside all those years, and trusting them had proven to be a horrible idea. What had Rafael said to me hours prior was right. I needed to forget fear.

I gathered my things, and with the duvet wrapped around me, I headed to my room. Sleep came too easy and I woke up the next morning when the door to the apartment banged shut. He'd spent the night. I'd managed my first night in Covington. Too bad it didn't reassure me.

After a little clean-up, I got dressed. I drank a tea and made my little grocery list. I posted a status update for Nate. I still couldn't bring myself to kill his nonexistent cat. A couple of hours after I'd gotten up, I called Rafa. He didn't answer, which I thought odd, so I went down the hall and knocked on his door. I needed to tell him I was running home to get some things, I didn't want it to seem like I was bailing. Why I cared was something I wasn't willing to think about.

The guy I'd seen the day before, Jimmy, answered the door with a crooked grin that could have been mistaken as a snarl. His gaze raked over me, the dirty thoughts in his mind practically jumping out of his eyes.

I cleared my throat. "I'm looking for Rafa."

"I'll tell you where he is...for a price."

"Really?" I rolled my eyes. "You're *really* starting your day stupid? I could make up any number of lies about you and he'll believe me." I gave Jimmy the dopey smile he deserved.

He winked and it was hideous. "Can't blame a boy for tryin'. Addicts offering to suck your dick for drugs gets pretty old after the first few times." Jimmy shook his head and continued, "Clean girl like you? Well, us boys, we notice that."

Jimmy pushed by me and sauntered across the hall. He may have thought his little swagger was impressive but to me it was just pathetic. He typed in a code for a door and it popped open. With a wave of his hand, he ushered me in then left without a word.

Right. The workouts. At least my presence hadn't actually been required. I was thankful for Rafa's lie.

Anton and Rafa were in only sweatpants and their chests glistened with perspiration. They didn't check to see who'd come in and Rafa ducked quickly out of the way of Anton's punch. They were definitely not holding back. The guy they called Scooter ran on a treadmill toward the back of the improvised gym and Jackson bench-pressed in front of him.

But my attention was to the fight in the middle of the dark blue mat. Rafa landed a blow on Anton's side then successfully blocked the counter punch. The offensive move lit something up behind Anton's creepy blue eyes

93

and his attack on Rafa intensified. Blow after blow landed until Rafa bent all the way down and took out Anton's legs with a swift circular kick.

Anton fell on his ass and laughed as he draped his arm over a knee. "That is so utterly Ricci. I can't believe I didn't see it coming. It's good, though. Keeps me guessing." His gaze drifted over to me. "Ah. Rainbow Brite. You make me some money today?"

"Working on it, boss." I'd been there less than twenty-four hours. How could I possibly have made him any money? But saying, 'No. Are you insane?' didn't strike me as a valid option.

"Jackson!" Anton called. "You're up." The bossman stood and dusted off his pants. Rafa grabbed a white towel from a rack holding dumbbells and wiped his face while he headed over to me. He wrapped it around his neck and jutted his chin in my direction.

"What do you need, baby girl?"

More of him sweating, that was for sure. Why did men look divine when they worked out?

"I, uh…" Needed to pull my shit together. His half-naked body was a distraction. I shook my head and a tiny smile on his clean-shaven face told me I was busted. *Damn it.*

I started again, "Like I said yesterday, I need to go get a few things and I wanted to tell you so that you didn't think I was running away or something."

"I'm not worried about that." He licked his lips and a confident power came over him. Was he so cocky that he thought one orgasm—okay, one fucking amazing orgasm preceded by mind-blowing foreplay—was enough to keep me around? He was a fool.

I laughed a little. "You're not afraid I won't come back?"

Rafa leaned in and the heat from his body engulfed me, intimidating me more than I wanted to admit. "No," he whispered, "Miss Marigold Pfeifer of Bay Ridge, I am not."

My heart stopped and the blood drained out of my head, leaving me faint.

He knows my name and where I live.

Everything.

All the power I'd been clutching onto with anonymity gone in a gut-wrenching poof. I had to remind myself to breathe.

It was one thing that he could find me, an entirely different one that he could expose me. And, holy shit — my parents.

But how? I'd been with him for most of the night. So when? Jesus. I thought back to the night before. He'd been so fucking calculated.

I reached up to slap him, but he caught my wrist.

"You used me." I yanked my arm away.

"*I* used *you*?" He chuckled. "You asked for it, baby girl. You said yes. It was quite clear."

"You're fucking sick." I hated him. It was all a game.

Rafa opened his arms, exposing his colorful tattoos. "I keep telling you. I'm not a nice guy. Just cuz you came on my face doesn't mean I've lost perspective."

"You're vile."

He beamed. "You probably shouldn't like kissing me so much then."

I crossed my arms and sent my best eye daggers. "That's never fucking happening again."

Rafa ignored the threat and waved his hands for me to leave. "Go home. Get your shit. Hell, bring your dog if you want. Then get your ass back here. We have work to do."

I turned around and marched to the door. "I fucking hate you, Goldie Locks."

"You know I want you too, right?" he called from over my shoulder.

Asshole.

I slammed the door behind me and did a proper pout against the wall in the hallway. I was screwed.

Chapter Nine

Rafa

I glanced at the door a final time and licked my lips. Miss Marigold Polaris Pfeifer had tasted way fucking sweeter than I could have imagined. The only problem was confessing I'd found out who she really was had probably ruined any chances for second helpings...or maybe not. She liked playing with fire. I'd known that before I'd laid eyes on her. It was too bad she couldn't see how fear was eating away at her. Too bad for her, anyway. I didn't mind how she'd 'coped'.

I walked over to the second treadmill and climbed up next to Scooter. The machine beeped several times until I found the speed I wanted, and I jogged at a rate just a little bit faster than Scoot. We were always doing that—one upping, proving who was tougher, faster, better. It was how we thought we stayed in Anton's favor—by being better than the next guy. Not very mature, but not much we did was.

As my feet and heart pounded at a steady pace, I caught Scooter checking my stats before rolling his eyes.

Without showing the strain the running was having on my body, I asked, "Can you get me a couple of desks and some decent chairs? We're officially setting up hack shop."

"Yeah," he panted. "No problem. I'll get them while you work the bench."

"Cool. There might be a grocery list, too." I shifted my gaze to Jackson and Anton sparring in front of us. Jackson, with his long arms and legs, had a height advantage, but Anton was getting the best of him, mostly because of rage. Anton had an internal power that the rest of us didn't. Before Leo had left, he'd given me private fighting and shooting lessons. He'd explained to me that the opponent's advantage needed to become their weakness in order to get the upper hand on them. He wasn't wrong.

That was what I'd done to Marigold. I'd used her own program against her. It was also how I'd gotten Anton to fall when we'd fought. He still saw me as the earner, not the fighter. He underestimated me. So had she. It was a powerful tool.

I ran for twenty more minutes, all the while studying Anton and his techniques. Yes, he was stronger. Yes, he had more pent-up anger than I'd ever seen. But he wasn't unbeatable.

Scooter had moved to lifting weights and I shut off the treadmill. Anton told Jackson they were done and we congregated around the bench where Scooter did his biceps curls.

"Right," Anton said as he wiped the sweat from his brow with a little white towel. "Goldie in the courtyard to start. Jackson, you and me are headed upstate for supplies."

It was funny that he referred to drugs as 'supplies'. He never said 'meth' or 'dope' or 'fucking poison', maybe because there was such a demand that he thought it was our duty to supply it. Or maybe he hated selling that shit as much as the rest of us did.

He continued, "Scoot, check those Bradford recruits and make sure none of them are using. Raf" — Anton's steel eyes narrowed and bore into me — "word on the street is that Jefferson has started to host the games. I want to know where. I want to know who is going. I want to know how much they are charging. Then I want to burn them to the fucking ground."

I nodded once. *Fucking Jefferson Manors*. They'd stepped up their game in the last month and taken full advantage of the rumors that we'd shot one of our patrons. Even though Mac had been a slimy fuck, he'd still been a regular at our poker nights. Taking him out had proven to be costly. It had given our regular players a reason to try Jefferson.

"Shower. Eat. And make me some fucking money today." Anton looped his arm around me and guided me to the door. For my ears only, he said, "So…Rainbow Brite. How long until she puts money in a secret bank account?"

"Hard to say." I waited for him to exit then crossed the hall to our place.

Anton typed in the code and our door opened. Jimmy, who I was sure was a worthless fuckwit, popped up from the bar stool where he was sitting and stood at full attention for Anton. *Kiss-ass.*

"Out." Anton pointed to the door with his thumb and Jimmy scurried like a rat. "How many eggs you want?"

"Four?" I shrugged.

"Sheila!"

In seconds, a pretty blonde came from Anton's room wearing one of his black T-shirts that hit her mid-thigh. Her hair was a mess and she hadn't washed off her makeup from the night before. It made black smudges under her brown eyes. I offered her a small smile, poor thing. She probably thought she was special to him, getting to spend the entire night, stay in his bed.

"Eight eggs. Scrambled." Anton grabbed her ass. "Then we're gonna have a repeat of last night."

Sheila bowed her head and ran a hand up Anton's bare chest before stepping away and digging out a frying pan from the drawer under the cooktop. I'd seen her before and she knew her way around our kitchen — another reason she probably thought she was special.

"I'll shower first." Anton disappeared down the hall to his room. For all the luxury we'd given the third floor of the building, we hadn't been able to fix the pipes. The hot water was the only thing we couldn't control. Two showers at the same time was a constant flipping from hot to cold and we'd just learned to live with it.

I opened the fridge and grabbed the orange juice. Sheila brushed against me as she reached for the carton of eggs. Anton's girls weren't exactly subtle. It was like they understood their time was limited, all the while hoping it wasn't. She was pretty, just not my type.

"I heard there was a new girl around." Sheila cracked the eggs in a bowl and tossed the shells in the sink. "That your girlfriend?"

Jesus. That hadn't taken long. But then again, the rumors traveled as fast as our drugs in Covington.

I reached for a glass then carried it around the counter and sat facing Sheila. While I poured the juice I said, "That's none of your business."

She shrugged and dumped the eggs into the pan. "Some of us girls are just wondering why there are certain ones who can earn money and why we can't. Fiona—"

I held up my hand. Fiona and Leo were off limits to anyone not on the top tier. We didn't talk about them. In fact, we acted like they were a figment of the outsider's imagination.

Sheila rolled her eyes. "It's just that we're not really afraid of Bradford anymore. Half those guys work for Anton now and the other half buy their drugs from you guys. We don't need your protection. So why are Covington girls still doing your dishes and folding your fucking laundry?"

It was an excellent point. I'd secretly wondered when the girls would wake up and realize we didn't have much to offer them. The problem was, we couldn't pay them. In the three months since Leo had left and we couldn't run the games, we'd lost twenty grand a week. We were nearly fucking broke.

I drank my juice then wiped my lip with my thumb. "No one is forcing you to be here, Sheila."

"I want a job."

I bet she didn't have the courage to say that to the man in the other room. I bet she was like many before her who had mistaken my light eyes and dimpled smile for kindness. But I didn't give a fuck about her or her friends who came and went. Neither did Anton. And the truth? The horrible, sick, honest-to-God truth?

There would always be another Sheila. Someone would always come around.

Not for money, not for affection. We weren't giving that to anyone.

Because they were attracted to the power. It was a sad fucking cycle—one I had seen since I'd started working the bench. The clean girls the crew slept with were just as caught up in it as we were. It was also why girls who didn't throw themselves at us were instantly hotter than those that did.

Sick, fucked, twisted. All were true. It was part of why Leo sought out Fiona and why I had the hots for Marigold. And Anton? He'd never settle down with a girl from Covington. He was from an actual crime family. Jackson and I sometimes joked that Anton would have an arranged marriage with the daughter of the devil…if he ever settled down at all.

It was another way we differed. I'd grown tired of fucking random girls quick. Maybe it was part of why I'd gotten into liking them hating me. Did that make me sick? Sicker?

Sheila stirred the eggs in the pan and the spray stopped from Anton's bathroom. I stood and said, "Then go get one."

I had my shower and dressed in my drug-dealing uniform of all black with the added flash of my baseball hat. I ate my eggs alone to the soundtrack of flesh slapping then left the dishes. It was sad that she would do them before she left, sad that she wanted to come back and even sadder that she might not be invited to.

The bench was busy. It was always like that after a storm. Our customers had gone too long between fixes and they were practically lined up all damn afternoon.

The sight of them — itching their scabs and shaking in their tattered skin — turned my stomach.

When I'd first started selling drugs, it had never bothered me. Every face was a stranger. No one had a name. But that had faded. Too soon, I'd known every person who wanted to score. I'd memorized what they wanted, how much they could afford and I could calculate just the right quantity to get them high but not let them overdose. Dead junkies didn't pay the bills. Over time, I'd also learned who their kids were or a fucked-up reason why they'd fallen into the life of an addict. Ignorance had been bliss, and knowledge was hell. I fucking hated working the bench.

So when I spotted a giant blue pit bull and his tiny pastel-haired owner towing a rolling suitcase behind her, I genuinely smiled. I sent a quick text to Scooter, telling him he was officially on duty and I jogged over to meet Marigold once she'd crossed the street.

"Hey, big boy." I bent down and scratched Spock behind the ears and he licked my cheek.

Marigold's glorious snarl crossed her face. "Don't suck up to me by being nice to him. I still loathe everything about you."

I grabbed the leash and started walking toward our building. "And yet you came back."

She scoffed, and I'd never heard anything hotter. "As if I had a choice." The wheels of her suitcase rolled behind her in a loud rhythm that was randomly upset by a crack in the pavement.

"There's always a choice, baby girl."

She stopped and cringed. "Don't fucking call me that."

I couldn't keep myself from taking in the sight of her. She'd changed her clothes and I could only think about what they would look like in a ball on the floor. She had on a short, white T-shirt with a kitten in a saucer, a black choker necklace, a tiny skirt that barely covered her cute ass and her combat boots. She was a gothic nerd and fucking beautiful.

"Eww." She frowned. "You know you are so fucking obvious when you think about sex. Your face goes all drool emoji. Stop it."

Spock tugged at the leash and smelled the gate to the park. He lifted a leg and pissed down the rusted pole.

"Does he need more of a walk?" I asked.

"No," she said with her top lip still turned down. "He just needs a little one morning and night. Otherwise he holds it, cuz he's a good boy."

There was some sort of dig in there about me not being as well-trained as her dog, which I'd never claimed to be, so I shrugged off her desired insult.

"You don't walk him or throw a ball for him to exercise?"

"Ugh." Marigold passed by at a quickened pace. "You are fucking worse than my mother, who is convinced you are a nice person and my friend, by the way. If she only knew what an absolute asshole you are."

Her rasp? Insulting me like that? I fucking loved it. She yanked open the door to the building and stomped through the run-down lobby then banged the call button to the elevator a few times.

I leaned in to her, and Spock sat at my feet. "That would require you to be honest about who you really are and what you do. I doubt that's gonna happen." I inhaled her sweet scent and she smacked me away.

"Did you just fucking smell me?"

I grinned.

"You have a problem. A serious, disturbing, warped problem."

The door opened and we entered the empty elevator. God, I wanted to kiss her again, slam her little body against the fucking wall and shove my tongue down her beautiful throat.

"Oh my God." Marigold shook her head. "You get fucking turned on when I insult you." She brought her palms to her forehead. "Does this mean that if I'm nice to you, you'll stop eye-fucking me?"

I shrugged. I wasn't sure. But damn, her side-eye game was hot.

The elevator dinged open and I unhooked Spock's leash. He followed us to her door while she typed in the code. Once in, Spock made the rounds and smelled everything while Marigold dragged her suitcase behind her.

She banged around in her room for a good fifteen minutes while the dog and I settled on the couch. When she finally emerged, it was with a sour expression on her face and her hands on her tiny hips.

"So tell me, Rafael Emmanuel Santos. How did you figure out my identity?"

Were we using middle names now? *Fucking bring it.*

"Your phone. You had entirely too much information on there." I gave Spock a final scratch and stood. "Come on. The desks are here."

"You said you got rid of my phone." Marigold marched after me down the hall.

"I lie, baby girl. You should have figured that out by now."

The gap between us grew. I missed her buzzy energy and I turned around to see that she'd stopped following me.

"Oh. My. God." Marigold stared at me with a fallen face. "You cracked my phone with my own program. Zero fucking morals or code. Unbelievable. Just when I thought I couldn't hate you more, you prove me wrong. Wow."

"Must we do this every time you figure shit out? Stop expecting that I'm going to do something nice. It ain't gonna happen."

She huffed down in one of the black chairs Scooter had brought in. The bed was on its side against the wall and the two desks faced each other. "I hate you."

"Just the way I like it."

Marigold rolled her eyes and logged into the computer in front of her. I sat opposite and opened the laptop.

Our banter could wait. We needed to get the ball rolling and make a profit. I swiped away my lust and said, "Let's just kill Nate's cat and make some money. Do you think you can handle researching a new target or will I need to do all the work?"

She typed at a fast pace and I decided that Arizona was as good as any state to try to find a small city or county that wasn't equipped enough to handle hackers. The only sound between us was our keyboards for a good hour.

"How much?" she asked in a cool, quiet tone.

"What do you mean?" I hooked my head around her screen.

"How much money do you want to make off of Zapata Falls?" Her eyes were slits and she stared ahead.

"A hundred grand?"

Marigold nodded once and let out a slow breath.

"Too high?" I asked. I had no idea what the going rate was. But ninety thousand dollars would put a smile on Anton's face.

"No," she said, still not making eye contact. "It's perfect. Not too high, not too low."

I stood and walked around the table. The download bar on her computer was halfway.

"They don't even know I'm in the system. Man, you would think they had a security wall or something. It's sad. Pathetic even."

My nerves stood at attention. It was the same sensation as when I stole something in public. Marigold spun around in her chair and looked up at me with heavy lids.

"Now we wait."

"How do you normally pass the time until they pay?"

She shrugged. "I'm not very good at that part. I usually get a bowl of cereal and stare at the screen."

A soft ding came from her computer. We officially had all Zapata Falls information. Marigold twisted back around and logged into a bank account.

"It could take a couple of days or a couple of hours. No way of knowing." She sighed. "Show me what you found."

It was all very anticlimactic. I wasn't sure what I'd expected but it wasn't her casual brushing off of the fact we were holding an entire town and its sensitive information captive.

"Couldn't we…" I scratched my neck.

"What?"

"I don't know, wreak a little havoc?"

Her blue eyes flashed, and she grinned. "Yeah, actually, we could. Pull up a chair."

Chapter Ten

Marigold

Rafa rolled his chair from the other side of the desk and scooted in next to me. My skin tingled at the memory of his slow, selfless touch from the night before. I hated that I wanted more, hated that I'd come back for it. But most of all I hated him.

He'd laid a perfect trap for me and I'd dove in head-first. Every action I took, every word I spoke was a lie. I'd lied to my parents about where I was and a job they thought I had. I'd lied to myself that there was some way to play criminal and it would be fun. And I was lying with every breath to think that I wouldn't end up back exactly where Rafa wanted me, where *I* wanted me.

I brushed the truth from my mind, instead playing the game of telling myself it was all normal. I sat there and giggled while we flipped all eleven traffic lights in Zapata Falls to red at the same time. I convinced myself that none of it mattered because I'd finally found like minds to share my perverted sense of humor. I tried to enjoy it, not analyze if I was becoming more or less of my true self.

The buzzer to the apartment rang and Spock barked. Rafa shot me a tight, soft smile. Up close, I could see just how deep his dimples were. Many a girl had probably fallen into those little pits and been gone for good. Not me, though. I was still holding out hope that I could fake my way through not being attracted to him, not internally gushing about someone with his looks actually kissing my nerdy ass. Those little swoons were locked down deep and I was trying like hell not to let them raise to the surface.

He said, "I bet that's your groceries. Scoot said he found your list."

I gawked, stared and ogled his backside as he walked away. His shoulders were broad, and his jeans hung low on his hips. He probably had one of those asses that was all muscle but you couldn't tell until you'd taken a proper squeeze. Yeah, his body was a fucking fantasy—one I could explore if I could just figure out how to do so without giving him more of the upper hand.

Because while I'd thought that Covington would be an exciting lifestyle change, I'd been naïve in the worst way. I needed to get back my power.

After some hushed voices, the door closed and bags ruffled. The thought of everything on my grocery list at reach made my mouth water and I went out to the kitchen where Rafa held a jar of Fluff.

I clapped my hands together in delight.

"You can't be serious?" He twisted the jar and studied the blue and white label. "This is basically just sugar. Oh no, wait, there's corn syrup, too." He peered back at me. "You know that's not a vegetable, right?"

I leaned into the doorjamb and flipped him off. "Why do you care what I eat?"

Rafa licked his lips and narrowed his light eyes. He really needed to stop doing that. "Good point."

Spock jumped up and put his front paws on the counter next to Rafa.

"Did you get food for him?" Rafa asked and scratched Spock behind his collar.

I pushed off the frame and walked over to the island. "He eats whatever. Give me that."

Rafa shook his head but handed me the jar of Fluff. I opened it and tore off the protective seal then reached for a spoon behind him. I banged the silverware drawer shut with my hip and the contents rattled inside. Then I dug fucking in.

"Mmm-m…" I closed my eyes and licked the spoon. The artificial vanilla sugar hit my taste buds and they instantly craved more. "So fucking good."

When I glanced over to Rafa, I could see it. That hot little haze that filtered over his amber eyes when he thought about sex. And I wanted him thinking about sex. In the twenty-four hours I'd spent with him, I'd realized his attraction to me was one of the few things I could use to my advantage. *Fool.* Did he really think I was some kind of nice girl who was above manipulating a man with sex?

I scooped out another bite of the marshmallow delight and was ready to make sweet mouth-love to my spoon.

But in a boring tone he said, "Listen… I got some shit I need to do. I'm meeting someone. You want to head out to that bar tonight?"

Wait. What? Where did drooly face and his fuck-me-eyes go?

I swallowed down the Fluff. To be honest, I did want to go out. It was part of my internal push to get myself into new situations. "Sure."

"Great. Call me if the money comes in. I'll leave you to putting all your shit food away."

I didn't want him to go. The entire reason I'd gotten myself into the stupid illegal mess was to have some fucking company. But he was out of the door before I could find an excuse to object.

With an exaggerated frown, I stored the bags of chips and candy I'd ordered. I found a big mixing bowl and filled it with water for Spock, who promptly drank half and slobbered the other half in a slimy puddle on the floor. I grabbed a bag of orange, finger-staining chips and thumped down on the couch. Spock and I shared our junk food and I promised to make him a juicy steak the next time I ordered groceries.

Between episodes of *Dress for Your Stress*, it hit me. I didn't have to stay where I was, alone. I had the code to my door. I wasn't a prisoner.

"Come on, big boy." I hopped up, washed the fake cheese off my fingers and grabbed Spock's leash. We rode the elevator down, and once out of the building, the warm sun kissed my face. The guy they called Scooter was at the bench surrounded by a lot of younger and skinnier crew members.

A scuffle in the park caught my eye. Lisa had her head tilted to the side and her arms crossed. A sour expression blanketed her face and she shook her head at the woman standing in front of her.

Live drama wasn't something I was used to, and I probably should have passed by without sticking my nose where it didn't belong, but I wanted to be Lisa's friend. That started with me having her back.

I walked over to the enclosed park and Spock relieved himself on the rusty pole at the gate.

"Puppy!" J.J. jumped off the swing and both women's eyes followed him to me.

Before J.J. could reach out for Spock, I bent down to be at his same eye level. "Hey," I said with a little smile. "Remember me?"

"L, M, N, O, P!" J.J. reached for Spock, who promptly sniffed then licked his hand.

"Just M. Anyway, not all dogs are as nice as mine is, so you should always ask before touching one, okay?"

"He knows that." The woman who had been arguing with Lisa scowled over me. Her eyes were bloodshot and her skin was transparent, as if she'd never been out in the sun. And she was skinny, too skinny. Her upper arms had no muscle and her shoulder blades stuck out of her white tank top.

"Come on, Junior," she said as she waved him toward her. "You can say hello to the dog another time."

"Bridget"—Lisa closed her eyes and whispered the name—"I told you. You can't have him today. Not like that. Let's not make a scene…for him." Lisa nodded to J.J. and I tried to distract him by talking about Spock. But I kept my guard up and ears open.

"Which *him*?" Bridget spat. "My boyfriend or my son? It's hard to know which one you're trying to steal from me. Oh, that's right. It's both."

Lisa's jaw shifted and she let out a slow breath. Damn, she was impressive at keeping cool. I would have smacked the bitch by now. Well, in the version where I was a badass and not a computer nerd.

Bridget continued, her voice rising with each word, "And you don't want to make a scene? Well, too bad Miss Holier-Than-Thou. This is my kid, not yours. He's coming home with me."

I grabbed my phone from my back pocket and sent two words to Rafa.

Courtyard. Now.

"Hey." I stood and smoothed the back of my skirt. "Maybe you two can go inside and talk this out. I'll stay here with J.J. until things are sorted."

Bridget's top lip curled as she scrutinized me through squinted eyes. "Who the fuck are you?" Then to Lisa, "Who the fuck is *she*?"

"She works for Anton." Lisa's words sounded more like a warning than fact.

"Doing what? Dying Easter Eggs?"

Oh, bitch was going to throw down like that? "I – "

"You what?" Bridget challenged, puffing out her chest. I had to admit her street sass was intimidating. "Mind your own fucking business." The glare she sent me was way more threatening than her physical frame.

I looked over to Lisa, sending sympathy and an apology for my lack of power.

Bridget turned to Lisa, I was a mere gnat that she'd swatted away. "You have no legal grounds to keep my son from me. Tell Jackson he can come and pick him up when he gets back from wherever the fuck it is that he goes. But until then, I'm taking him."

The gate to the park banged. "Hey, Bridg. What's up, mama?" Scooter stepped closer to us with a soft smile on his face. I bent down and spoke in hushed tones to J.J. and Spock. Bridget was going to be handled, of that I was sure. Maybe Rafa wasn't there in the flesh, but he'd gotten my message.

"Come on," Scooter said and motioned for Bridget to join him.

She gave a final set of stink eyes to Lisa but walked toward Scooter. Lisa let out a sigh and raked her hands over her face. A second later, any stress she'd shown was replaced with a warm smile as she crouched down next to J.J., who was still busy petting Spock between sloppy kisses.

"Looks like you made a new friend, sweetheart."

I showed J.J. all Spock's tricks — sit, down, up, paw, other paw, until Lisa told him it was time for his snack. I accompanied them upstairs and didn't hesitate to agree to a cup of tea with Lisa.

We sat at their table and Lisa beamed as J.J. giggled while he 'accidently' dropped a few apple slices on the floor for the dog. Spock was in dopey dog heaven. I sipped my tea in awe of Lisa. She was one of those women who had silent strength. There wasn't anything bold or bitchy about her, two qualities that were often confused with inner fortitude. It was her softness and backbone that whispered she could be trusted. She was a beam of good amongst so much bad.

J.J. hopped down from the table and went to wash his hands without being asked. After, he led Spock down the hall to his bedroom.

"I don't think J.J. is the only one who made a new friend." I rolled my eyes but smiled.

Lisa let out a long exhale. Maybe she'd been holding it since the park. "I tell you what. It's not easy to make them. Junior was friends with a little girl who moved away and he's been a bit of a loner since then."

I probably shouldn't have asked but I was hoping to build a bridge that I might get to use one day. "What's the deal with his mom?" I kept my tone hushed.

"She's an addict. Wasn't always, though. She used to be fucking gorgeous. I think she started using as kind of a revenge against Jackson—a way to pull him back into her and J.J.'s life. But she got hooked." Lisa stared at her empty mug and flicked her thumbnail on the handle.

"Thank goodness that little guy has you. And the big one too."

Lisa leaned in and whispered, "You know what's sad? She didn't even really want to be with her son. The crew gives her a free fix for not throwing a fit in front of J.J. She does it every time Jackson is away."

That was sad—fucking depressing, actually. Had I enabled it with my message?

"Does J.J. understand it?"

She looked up, glanced to the hallway, then back to me. "I don't know," she said through a frown. "Sometimes I wonder if I'm not just being selfish, trying to give Junior the loving female role model I never had. And I know I'm being selfish about his daddy."

"Your eyes light up when you talk about him."

She scoffed out a laugh. "Oh, you want to talk about sexual chemistry?" she teased.

I scrunched my face like I'd taken a spoonful of disgusting medicine. "If I say something, do you promise never to repeat it?"

"M"—Lisa tilted her head and raised her eyebrows—"I am surrounded by men. They grumble, scratch their asses and think it's hilarious if they beat the shit out of each other. I'm loyal to Covington, yeah, but I'm also a girl who likes some dish. Serve. It. Up. I'm starving for gossip."

I pointed my finger at her like a warning—which was funnier than threatening—I'd proven I had no street game. "Not a peep."

Lisa zipped her lips and tossed the imaginary key over her shoulders while fighting a grin.

"He's so hot." I shook my head and closed my eyes. "So fucking hot."

She laughed and I didn't even care.

"You don't get it," I continued. "My world? It's all dorks and geeks. They are either super skinny or super fat. Find the oddball with the normal body and he wants you to call him Jon Snow. Rafa is a body builder with a nerd brain. It's…weird."

Lisa sat back in her chair. "I have no idea who Jon Snow is, but I'm just going to go out on a limb here and say it's possible you actually like weird."

I faked a snarl…but she was right.

Her gaze tightened. "How did you two meet, anyway?"

"Online. He actually had a crush on me."

"So it's mutual?" Lisa shrugged with a little shake at the end.

"I loathe him. He's an asshole and a perv."

I was expecting Lisa to laugh or tell me I was full of crap. Instead, she worked her jaw then said, "I grew up here. I know everyone. Rafa came a few years ago. I think he met Anton in jail or something. Anyway, he's not like them and yet he is. It's hard to explain."

I thought I knew what she meant. Maybe that was what I'd been picking up on from him all along. He wasn't like anyone—not fully anyway. Rather, he had distinct pieces that fit into multiple puzzles.

Lisa continued, "Take how he is with Junior. You think Anton or Scooter or any of those other guys give a shit about that beautiful little boy?" She shook her head.

We sat in silence for a few moments. Maybe she was counting all the examples of her point like I was.

Finally, I said, "He's bad *and* good."

"Aren't we all?"

Yes, I supposed we were. And if I took my own self as an example, those proportions were in constant flux.

I tapped the table lightly. "Thanks for the chat."

"Anytime. Good luck getting your dog back." Lisa lifted her hands in surrender. I was on my own.

"Good luck explaining to your man that you need to get a puppy for Christmas."

Lisa's regard turned solemn. "Why? Where are you going?"

I admired the challenge she carried in her tone. After all, why would she open up to someone who was here today and gone tomorrow?

"You want to take J.J. and Spock for a long walk by the river tomorrow morning before it gets too hot?" I asked.

"Sounds nice."

Without too much fuss, I was able to get Spock out of J.J.'s dinosaur-themed room and back down the hall to my apartment. I checked the bank account and didn't find any activity. Instead of working on a new profile, I finished the bag of chips from earlier and watched a documentary about 3D printers being used in Africa.

Chapter Eleven

Rafa

I sat across from my cousin Juliana in the back table of her hair salon. Her light eyes matched mine and her dark, naturally curly hair had been straightened. It shined all the way down to the middle of her back. As far as I could tell, she only had one fault—incredibly shitty taste in men.

Her current asshole was in the Jefferson Manors crew, and the slight blue on her cheek was almost perfectly hidden under her flawless makeup—unless a person knew what to look for.

I'd stopped trying to figure out how she could pick the one asshole who wanted to use her as a punching bag in a line-up or how that one prick knew how to seek her out. But ever since Juliana had been seventeen, she'd been in abusive relationships. Our family had tried each time to help, but her pattern was her own. I loved her, wanted the best for her, but I couldn't live her life for her. Part of me wondered if she would ever be able to have a functional relationship. Juliana was beautiful, but holy hell the little mama loved her Brazilian drama.

I slid her five one-hundred-dollar bills folded in half. "I need to know who is going to their games and where they are."

Juliana crossed her arms and stared at the cash. "One condition."

Alarm bells rang in my head. Her conditions usually ended with me doing things I hated, like when we had been fifteen and she'd died my hair white. That shit had stung like a motherfucker and I'd had to shave my head when my black roots had started growing out. Or pretending to be her boyfriend to make some idiot jealous... That had been seriously fucking weird and given me the heebie-jeebies for months.

But I needed the information and she was the best mole I had. I hated that it put her at risk, but I didn't have any other clue as to how I could get what Anton wanted. So whatever her condition was, I would do it. I would hate it, but I would do whatever she asked.

"What?" I asked, already tasting the bitter bile rising from my stomach.

"You have to take Angela on a date. She won't stop talking about you and I need you to show her what an ass you are so she'll shut up about it." Juliana rubbed her temples.

I dropped my head back. Yeah, it was not going to be fun. "Who's Angela?"

Juliana leveled me with a sneer. "You can't be serious."

"And yet, you know I am."

The eye-roll of a Brazilian woman could probably win some kind of competition. It had disbelief, ridicule, attitude, sass all in a flash of white and was complete with a subtle head wave. Juliana was the master and it actually made me smile.

"Raf, she's the girl you passed on your way in here. She's worked for me for three years. You honestly didn't know her name?"

No, I didn't. I wasn't attracted to my own kind. Girls from my neighborhood and culture didn't stand out to me. It wasn't that I didn't see or respect their beauty. I loved a lot of them. But I had a different taste. Besides, they tended to be gossipy, and I didn't want my private life to be part of their discussions while they chopped and colored hair. *No, thank you.*

I shrugged. "Sorry?"

Juliana slapped the table, her hand landing directly over the money. "Just do it." She slid the cash closer to her then stood and stuffed it in the back pocket of her dark blue jeans. She turned to walk out of the back room then stopped.

"There's an English or Scottish guy. Stevie says he has a funny accent and is always doing an impression of him around Roarke. You'll get the rest of your information once you've broken her heart." Juliana pointed into her salon.

"Why would you want me to do that, anyway? You know how I am."

"I told you. I'm tired of hearing about it. The only way to shut her up about my hottie cousin is for you to show her your blackened soul."

"Ouch."

She tucked her chin and widened her eyes. "You denying it?"

There was a dramatic sigh dying to make its way out of me but I pushed it down. "Okay. Which one is she again?" I peered through the beaded curtain over Juliana's shoulder. There were three stylists busy at work with caped women in chairs.

"The first one." Juliana pointed her long nail.

Angela was pretty and she had perfect curves. Any man would be lucky to go out with her. She just didn't do it for me.

"Locations, Juliana. I need locations."

"Have I ever let you down?" she asked with a wry smile. We were both hustlers. Always had been.

"Not once."

My phone vibrated in my pocket and I pulled it out. Scooter's name flashed on the screen.

"Hey," I answered.

"Where you at?"

"At my cousin's."

"Which one?" he asked. It was a valid question. There were a lot.

I smirked at Juliana. "The one that's a pain in my ass."

She snarled and flipped me off then walked back to the salon.

"Anyway," I went on, "what happened in the courtyard? What did M need?"

"Fucking Bridget." Scooter groaned. "It's like clockwork. Jackson's not around and she fucks with Lisa."

I rubbed my neck. I hated that J.J.'s mom used her little boy as bait to get a free high, but what the fuck else were we supposed to do? Jackson was clear that when he was away, J.J. was to stay with Lisa. It hadn't been the first time Bridget had acted out her baby-mama drama. For criminals, we were far too hopeful she wouldn't pull her stunt again.

"And M?" I asked.

"She went in with Lisa and the kid a couple of hours ago. Listen, I'm putting Jimmy on the bench tonight. You good with that? Anton's not picking up."

Right. We had to start seeing who could handle the bench and who couldn't. Jimmy had been a Bradford boy and converted to Covington. Did I trust him? *No.* But then again, the list of people who I did was fewer than the fingers on my left hand. Besides, Anton had tested him before.

The future of the crew meant delegating certain responsibilities. And with Jackson and Anton away, Scoot and I couldn't do it all.

"Yeah. Let's see how he does. You're around, though, right?"

"Gonna Netflix and chill." Scooter's life had taken a boring turn since his girlfriend had suffered at the hands of the BTs. We'd gotten our revenge, but the damage to her couldn't be undone. She stayed home with the curtains drawn. I couldn't even remember the last time I'd seen her.

"That sounds incredibly lame, Scoot. But good, cuz I'm going out."

"Let me guess. Your cousin's?" He laughed.

"You know it."

We hung up and I stood behind the beads and internally bitched, moaned and whined to myself for agreeing to Juliana's condition. I didn't want to waste my time or Angela's by going on a date that would be pointless. There was nothing she would be able to do to make me like her. Already, the fact that she'd been talking about me to my cousin was more of a turn-off than she could imagine.

I wasn't into fucking anyone stupid enough to want me. Most of the time women prejudged me as the bad boy with muscles, and they were convinced they could change me into a better man. There were a lot of problems with that, mostly because I didn't want to be a better person. I liked my lifestyle and had no intention of reforming. So me and their white picket fence and a steady paycheck to buy their high heels wasn't going to happen.

The other thing that bugged the shit out of me was how surface it all was. Girls like Angela never really wanted to know what went on in my brain. In honesty, they probably shouldn't. Maybe my soul had been charred. For whatever reason, some girls were attracted to the mystery that went along with being a criminal.

But I needed to get Anton his information about the games. So I would whore myself out for a movie then ghost her. If I was lucky, maybe she would slap me. I did like a nice slap in the face from time to time.

I hung back until Angela's client was under the dryer and she was alone at the reception desk. I sauntered over and stood opposite her.

After a little dip of my head, I said, "Hi," in the breathiest, cockiest and fakest whisper I had.

Her soft smile was nice. It really was. "Hi, yourself. Funny how you waited back there until the exact moment I had a break."

"Just getting my confidence up," I lied.

"Oh, yeah? What for?" Angela dug her top teeth into her bottom lip and released it all slow like.

I reached for my phone and hit new contact then nudged it toward her on the counter. "Can I get your digits?"

She smirked and her dark eyes glittered. "Is it always this easy for you?" She took my phone, thumbed in her number, then before I could get it back, she sent herself a message so she had my number too. *Clever.*

"I don't know what you're talking about." I took my phone back and shot her a wink to seal the lie then got the fuck out of the hair salon.

It was dark when I got back to Covington and I stopped at the bench to check in with Jimmy. He had three other guys with him and I was glad to see that they weren't all Bradford converts.

On the third floor, I knocked gently on Lisa's door. She opened a crack behind the chain before closing again then pulling the door wide with a small smile.

"You two okay? I heard about Bridget. Jackson will be back in the morning."

Lisa nodded slowly then smirked. "Junior fell in love with your girlfriend's dog."

Wise ass.

"She's not my girlfriend." My words were too quick, too much of a protest. What the hell was that about?

Lisa's eyes twinkled. She was all happy and shit that she'd struck a chord.

"You kiss her yet?" A small smile pulled at her lips.

"I don't remember you being this nosey."

Lisa crossed her arms. "I don't remember in the years and years I've known you, you ever having a double date."

What the who now? I propped my hands on my hips and shook my head. "I didn't go on a double date. I didn't go on any date."

"Raf, if eating a meal together then making out isn't a date, then what is?"

I opened my mouth. There had to be an objection inside me to what Lisa was saying but it didn't come. *Shit, shit, shit.* I snapped my mouth shut and turned around.

After one step, I spun around before Lisa could close her door. "Did she tell you we made out?" I shuddered. Even the sound of it sounded like middle school.

"Nope. You just did."

Lisa waggled her eyebrows and I thought I might be sick.

"Have a good night." She closed the door.

I marched halfway down the hall and punched in the code to M's place. The door popped open. M was on the couch watching something on the television and Spock poked his head up and wagged his tail. I would have greeted him with a scratch or something but I had other pressing business.

"You didn't think last night at Lisa's was a *date*, did you?" I shuddered again.

Marigold's face wrinkled like she was smelling a dead fish. "Eww. No. Gross. We don't even like each other."

"And what happened after?"

Her nostrils flared. Jesus Fucking Christ she was gorgeous.

"That was you just helping me not think about the storm. Raf, you're not going to get all mushy and shit, are you?"

"No. I don't even know how to be that way." I let out a long breath. *Phew*. She didn't think it was a date either. "Okay, good. I'll pick you up in an hour."

She smirked. I could have kissed it off her smug face. "For another non-date?"

"Fuck off." I said and it came out just a hair too defensive.

Marigold saluted me and laughed. "Aye. Aye. Captain Caveman."

I left. It was possible that I stormed down to my place. I may have even slammed my door shut. Then I definitely threw myself on the bed like a teenage girl and screamed into my pillow.

As I got ready to go out, I reminded myself that I always wore cologne and styled my hair. It wasn't for her. It was routine. And God bless her incessant babble about some documentary she'd watched earlier in the day as we drove downtown. It was a needed distraction to how pretty she looked in her thigh-high white socks that had two stripes at the top. And thank fuck for me having to keep my hands on the wheel, because they were fucking dying to touch her right above those stripes and find out what was under her tiny black pleated skirt. How I kept my eyes on the road and didn't stare at her white button-down nerd shirt and ponder how she'd made something so plain hotter than hell was a mystery only the universe could solve.

I got lucky and found a parking spot on the street opposite my cousin's place. Inside, his modern tapas bar was crowded, but there was always a table for family. Moombahton beats pumped through the speakers and the small dance floor was packed with people swaying their hips and shaking their asses. I nodded to Carlos behind the bar and he pointed to a low empty table with a reserved sign on it.

With my hand on M's lower back, I led her to it. It was only when we sat down in the short blue velvet chairs that I saw her ear-to-ear grin. Yeah, I had to agree. Carlos's place was a great escape from the gloomy courtyard of Covington Heights.

A waitress brought over two caipirinhas and I winked at M as we tapped our glasses. The tart, cold liquid gripped my tongue and warmed my soul. I was normally a beer guy, but I couldn't resist a Carlos Capi.

"That's strong. *Shit.*" M shivered and placed the drink back on the table.

"You want to dance?" I asked. From the second I'd heard the music, I was sure my heartbeat had synced with the bass and my bones we calling me to move.

M's face dropped and she shook her head. "I can't dance. And doing it in front of you? Way too much ammunition for you to make fun of me. Nope. No way. But if you want to, feel free. It's not like we're on a date." She'd raised her voice to be heard over the music.

"You don't mind?" I wanted her to mind. *Shit.* But then again, maybe dancing with another woman would prove that we weren't, in fact, on a date.

M took a cautious sip of her drink. "You're a free man, Raf."

Chapter Twelve

Marigold

That motherfucker actually got up and asked another girl to dance. And she was gorgeous. She had everything that I didn't—long auburn hair, ample cleavage on full display and dark blue jeans that were a second skin. How she managed not to tumble over in her insanely high heels made me respect the hell out of her.

But I fucking hated that bitch and her graceful, seductive moves. Anger burned in my stomach and I envisioned a new way to murder her each time her perfectly curvy hips swayed to the beat of the music. I sat alone and tried not to stare. I sipped my drink and convinced myself I wasn't jealous. Why would I be?

"Is this seat taken?" a deep voice asked.

When I looked up, a thinner, cheaper version of Rafa met my eyes. I smiled, hoping it would be mistaken for kindness and interest.

"It is," I said. "By you."

He sat and introduced himself. It was hard to hear much of what he said but it didn't matter. Rafa's narrowed amber eyes were all I needed to know my mission of throwing his childish, petty act back in his face had been accomplished. I laughed in all the right places. I even put my hand on the guy's thigh for a brief moment. My grin was wide. Every overly friendly and flirtatious act served as bat signals to Goldie Locks on the dance floor that two could play his stupid game.

But — probably because Rafa was an asshole royale — he kept dancing. The little moves he made with the beautiful woman fueled my hate for both of them — his sexy smirk when she ground her fantastic hips into his thigh, his fucking hand on her ass, the giggle I couldn't hear but could see. Every second he chose her over me flickered as another bright spark to light my blazing fire of rage.

And yet, even though I would catch the fractions of seconds when Rafa glanced at me and the guy, he never stopped dancing. The worst part? He was fantastic — smooth, skilled, sensual. I would have tripped or fallen at least four times per song. He was more than a natural. It was an amplified version of all his best qualities.

It must have been an hour later when he finally came back to the table dripping in sweat. He raked his eyes over my new friend and said, "Thanks for warming my seat. You can fuck off now."

"Oh my God," I sneered. "You can't just say shit like that. We're having a conversation." My objection was just as much of a lie as me faking interest in the guy who'd been talking my ear off for the better part of an hour. Deep down inside that was exactly what I'd wanted Rafa to say.

Rafa did one of those half long blinks, half eye rolls in my direction. "Let's go." But his words weren't an order. They were an invitation that made energy buzz beneath my skin.

I worked my jaw in a feeble protest but stood. I didn't even bother to say goodbye to the pawn I'd used. Rafa sent the peace sign to his cousin behind the bar and steered me by the elbow through the crowd. When we got to the street, I yanked my arm away — another pointless sham in my fake rebellion — and climbed into the car with a *humph* for good measure.

We drove back to Covington in silence, which only thickened the tension. I'd never been so lust-filled. It was lucid, pure and all-consuming. I didn't understand what was happening to my body and brain and was afraid that if I did, the connection we had would instantly be broken. The only thing I was sure of was that I wanted him more than I had before, which was fucked-up and illogical.

I stomped all the way back to my apartment, Rafa never saying a word. I jabbed in my code, and when the door clicked, I smacked it open. Spock barked but then wagged his tail when he caught sight of us.

With my arms crossed, I marched to my bedroom. Rafa sleeked behind me. There was far too much swagger and confidence in his quiet stalking. Calmly, so fucking calmly, he closed the door to my room and the short hairs on my neck stood at attention. Between my legs, I clenched in anticipation for what he would do next.

I turned around and snarled. "I hate you."

He smiled with half of his face, a dimple creasing in his lifted cheek. Rafa reached out and tucked his hand into the waistband of my skirt then he jerked me to him. I had to close my eyes. His bold stare was more than I could handle. My own eyes would have signaled my defeat, my unavoidable undoing.

The draw to him overwhelmed me. It heightened all my senses, put me on red-alert. When the tip of his nose brushed down my jawline, I wouldn't have been able to state my name. I was unrecognizable, inside and out.

His warm breath on my skin fogged over any final thoughts of abandonment. He whispered, "If you want to stop —"

I pulled away, but didn't make it too far. His hand was still dug into my waistband. "Don't even fucking think about it."

Our lips met and gone was the thoughtful, delicate Rafa of the day before. Our tongues twirled and clashed together in a twisted game of pain and desire. The hand that had been in my waistband drifted up my skirt and I instinctively opened my legs a little wider. A faint, traitorous moan escaped my throat and he dipped a finger inside my underwear, only to find how fucking ready I was for him.

Rafa sucked down my neck, grazing it with his teeth as he made his way to the collar of my shirt.

"Rip it off," he said with a rasp.

Fuck buttons. Buttons were stupid and took far too long to undo. I reached up to my shirt and pulled as hard as I could, ruining it and desperate to follow any order he was giving. *Jesus Christ, who am I?*

As he guided me backward to the wall by leaning his weight into me, he managed to take off his own shirt. Rafa powered into me, his erection pressing against my thigh as he cupped my breast under my black bra before pinching my sensitive nipple…hard. I yelped, which made him smile and do it again while he reclaimed my mouth. There wasn't a cell in my body rejecting him. In fact, they were more alive than they'd ever been and begging him never to stop. I was higher than when I stole, far more alive than when I created a new successful virus.

I dug my nails into the tight skin of his back and the thick muscles below protested my intrusion. Rafa pinned me with one hand on my wrists and the other one still between my legs, working a vicious pace on my clit. The rise of my release appeared out of nowhere and I felt unprepared for its arrival.

My orgasm consumed me, crashing hard at my base then washing over me like a tidal wave. It was savage and shocking, over too fast, a memory too soon. Rafa let go of his grip and in the haze of my stunned state, I barely registered the rip of a condom and the hissing unzip of his jeans.

He whipped me around to face the wall, yanked my underwear down and flipped up my skirt. He was inside me within seconds and his fast and furious pace made me dizzy. His girth stretched me, the pain immediately taken over by carnal pleasure. A perverse desire awoke in me and I cried out, "I hate you!" not caring that it was a complicated half-truth.

His tight grip on my hips burned and I braced myself, fearful he might knock me through the wall. Our skin slapped violently together and echoed over our airy gasps. He was relentless and unbridled. But it wasn't him that worried me. It was the ravenous, insatiable hunger inside me, the bottomless pit of unreasonable need that lapped up every drop of life he presented.

I'd found some strange union with a kindred soul who was as equally degenerate as I was. We only functioned in society because we chose to, not because it allowed us in.

Rafa grabbed my shoulder, taking away any stability I'd had. He thrust harder, deeper and I whimpered out a plea, not sure if it was to stop or keep going. He hardened inside me before letting out a rage-filled groan.

I flattened both palms against the wall and sucked in air that seemed to stop at my throat, never quite reaching my starved lungs. My mouth was dry, my underwear bound my ankles and my mind spun in a million directions. I bent my knees and dropped to the floor then turned so my back was supported. A cool drip of sweat streaked down my temple.

"You okay?" he asked. Did he truly care?

I nodded then dropped my face into my hands. Rafa held his pants and walked off to the bathroom. The toilet flushed and he ran the tap.

Was there a way to process what we'd just done? The fact that we'd both been one hundred percent into it? That our inner freaks were mirror images?

When he came back in the bedroom, he swiped his T-shirt from off the floor and studied me with narrowed eyes.

"I'm going to—"

Oh no, he was going to bail on me. *Fuck that.*

"Listen," I started. "I get that this is what you do, probably more often than not, but I need a minute to sort through what the fuck it is that we just did."

Rafa frowned. "I was going to say, I'm going to walk Spock and grab a change of clothes."

Okay, so I'd been wrong. I'd been sure he was going to leave me in the puddle he'd created—not that I would admit it. "Oh, look who's Mr. Presumptuous. You think I want you to stay?"

Rafa squatted in front of me with a soft smile. "What we just did was a little bit fucked up. If I leave you alone all night, that beautiful brain of yours is going to find hidden meaning in something every time you replay the last thirty minutes in your head. I don't want to send you the wrong signal."

There was a kindness in his eyes that twinkled for a brief second before realizing it didn't belong there, like a diamond in an otherwise black mine. It was the sort of thing that I understood to be more dangerous than his criminal side.

But I dared search it out again. In a soft voice, I asked, "What signal do you want to send?"

He pursed his lips. "Just not the wrong one." Rafa pushed on his knees and stood, then threaded his arms through his shirt. "I'll be back in a bit. I need to check the bench anyway."

He stopped just before opening the door. "Take a bath. Don't over think this, Marigold. We can talk about it when I'm back."

Did I like that he'd used my name? I didn't know. Up was down and down was sideways. He closed the bedroom door behind him and I stared down at my black underwear still tangled on the top of my black boots. I violently kicked off the menacing lace, a proper tantrum taken out on an undergarment.

My life had gone from a secret, quiet existence to a high-speed train in forty-eight hours. I'd sought out danger, found it and discovered it was more appealing up close and personal than I'd bargained for. But why? Why was I so mangled in my brain that I took pleasure from stealing?

I decided to follow half of Rafa's advice and drew a bath. But the overthinking part was unavoidable. My mind zinged through a thousand different judgments of myself and of him. If I didn't hate him, it didn't mean that I liked him. I sure as shit wasn't indifferent to him. Maybe he was just a vehicle to my addiction of social chaos.

I slipped into the tub. The hot water steamed around me and fogged the long mirror on the opposite wall. I rubbed my temples and closed my eyes. Covington Heights was changing me, *had* changed me. It allowed me to be totally selfish, reckless. Maybe I needed to check back in with my parents. But then again, I'd been miserable there.

The question wasn't if I'd changed for better or worse. It was if I liked how I'd changed, what I'd become in a short amount of time. The sad answer was yes. All the years of hiding from society hadn't made me fear it. It'd made me loathe it. Covington Heights was not that society. It was a place to blossom into my most audacious self.

But there was one tiny problem. I could never show that person to my family. The disappointment would drip from my father's eyes. He would blame himself for my wicked ways. He would be wrong, though. My parents may have made my body, but it was me who had warped my mind. Years of solitude had allowed me to justify actions and go unchecked.

And at one point, my lies would be uncovered. They always were. Then my parents would ask me to make a choice—to murder the happy beast inside me so I could live a proper, legit life or be done with them forever. My mother wouldn't have it any other way.

The door to my apartment opened and closed and I turned the drain to the tub and got out. After drying off, I found some fluffy, lavender pajama pants and a tight cropped white tank top. I didn't bother drying my hair or putting my makeup back on.

Spock greeted me with his ears back and tail wagging as soon as I came out into the living area. A red-and-white pizza box sat on the counter and I was sure I smelled some form of bacon.

Rafa had showered, his hair was still wet and it glistened under the spotlights above the kitchen island. His clothes were casual, baggy training pants and a tank so tight the ripples in his stomach poked out like little hills. He held a clear plastic bowl of salad and chewed while he leaned against the counter, his legs crossed at the ankles.

"Did you buy me bacon pizza?"

He finished his bite and licked the inside of his mouth before answering. "I imagined the unhealthiest meal I could and bought it."

"Are there fries on top?" I lifted a shoulder and grinned.

"Jesus Christ, you have problems." Rafa shook his head and pronged more lettuce.

"Thank you."

I slid into a barstool opposite him and swiveled the box toward me. Drool puddled in my cheeks. There was enough to have cold pizza for breakfast. *Jackpot.*

We ate in mostly silence, only judgment and objections from Rafa when I gave my crust to Spock, who had been sitting next to me patiently waiting for his reward.

Rafa tossed his empty bowl into the trash then propped his hands on his hips. "So. Do we need to talk about what that was?"

I wiped a little grease from bottom lip with the back of my hand. "Hate fucking. I totally get it now. We hate each other and we accidently had sex." I shrugged.

"Yes and no. We both know it wasn't an accident."

It was odd, the candor of it all — quite the opposite of how I'd been living. Honest public life, deceitful private. In Covington we betrayed publicly but were truthful behind closed doors.

He continued, "The question is, do you want it to happen again?"

I furrowed my forehead. "Like right now?" Pretty sure round two was off the table for a few hours while my downstairs girl had a break. Did he know what he was packing?

A pained look spread on his face. "That's not really how it works."

"Oh, Christ..."

"See. We kinda have to be pissed for it to be hot like that."

Holy shit. He was right.

"And if you want to hit me, it's totally cool. Fuck, when you said you hated me, I practically came right then. So hot, M."

I closed the pizza box and walk over to stick it in the fridge. In his ear I whispered, "You're the one with problems, big boy."

He bit his bottom lip and grinned from ear to ear as he nodded. Jesus, his eyes even twinkled. *Psychopath.*

Chapter Thirteen

Rafa

"I'm going to work for a bit. Thanks for the pizza." M walked down the hall to the bedroom where we'd set up our workstations, and Spock followed her. Her tight little ass shifted from left to right in her lavender pajama pants.

I didn't know what to do with the part of me that liked the softer side of her. She didn't have any makeup on and the pure version of her was pretty in a way I wasn't prepared for.

The sex had been hot, no real mystery there. Problem was, now we were chasing the dragon. We would have to find new and unscrupulous ways to piss each other off. Hate had a way of withering away in the face of pleasure.

I pushed off the counter and walked down the hall. Marigold had headphones on and only glanced at me as I sat opposite her. My phone vibrated in my pocket and I knew without looking that it was Angela. Lord, I hated eager. But the sooner I showed her my true colors, the better.

M's eyes narrowed as she stared at her screen before a heavy, long blink.

I cleared my throat. "It's late. You had a long day."

She let out a long breath. "Are you gonna stay?"

There had been one thing I'd figured out about M without the help of her phone. She didn't like being alone. I nodded once. It had been true what I'd said earlier. I didn't want to give her the wrong impression. I just hadn't quite figured out what impression I did want to give her. Maybe I didn't want her to think I'd used her. I needed her to understand that what we'd done was mutual.

M stood and stretched, her tone stomach on full display. "You're not going to spoon me or some fucking sweet bullshit like that, are you?"

I shrugged and frowned. "How else will I cop a feel of your perfect little tits?"

"Great. We can add 'pervert' to your list of nicknames." Her tone was flat but I hadn't missed the small smile from the compliment.

"Damn straight." I smacked her ass as she walked by which caused her to jump.

Spock sensed our playful nature and hopped up from where he'd been sleeping next to the desk. He wagged his tail and pranced down the hall with us to the other side of the apartment where he jumped on the bed and did a proper play bow and a sparkle gleamed in his light eyes.

I tapped his shoulders and let him tackle me until he had me pinned and licked my cheek. Marigold stood in the doorway of the bathroom shaking her head while she brushed her teeth. Spock released me and curled up at the end of the bed. I stood then wiggled by M, taking one more squeeze of that ass.

With a snide glare, Marigold spit into the porcelain sink. "You know I'm not having sex with you until I hate you again. Consider it penance for being adorable." She shivered and wiped her face with a towel then threw it on the counter.

I loaded my brush and said, "Sounds more like a reward for bad behavior. I suddenly have happy thoughts of force-feeding you vegetables."

She scoffed. "That would probably do it."

As she climbed into bed, I finished in the bathroom and turned out the light. It was odd having her in my old bed—the number of times I'd wondered what she had actually looked like when I listened to her videos, the fantasies I'd had about her rasping out my name with desire. For all the day-dreaming I'd done about Majel213, I'd never expected her to fit so perfectly into my life. We liked the same things, had the same warped view on the world. We even had the same dry sense of humor.

I walked over, stripped down to my boxers, lifted the covers, then slid in. She'd taken off her pants and was in just a thong and the little tank top. It was the best kind of torture I could imagine. I rubbed my hand around her smooth ass then up her stomach where I absolutely copped a feel of her left breast.

She had that sweet smell that I was beginning to suspect was just her. I nuzzled closer and there, in the safety of the dark, I had to tell her. "You're fucking beautiful. You know that, right?"

"Shut up, asshole." M sleeked her hand into mine and interlaced our fingers.

I kissed her bare shoulder. "You know insults make me horny." I wiggled my dick into her ass crack. Then my mind went to all kinds of dark and wonderful places. *Damn her.*

Marigold flipped around and straddled me. She hovered just above my lips and whispered, "You have the prettiest eyes I've ever seen." She placed the softest, most gentle kiss I'd ever gotten on my mouth and held it there. The next move was for her. I had no idea what she was getting at.

Slowly, she drew back. "Now let me fucking sleep." Off she climbed and back on her side with her ass pressed into my hip. She spooned her pillow while I laid on my back and stared at the ceiling. Had she been serious? Was it some sort of revenge compliment? Jesus, we were fucked up.

After a few hours of tossing and turning and my mind not being able to settle, I crept out of bed and went back to my place. Anton didn't like it when no one was in the king's castle, so it was good to be there when he got home, even if I was sitting on my ass watching sports highlights from the night before.

He tossed a key fob into a drawer and nodded his hello. "Ready to get your ass kicked?"

"Always." I pushed the power button on the remote and hopped up. "Oh. We put Jimmy on the bench again. I'll check in with him after we work out."

Anton let out a slow breath then said, "He was the best choice, but I don't trust him yet. Count everything three times."

We headed over to the gym and went straight to the treadmill.

After five minutes, we found our strides and Anton glanced at my stats. "How's my new business venture?"

I'd wondered how long it was going to take him to ask. "Should get payment today. We've already started targeting a new town." I did my best to hide my worry. Anton couldn't see the long game in hacking. He needed instant gratification.

Warm-up complete, we switched to weights and my lack of sleep began to show as I struggled with the bench press. Anton spotted me and the bar clanked as we put it back in its spot over my head.

He narrowed his light eyes and smirked. "You fucked Rainbow Brite."

There was no point in denying it, but that didn't mean I was going to talk sex shop with the bossman. Besides, I'd heard plenty through the walls of how he liked to get off. My darker side was better off in the shadows.

"This gonna fuck up your earnings?" He crossed his arms and peered down at me.

"Not a chance, boss."

The door opened and Jackson sauntered in. He stretched and yawned. "Morning."

"Jesus Christ, you too?" Anton shook his head. "My whole crew falling apart in front of my eyes due to pussy. For fuck's sake."

Jackson shot me a questioning glance and I shook it off in a 'I'll tell you later' gesture that we'd come to understand between us.

Anton turned back to me and asked, "What did you find out about the games?"

"I'll know everything in a week." I clasped Anton's outstretched hand and curled up to sit.

"Let me guess. You have a cousin working on it." Jackson smirked and reached for the jump rope from the plastic box of accessories under the wall of weights. "How you payin' for your info this time?"

Over the years, Jackson had learned about the many different forms of currency in my family. I'd worked as a bouncer in a few bars in exchange for free drinks, I'd roughed up a few boyfriends and I'd even helped steal a car. Cash and conditions… That was how my web of cousins all over the city functioned.

"I have to go on a date and prove that I'm an ass." I hadn't had the courage to get back to Angela after her mildly obsessive text messages. Also, I'd been kinda busy with the woman who did know how to float my boat.

Anton and Jackson laughed.

"What?"

Jackson dipped his chin. "You, Goldie Locks. You have a type. It's a crazy type. It's like you can smell who will be the most jealous woman in the room, then you proceed to push on that button until the poor girl can't take it anymore. You don't think it's a coincidence that you found M and now you *have* to go on a date with someone else. I love you, man, but your love life is based on stupid drama."

"First of all," I said, then stood with my hands on my hips, "I think we can all agree that I don't have a *love* life —"

"Oh for fuck's sake. I can't listen to this girlie shit. Raf, go check in with Jimmy and text me. Jackson, warm up. I need to hit somebody."

I fake-snarled at Jackson and left the gym without objection. After a quick shower, I dressed in the Covington uniform of black jeans and a black tank top, threw on my tattered baseball hat and took the stairs down to the second floor, not stopping to check on M, even though a part of me wanted to.

I knocked on Jimmy's door, and when he didn't answer, I called his cell.

"Hey, man. Had a late night. You need me?" Jimmy coughed through the phone.

"I need the money you earned and your numbers. Open your door." I hated training newbies. Delinquents were never very good about following the rules.

"Sorry, man. I'm not home. I'll be over in ten minutes."

Ten minutes? Was he fucking kidding me?

"Where are you?" I kept the annoyance out of my tone. Staying calm was the only way to control the situation and show the new jerk-off how the ranks worked. He was lucky I wasn't the bossman. Not being home when it was time to collect money would have ended with a smack on the face in front of a group of people.

But I had other motives. I needed someone to replace me on the bench. So did Scooter and Jackson. We were fucking tired of selling drugs.

"Just down the hall. I'll be right there."

Street smarts and intuition were muscles that strengthened simultaneously. I knew where Jimmy was. Problem was, I didn't think Jimmy knew where he was. After a long exhale, I walked down to apartment two-twelve and knocked on Bridget's door. The faint smell of burnt plastic seeped out and my stomach turned.

With a fist, I pounded just below the number. Jimmy's only saving grace would be if he hadn't used.

Bridget answered in a dirty tank top and her underwear. Her frail body was a shell of what she'd once been. It was a fucking shame.

Across the room, Jimmy stood and put his dick back in his pants.

"You think I have ten minutes to wait while you get your dick sucked?" *Unbelievable.*

On his way out he stopped in front of Bridget and shook a finger in her face. "Your payment is not complete. I'll be back."

I shoved him through the threshold and he stumbled. "Take it easy, man. My count is legit."

It would have been easy for me to order him to forgive Bridget her debt, whatever it was. But that would have been an act of kindness when I needed to show our new recruit who was in charge.

Jimmy fished out his keys and opened his apartment. It was clean, hyper-organized even. He didn't have a roommate. It had been a negotiated point when he'd come from Bradford.

I sat at his kitchen table, also spotless, and he went to the back bedroom. Two minutes later he came out with a wad of cash.

"Busy night." I had to admit that I was impressed and the bossman would be pleased. Jimmy's little indiscretion with Bridget would not get reported. Money mattered, bullshit didn't.

"I guess the customers liked seeing a new face. Maybe some of the Bradford peeps are happy that I'm being folded in."

His confidence, while gag-worthy, was what we needed, so I let his attitude slide.

I checked the sheet that Scooter gave at the beginning of each shift and counted out Jimmy's share after verifying that he'd sold as much as he'd said.

"A few more pulls like this and I'll be moving upstairs."

He might. After all, he had all the qualities of upper management, minus some muscles.

"You need to bulk up. How often do you eat?"

"Breakfast, lunch, dinner…like a regular person."

"Nah, man. You need to fuel the muscles every two or three hours if you want to gain weight. Until that happens, you'll be stuck down here."

Jimmy face scrunched up. "I need some pointers, I guess."

I could relate. I'd been in the same boat. I'd known how to work out, but it was Leo who had taught me how to fight and shoot a gun. Jimmy was probably a good scrapper. He just was missing the power behind it.

"I can meet you at the gym this afternoon. We can write out your diet and start talking about a routine."

"Really?"

I stood and tucked the money into my back pocket. "Yeah. Really. I don't know how things were at Bradford, but we support each other here."

"Three o'clock?"

"Sounds good."

I headed for the door, I needed to get Anton his money then figure out when the fuck Zapata Falls was going to pay us. Plus, Angela… I had to deal with her sooner than later. Getting that over with would mean my end of the deal would be done. Loose strings and unpaid debt weren't my thing.

"Raf?"

"Yeah?" I stopped and looked over my shoulder.

Jimmy rubbed his neck. He had a hellish beast with horns tattoo up to his ear. "About the Bridget thing…"

"Keep your nose clean and the money coming. That's all I care about. But I wouldn't make a habit of trading sex for drugs. It gets fucking depressing."

A knowing frown crossed his face. "What about the new girl on the third floor?"

"All women on the third floor are off limits. You know that."

"Right. I just wondered now that I'm kinda moving up…"

"You haven't moved anywhere yet. Don't get greedy after one night." I glared at him.

And stay the fuck away from Marigold.

Chapter Fourteen

Marigold

Lisa and I walked along the wide path next to the river. The cool air could almost make one forget about the pollution one block east. J.J. held Spock's leash with a massive grin, the scooter he'd brought had been long forgotten.

My new friend Lisa—yep, I was going there—carried the metal kick scooter in the crook of her elbow, admired the boy and dog in front of us and said, "I am going to be in so much trouble with Jackson. You and Spock better not leave us."

There didn't seem to be a point in empty promises, so I gave her a different nugget to savor.

"You want to know something sick and horrible?"

"Duh." Lisa quirked a brow.

"Okay but girl code here. No telling the sausage stew of Covington. And no thinking shitty of me."

Hack

Spock sniffed the base of a tree and we came to a halt. In a low voice, Lisa leaned in to me and said, "M, my boyfriend feeds the habit of the mother of the child who I love like my own. If you don't judge me, I'll offer you the same pass."

I didn't judge her. Lisa was stuck and doing the best that she could. She was a gem of goodness. I was more worried I would taint her gentle ways than think poorly of her choices.

"So, a bit of background," I started and we walked south again.

Lisa's eyes lit up and she let out a tiny *squee*. Yeah, girl-talk was dope.

I grinned. "Rafa took my phone and hacked it the first day we met. He found out my identity—everything."

"Not surprised… He likes shit like that."

I lifted a finger. "Here's the thing. I'm rather vengeful. I paired his phone to my laptop and now I get all his messages."

Lisa's brown eyes widened. "That's naughty. But paybacks are hell, right?"

The bile stewed in my stomach. "There's only one problem."

"Let me guess. It has nothing to do with Covington business."

I frowned. Yes, it was wrong to spy on Rafa—but he'd started it! And yes, when one goes snooping around, one might not like what one finds. *Blah, blah fucking blah.*

It made perfect sense that Rafael had a woman lighting up his phone. He was the epidemy of a hot bad boy—the kind of asshole who fueled fantasies. It was common knowledge that bad boys were the best kissers, and well, the best kissers did other shit pretty fucking spot-on, too. Point proven the day before. Hell, I was happy Lisa hadn't called me out for walking funny.

I scrubbed my cheeks. "It's horrible, Lisa. The jealousy is eating me alive."

She shifted the scooter to the opposite arm and crinkled her brow. "So you like him?"

"No! I hate him. I just don't want anyone else to have him," I whined.

She laughed. It wasn't mocking or in jest. The light chuckle carried a wave of understanding. "You poor thing. You're just as fucked up as he is."

I fake-wept. "I know and it's equal parts freakishly comforting and deeply disturbing."

Lisa draped her free arm over my shoulder and tugged me close. "Consider the possibility that you've met your match, girl."

I whimpered. I didn't want to have met my match. But, what did I want?

"I hate him," I said for good measure.

"If you say so. Come on. Let's head back. I have to watch another kid this afternoon and I need to start lunch." She let me go and called for J.J. to turn around.

There was a distinct feeling once I hit the territory of Covington Heights. Eyes followed me, energy hummed in my ears and the walls of the buildings seemed taller. I'd noticed it the first day, but each time I left and came back it was the same. There was nothing safe about the neighborhood.

I said my goodbye to Lisa and J.J. — who was kind enough to return my dog to me — and let myself into my apartment. Rafa wasn't there, not that I had expected him. But that didn't mean I couldn't find out where he was and what he was doing.

With a little bounce in my step, I grabbed a soda from the fridge and headed to my workstation. I flopped down and cracked open my laptop. Damn it, spying was fun. All the nerves in my body lit up and tingled.

They went immediately limp with one quick read of his texts.

Stop making me wait. Besides, you promised Juliana.

Tonight?

Perfect. Will you come and get me after work?

Sure. Then we can go up the street to Manny's. C U then.

X

I did a search for Manny's in the city and found several, which brought an annoyed *humph*. Also, Rafael knew where the girl worked and the neighborhood well enough to place Manny's just up the street from where she was.

The little strum sound my fingers made on the keyboard slowed as I thought it through. There had to be a clue in her text. Who was Juliana? Rafa talked about his cousins. Maybe they were related. I did a social media search for Juliana Santos and found a stunning brunette who had the same light eyes as Rafael and owned a hair salon not far from Covington. Then I went back to my Manny's search and found one that was literally on the same street as the salon. It was a Cuban restaurant that boasted about its famous chicken and beans.

Boom. Mic drop and all that other shit. Jesus, I was a proficient stalker. It hadn't even taken me fifteen minutes. Also, that chicken and beans sounded damn good. Too bad I would refuse to eat it for the rest of my life.

I spun around and around in my chair, using the table in front of me to go faster. Only children were notoriously bad sharers. One time, in a park not far from my house, my mom had offered some of my apple to a little boy I'd been playing with on the slide. According to my mother, I threw myself on the ground in a tantrum that had included me banging my fists and cheeks turning red as tomatoes. It was a pretty accurate assessment of how I wanted to react to Rafa with any other woman.

Which was utterly ridiculous. He wasn't mine. I wasn't his. Still… I wanted him, and he fucking wanted me.

I stopped spinning and stared at the blank wall. What did I have that Angela did not? What was my advantage? Where was my angle? I reread their exchange and a devious grin curled my lips. I had hate.

"You look fucking spooky."

I startled. I hadn't heard him come in.

"Bad dog," I scolded Spock. "You're supposed to protect me."

Rafa leaned into the doorway. With his dark jeans, black tank and light eyes, he was the one who was spooky. *Spooky fucking hot. Yeah, fuck you, Angela.* I'd had a taste of him and was going back for more. No apple or dick-sharing for me.

Spock wagged his tail all the way over to Rafa, who bent down and rustled his head. I didn't like him being nice to my dog. Come to think of it, I didn't like him being nice at all.

I frowned. "I hope you came to work. Zapata Falls still hasn't paid and I'm starting to get nervous." *And maybe just a little afraid that they won't pay.* Then what would I do? I didn't seem like the type who they would want to work the bench. There was no way they wouldn't make me pay for the apartment or my food.

"Ooo. Cranky Marigold. Hot." He stood and dusted his hands on his thighs. Rafa took off his hat, smoothed his hair, then secured it back on his head with a shaping of the bill. "Sorry to say you're going to have to fly solo today. I have to work with an underling then I have a meeting."

A *meeting? Really? With a girl who sends an 'x' for a kiss?* I crossed my arms and swiveled the chair in his direction.

Rafa's face tightened. "Are you mad at me?"

Yes. Wasn't that the entire point? "Always." I shrugged.

He licked his lips then rubbed them together slowly. Maybe he was trying to figure out my thoughts. Maybe he was trying to remind me that his kiss was the sweetest of Satan's fruit. Didn't matter. I wouldn't give up my game.

I rolled my eyes and turned back to my laptop. "Suit yourself. Besides, you don't really help much anyway."

He let out a light scoff. "You want me to walk this beast?"

I quit out of the message application and logged into my new fake profile of Jan Kozak who trained Border Collies and wore men's sports T-shirts tucked into her mom-jeans. "Nope," I answered without meeting his gaze. But I'd popped the P too much and my aggravation rang a little too true.

Rafa sauntered over to me and leaned down. That fucker copped a feel of my right breast. My senses awakened and damn it if warmth didn't radiate from between my legs. *Really, Marigold? One fucking touch?* Some hot breath on the neck from a muscle-headed asshole and I was sex jelly. *Pathetic.*

I ground my teeth.

Rafa twirled his warm, wet tongue around my earlobe and I shivered. I knew what that tongue could do. Slow, fast, soft, hard — it was diabolic.

He whispered, "You're hot when you're cranky."

"Fuck off." I batted his arm and jolted away from him.

"I'll be back after my meeting tonight." He righted himself. I would have bet a hundred bucks that there was some kind of cocky smirk on his gorgeous asshole face.

"Don't bother." My tone was glib. And because I was an immature idiot, I added, "I have a date."

Oh, how the energy shifted. Rafa spun my chair so I faced him and he looked down at me with angry eyes and a titled head. *See? Doesn't feel so nice, right?* Except I was lying like a dog. A stupid dog.

"You have a *what* now? No one here is allowed to even look at you."

Telling untruths was so much easier online. There was a record and you could refer back to what you'd once said to make sure not to contradict it. In person? Just a teensy bit more difficult, especially on the fly.

"Relax. It's with an old friend." What would make him super-crazy? I fought my smile. "Yeah. My dad had this friend… 'Had' being the keyword in *that* sentence." I faked a little snort. "Anyway, sometimes we like to see each other again." I shrugged.

The snarl on his face was perfection. "I'll have you followed."

"Fun." I waggled my eyebrows and turned to spin around.

His hand stopped my forward motion and he leaned down. Rafa's amber eyes bore into me and my skin tingled. "Don't fuck with me, M."

He didn't mean it, not really. Deep, deep down? He was begging for me to fuck with him. I'd heard the pleas since the day we'd met. He wanted to be messed with, challenged. His desire to play the feckless game was as strong as mine. It burned between our eyes as we glared at each other with equal parts lust and confrontation.

We were locked in a battle of wills, electrified and motivated. The defiance seethed between us until I finally spoke. "You can't tell me what to do, asshat."

He frowned, his lips were poutier than ever, his nostrils were flared out and the crease in his mouth nearly touched his chin. It was so exaggerated that I almost giggled.

"Be home by ten." He pushed off the chair and it swung from side to side.

A curfew? That made me laugh out loud. I dropped my head back and practiced a cackle.

"I'll see you then." Bless the beast. He was serious. And Lord Almighty, I had hit the jackpot. He was as much as an immature, jealous fool as I was. He stomped toward the door.

"Not if I see you first," I sang out in a childish voice.

Rafa stopped, turned and lifted an eyebrow. "Really?" The disappointment in his tone was perfect. He'd bought my mirage of lies because they matched his own behavior. It was reverse projection. *So, yeah, really, fucker.* I was going to see you first.

As he crossed the threshold, he spat out some kind of warning about ten o'clock but I paid him no mind. I'd won our little battle of the wills and I was marking my point on the scoreboard while I could.

I worked the entire afternoon and had a bag of chips for lunch. Then I got ready for battle. I painted my nails black and put on my sexiest bright pink lingerie. The cut-offs I'd been too afraid to wear in Covington because they were hella short were the perfect match to my cropped white tank and thin black suspenders, fishnets and combat boots on the bottom and my multicolored hair styled to perfection on the top of my head. My makeup was as dark and as serious as my mood. At seven-thirty, with the map of how to get to Manny's locked into my brain, I gave a kiss to Spock on his pink nose and headed out.

It didn't take long to get noticed by the crew. The third floor was empty but the whispers started in the lobby. They floated behind me as I pushed through the front doors and got closer to the bench.

A thick brick wall of muscles stopped me before I could pass. Chilling blue eyes peered down at me. "Where you headed, Rainbow Brite?"

My heart thumped loud and fast. I froze. "Hey, Anton. How's business?"

How's business? That was my small talk? I was doomed.

"You tell me. You make me some money today?" He tilted his head ever so slightly and cocked a brow.

"Working on it. Worked all day, actually. Just meeting someone for dinner. Wanna join?" It was probably wrong that I was wondering if humiliating Rafael in front of his boss might get me fucked harder. But then again, so little I did or thought was right.

"Raincheck. I have a family thing. But" — he scanned his crew — "Jimmy will go with, just to make sure you get back okay. Can't have anything happen to my newest source of income, can I?" He winked. It wasn't playful or flirtatious. It was a threat, plain and simple.

I told myself to breathe. Getting my ass to Rafa's date was mandatory.

I cleared my throat. "I'd love to have him." I grinned. "Come on, Jimmy."

Anton's suspicious eyes followed us out of the courtyard and we stopped at the corner to wait for the light.

"Oh shit. I forgot to tell Rafa something and I left my phone upstairs. Can I borrow yours? He's gonna be pissed. Shit." I held out my hand and bit my lip.

Jimmy was tall, a bit on the skinny side and in need of a new bullshit detector. He dug out his phone, punched the code and I quickly went to the browser and downloaded a virus to scramble it. *Sorry, sucker*. I didn't need him to give Rafa and Miss Angela a heads-up that I was going to piss on their Cuban chicken parade, so no communications possible for Jimmy. *Bye-bye, cell signal.*

I brought the phone to my ear and smiled to my escort. He wasn't bad-looking, just not smart enough for me. The light flicked and I walked at a brisk pace, forcing Jimmy to follow. I mumbled some stupid conversation into the phone then pretended to hang up and handed it back to him.

"Where we going, anyway?" he asked as he stored his now worthless phone in his back pocket.

"You'll see. It's not far. Thanks for coming with me, by the way. I hear these streets are dangerous." I oversold my fear, because after the exchange with Anton, I was invigorated. I was alive.

Three blocks later I heard the very distinctive, "What the fuck?" from over my shoulder.

I turned and shrugged. "Sorry 'bout that. I guess you can either go back for a new one or follow. Up to you."

Jimmy sighed. "You know I thought you were hot. Now I just think you're a sneaky bitch."

"Thanks!" I smiled.

Twenty streets north and six west—all that time to build up my bravado. Each step I'd taken toward Manny's, my swagger increased. Because I had the key. I had hate.

The small restaurant was in the middle of the block. It had a red awning and a red florescent sign in the window that glowed 'Open'. I didn't reach for the door right away. Instead, I narrowed my eyes and peered through the glass.

They weren't hard to spot. The only thing missing was his baseball cap. Angela was as predicted in my mind—fucking beautiful from head to toe. Rafa's back was to the window and his date batted her eyes in a shy gesture while she took a sip of her beer.

Jimmy's energy crowded mine as he peered over my shoulder.

"Oh, fuck me," he said under his breath.

Chapter Fifteen

Rafa

Angela twirled a lock of her dark, long hair and leaned back into the booth. I was pretty sure it wasn't by chance that her biceps pushed into her breast and plumped her cleavage. My brain was screaming for her to stop being so obvious because my balls were shriveling with each over-the-top, not-at-all-bashful blink.

Juliana had better keep her end of the deal. Plus, while I had my doubts Marigold was on any kind of date, I did want to know who she was meeting. Anton had sent me a text that he'd sent Jimmy with her and I didn't know if that made it better or worse. Then again, I'd taken him under my wing, so trying anything on her would jeopardize his rising ranks. I wasn't sure he'd throw those dice.

The waiter came over and cleared our plates. It really was the best Cuban food Uptown. Lucky for us only the locals knew about it. I rubbed my cheek, then my neck. *How am I going to get out of this Angela situation?*

"So, I just want to say," she started in a quiet sugary voice, "that I know what you do and I'm okay with that. I'm not looking for a nice guy with a job Downtown. That's not how I...like things."

Oh boy. Here we go, down the road of 'nice girl wants bad boy'. Why did they all think we wanted them back?

"Listen—"

Someone cleared their throat over my shoulder and Angela's eyes went wide. My nose recognized M before my ears, sweet like the best candy in the shop. I had no idea how she'd found me, but it explained everything—the what-had-become-apparent-in-a-flash lie about her on a date with someone else, her hot crankiness and challenging spirit of the afternoon. And damn if it wasn't her blue eyes burning fucking holes in the back of my head.

I hid my mouth because I was sure I was grinning from ear to ear. Marigold had just solved two of my biggest problems. One, how to get rid of Angela. And two, how to land Marigold back in bed with a fire in her belly. If I hadn't been so committed to hating her, I would have confessed to liking her.

"Stand up, asshat." *God damn, the rasp, the anger. Fucking bring it all, little mama.* I dropped my head, wanting her to think I was caught.

"I said, stand up."

I turned my head and let it rest on my knuckles. "Why would I do that?"

Her chest rose and fell in short breaths. Jesus and every Mary, she'd made an effort and it had worked. A dark pink bra strap peeked out at her shoulder under a skin-tight and far-too-short tank top. Her midriff was exposed, and fucking hell, those cut-offs were barely existent. She was the most sinfully divine creature I'd ever laid eyes on. Any damage Angela had done to my libido in the prior hour was wiped away.

Je-sus. Marigold Pfiefer was the girl of my dreams. I was sure of it.

"So I can slap you." Her tone was too casual, too matter-of-fact — probably designed to lure me into a web. But did she think I would mind going?

Angela scoffed. Poor thing. She didn't understand she was a bystander. That was probably my fault. I'd had to lead her on a bit. Then again, she'd been warned.

Slowly, I dragged myself up to standing.

"Hold still." M's voice was just above a whisper. "This is gonna sting."

"Uhh…" Angela still searched for a place in the confrontation. I held up my hand and she quieted. She probably hoped it could still go her way.

Marigold's mouth was slightly open, her tongue pressed against the back of her teeth. She flicked her eyes around the restaurant, holding them a beat on Angela, then focused back on me.

"Ready?" she rasped.

Fucking every level of hell yes I was ready — my dick had come alive at just the whiff of her.

She tightened her expression. I could have stopped her hand in a flash, could have grabbed her wrist and pinned her against the booth in less than a second. But then she wouldn't have won her pissing contest, and besides, I didn't want her defeated. I wanted her unbridled passion.

The actual slap barely stung, but the rage behind it? Intoxicating. I flicked my head to the side at the end of the contact to make it seem like she'd gotten me better than she had. Compared to the blows I'd taken from the crew while we trained, Marigold was like a kitten swatting a string of ribbon.

For good measure, I rubbed my cheek like it'd hurt. I even shifted my jaw around a little. "You done?"

"Just getting started. You?" She shot her eyes to the table.

"Done here." I reached into my pocket and pulled out more than enough cash to cover the bill. I threw it on the table without looking at my date, who was mumbling something about me being a royal asshole.

Marigold eyed Angela one more time then did something I hadn't expected. She stepped up. "Listen, Angela. You're best not sending anymore texts or pics or what the fuck ever." M's nostrils flared. "I don't share."

I grabbed M's wrist and yanked her to the door. She'd made her point, but she was no street rat. Angela had probably thrown down with some bitches in her day. She would eat Marigold alive. It was one thing to hit me. It was quite another to get into a cat fight with a girl from the projects.

Jimmy stood at the door, pretending he hadn't seen a girl just slap me.

"Walk her home," I barked and thumbed over my shoulder.

"No problem, Goldie. But uh, just so we're clear…uh…she doesn't live on the third floor, right?"

Damn, Jimmy, picking up scraps left and right. But then again, if Angela was willing, why the hell not? Only thing was, Jimmy had a past with a less than disciplined crew and Angela did work for my cousin. "*Walk* her home."

A quick sour look passed over Jimmy's face. No one liked taking orders. I got it. But if he was going to rise up to be in the upper crew one day, it would be on our terms — not his. He nodded and I hoped the brief interaction hadn't done anything to dwindle the fire between M and me.

Out on the street, night had started to fall. I tugged at Marigold's wrist but she stopped in her tracks.

"I meant what I said." She yanked her arm away and crossed it over the other. *Pouting with rage, fucking gorgeous.*

"Good. For the record, I'm not very good at sharing either. So that's settled." I crowded her space, but she stood straight, not giving me an inch of surrender. I leaned down to the exposed nape in her neck and dragged my bottom lip up to her ear. "You hack my phone and been reading my messages?"

"Yes." There was still some spite in her tone.

Good. Let's keep it going.

"I don't owe you anything," I said and found myself drunk on her scent.

She stepped back and narrowed her eyes. "Then don't fucking give me anything."

Before I could reach out for her, she dropped her shoulder and maneuvered around me and was halfway down the block, her arms still crossed and her pace brisk. I followed — *What else am I going to do?* — but kept a distance between us. In the small space of her hot little ass and my raging hard-on, we walked all the way back down to Covington.

In the courtyard, the entire crew — including Anton, who was holding court at the bench — smirked at me as I walked by. Yeah, yeah, yeah. They could fuck off.

They had no idea how hot it was about to get on the third floor.

Spock wagged his tail from the couch but grumbled when neither of us greeted him with more than a glance. Marigold slammed the door to her bedroom before I could get there, but she didn't lock it. I adjusted my junk, counted to ten to make her worry I wouldn't come in, then entered. But me? I locked that damn door.

It was hard to know if the little flicker in her eyes was curiosity or fear. I wasn't looking to really scare her, just keep the stakes up so the payoff was bigger than the previous time.

"You all done with your big show?" I asked in a casual, bored voice then stretched my arms over my head.

"Just getting started." M threaded her thumbs under the straps of her thin black suspenders and guided them off her shoulders so they hung below her waist. She stepped toward me. "One thing, though. For clarity."

"Oh yeah? What's that?"

"No one fucking else. You and me until there's no more you and me." There was a weight to her words, a meaning heavier than I'd known. I suspected she'd had that same gnawing rub I'd had since we'd met. That I'd found someone, finally, who didn't just see me...a person who understood me and didn't run for the hills. But deeper and far more frightening—there was the acceptance. It somehow meant more that she'd liked me sight unseen when we'd chatted online. It was stupid, but it was true.

Her eyes raced over mine. Perhaps the internal struggle for her was harder. It had been a quick realization, our warped bond. Maybe she was in shock from it all. But it would have been entirely out of character for either of us to take something slow. We saw what we wanted, and we nabbed it. Simple.

I looked away for a long blink. It was our last chance to catch our breath, the final moment of incertitude.

But Marigold Pfeifer would have none of it. She crossed the room and peered at me for a long exhale. Then, bless her wicked heart, she slapped me again. The crack echoed between the otherwise silent walls. That time I caught her wrist and twisted it behind her back.

Heat spread like a wildfire over every inch of my skin. My dick strained against my fly and I pushed it hard into her ass. But she didn't whimper or tense. No, not my Marigold. She relaxed, like my tight grip was the warm bath she'd been waiting for at the end of a long day.

Through gritted teeth, I said, "Just us." I pushed her to the bed and she stumbled a little. Maybe it was for show, maybe not. Our lines of reality and fantasy were officially blurred. "Get undressed."

She shot me a dirty look but sat on the bed, unlaced a boot then threw it at me. I ducked and she missed but the second one skimmed my head seconds later. I kicked off my own boots, pulled off my shirt and dropped my pants before stepping out of them. Only my black boxers remained.

Once she'd gotten down to the skimpy dark pink lace, I said, "That's enough." I walked over to the bed and shoved her down but she propped herself up on her elbows. All night. That was how long I was going to tease and torture her gorgeous little body.

I said, "I bet you think this is going to go all fast and furious again. Maybe this time you might even get a couple fingers in your tight ass while I fuck you from behind."

She clicked her tongue. "You have other plans?" M pushed up and slid her knees behind her. She pressed her palms into my abs then my chest before glaring at me. "Because I want what's mine."

She kissed down my pec, twirled her warm tongue around my nipple and bit. Hard. *Yes.*

With one hand on my ass, she urged me closer while the other trailed down my stomach. Her fingers played with the waistband of my boxers, her thumb casually brushing over the head of my cock as she continued to suck and tease my nipple.

Her slow, deliberate movements of hand and mouth lulled me into a trance. My brain buzzed and I had to steady myself with her head and shoulder to remain upright. I was dying for her to grab my cock and yet didn't want to rush the build-up.

With both of her hands on my stomach, she clawed her nails into my abs before yanking down my pants, my erection springing free. I was too dizzy and shocked to know how I landed with my back on the bed and her hovering over me.

A devilish grin from the gorgeous woman on top of me was the last thing I saw before I closed my eyes and dropped my head back in full surrender. If that is how she was officially staking her claim, she might have to remind the world I was hers until the end of time.

M nipped, licked and sucked her way down to my cock. She wrapped her hand around the base of the shaft and took it in her mouth without letting her lips touch. In a slow, painful yet deliciously torturous trail, she raked her teeth upward. But once she reached the tip, she swiped her tongue all the way around, sucked hard and repeated. She worked my shaft at a pace that matched her mouth, the saliva dripping down acting as a perfect lubricant.

She was taking her fucking time, keeping me hard but in no rush to make me come. She cupped my balls and tugged too much and just enough, teetering me on an edge she'd somehow mastered.

I lost track of time, location and maybe even a bit of my consciousness. I was nervous and safe, my favorite place. When her mouth took charge, I was sure I was going to blow. But the pressure she gave the space between my sac and my ass was the button to the countdown of my explosion. She sucked hard, fast, furious. She gripped my balls, massaged them, tugged and did it all over again.

My cells and all my energy swarmed together like a whirlpool at my base, spinning around her and what she was doing. They hummed until they shrieked to be let loose. I gripped her head and wove my fingers into her short hair. I thrust her down one last time on my aching cock as I came hard in the back of her throat.

Every muscle in my body froze before I twitched like I'd been electrocuted, the only thing grounding me my grip of her head. When I fell limp, spent and the best kind of used-up, M hummed over my cock, swirled her tongue around the shaft and gave a final suck that made me scream.

With a small thump, my dick flopped on my stomach, the cool air of the room already luring it back to its flaccid state. She stood, wiped her chin with the back of her hand and raked her eyes over me before toddling off the to the bathroom.

Yeah, point made, Miss M. I don't need anybody else.

A few minutes later, I hadn't moved and she came out in sweatpants and a tank top.

"We're done?" I asked, hating the little creak in my voice.

"Yup. Gotta walk Spock." M crossed the room and opened the door. She looked over her shoulder and grinned. "Wouldn't want anyone to think you're a gentleman."

Chapter Sixteen

Marigold

He was still naked in my bed when I got back from my walk with Spock. The covers were under him as if he'd hadn't moved a muscle. I admired his confidence. I would have snuggled up and hid myself away, but not because I wanted to run. It was the chase I was after.

His eyes were closed, but his breath was too forced for him to be asleep.

"You're not going home?" I kicked off my boots.

Spock jumped on the bed and Rafa turned to the side, finally showing some modesty. I waited for an answer, but one never came. Was he brooding? Thinking?

"Suit yourself," I said with a sneer. Deciding whether him staying pleased me or annoyed me was too much effort. He could make the choice and I would deal with it—but after a little work. On the way to the other side of the apartment, I grabbed a soda from the fridge and popped it open once I'd gotten to my desk.

I logged into all my programs and fucking finally Zapata Falls had paid their ransom. I unfroze all their servers like we'd never been there, the equivalent of a thief tiptoeing out the back door in the middle of the night, sack full and swung over his back. I was just missing the mask and striped shirt. We'd gotten plenty of data, even some personal credit cards — not that I would be using them to deliver a pizza to my front door. I was reckless but not stupid.

With a few clicks, the online bank account popped up and I verified the deposit. One hundred thousand dollars. My lips twitched. That should have been all mine. It sat in the virtual world, hidden in crypto currency waiting for Anton to do what with it? Sell more drugs? Breed more criminals? Not that I could judge… I wasn't an outstanding citizen by any means.

But even so, the balance of the account pestered me like a chicken pecking at corn on the ground. I'd been the one who'd done all the work. I'd set my scheme into place long before I'd heard of Covington Heights. Why was it that I was sharing my loot?

Right, because I'd walked into a trap I'd laid for myself. My curiosity and fake swagger had wanted to be a part of something — anything. But, other than Rafa, I wasn't. There were no female members of Anton's crew. Even Lisa was an outsider to their business. Anton acted more like he owned me than respected anything I could do. Hell, he hadn't even bothered to ask me how I was going to do anything. All his trust was in Rafa, not me.

I transferred the agreed-upon ten percent into one of my own accounts and logged out of everything. The next target would have a higher ransom. Rafa just wouldn't know it. Then I would make what I should. My work with Covington would be like a little vacation with hot sex. Because I was starting to realize I was going to plan an exit strategy.

My phone lit up with a new message. My mom had been checking in with me ever since I'd left. She said she missed Spock and was worried I was only feeding him 'fake crap'. She and my dad were the only wrench in my spokes of an otherwise brilliant criminal life. I sent a text back that I'd try to come home in the next few days with some smiley emojis to make her believe I was happy. I tossed the phone on my desk and swiveled in my chair.

Was I happy? I sure as shit was afraid I'd bitten off way more than I could chew.

A little real-life excitement... That was what I'd wanted. Well, Rafa was definitely helping with that goal. Make new friends... I thought Lisa and I were starting something. Be who I was without judgment? Total check there.

The change I'd craved had come. Why was I resisting the free fall? Why did I think I had to leave?

I powered everything down, nabbed my phone and headed for my bedroom. A sliver of light from the window drew a light blue line across Rafa's bare stomach. Funny, he seemed almost docile on his back. Our eyes met for a long hold.

"Money came," I said in a flat voice.

"Anton will be happy." He was quiet, reserved. It didn't suit him.

My eyelids were heavy as I crossed the room. "What about you? Does it make you happy?"

Rafael rolled to his side and lifted the covers but didn't answer. His arm stayed in the air as I undressed and his light eyes scanned my naked body. I crawled into the bed and he tucked the covers around me. His warm thighs were the perfect landing for my cold ass.

"So we're doing this, then? Fucking spooning? You and me?" I sighed out my disgrace in both of us. We were suckers. Fakers, suckers and I guessed angry lovers to boot.

Spock stood at the end of the bed and jumped off, panting. But that didn't mean that Rafael uncrowded my space. Under the covers, he slinked an arm up my stomach and I couldn't decide if I was relieved or disappointed when he didn't kiss my bare shoulder.

My mind started spinning with what the hushed moment meant. A childish thought made me smirk and almost giggle. Was Rafa my boyfriend? *Dear God, no.* But whatever it was that was transpiring, one thing was clear. The gentle side of us? It was a secret.

And with that knowledge, a sense of safety blanketed me and some tension released from the top of my shoulders all the way down my back. My guard was down, but so was his.

He brushed his thumb back and forth over my ribcage and I closed my eyes.

"I need to see my parents. They're not used to the separation."

Rafa hummed. The low vibration warmed my neck and penetrated into my skin. His energy was drifting away. Actively hating each other was exhausting. And yet there we were, intertwined like we'd been together for years, neither of us objecting.

"I'm going to take Spock. We'll be back by the afternoon." Even as I whispered the words, I knew he'd never agree. The timing was too suspicious.

"I'll take you. It's the only way."

The thread of hope that I'd be able to go home and come back unsupervised faded as he tugged me a little closer. I chewed my bottom lip. He would have to meet my parents, see their crazy. He'd want to see my basement...

"Don't overthink it, M. Let tonight be tonight and tomorrow, tomorrow."

His breathing slowed and his grip loosened. I was kinda surprised he didn't make another move, but then again, we weren't mad. I put the following day out of my mind and savored his strong arms around me. While horribly superficial, I liked that his body was tight and his muscles thick. In one of the most dangerous neighborhoods in the city, the security of his physical lock was a welcome sensation.

I yawned and nestled in deeper. He was right. Tomorrow would be tomorrow.

A deep sleep took over, and when I woke, he was gone. The blade of moonlight from the night before had warped into the yellow sun. It was going to be hot, and the air was heavy. I would need to take extra water for Spock on the train.

I stretched, liking the fact that I could be naked in bed. It wasn't a luxury I'd allowed myself at my parents' house. We had no locks on our internal doors. But I didn't know if one of the crew would be lingering in my kitchen, so after I rolled out of bed, I threaded my legs through my pajama pants and found an oversized T-shirt I would have normally slept in.

After a few blinks, it occurred to me that Spock was also not in the room, and I couldn't help but smile that Rafa had taken responsibility for my dog right away.

Coffee. I needed artificial energy to face my parents. I gave myself a little shake and headed for the kitchen. Once there, I loaded the coffee machine and watched it percolate drop by drop. A little hum erupted after a tuff of steam and the roasted blend began to wake up my brain.

I leaned on the counter with my forearms down, cup in hand, waiting for the coffee to make its final perk.

A tiny creek and pop came from the door before Spock shot through. He didn't even look at me, just went straight to his water bowl and lapped it up, drool and excess water puddling around the dish.

Rafa, full of sweat, and—mother of mercy—shirtless, followed with a green apple lodged in his mouth. He took a crunchy bite and worked his jaw with a wide smile.

I glared over at him. He was entirely too perky for the morning.

Rafa swallowed. "Hey there. You know that shit is terrible for you, right?"

"Fuck off."

He wiggled his eyebrows. "Mmm-m. Cranky. Bring it."

I flipped him off, which only brought out his annoying dimples.

"So, I transferred the crypto to a new account where only I have the password. Don't freak if you don't see it there."

Well, fuck me. That was a smart move. *Respect.* I poured my coffee, added three teaspoons of sugar and opened the fridge for the cream. Spock finished lapping up his water, walked over to the side of the couch and lay down, still panting.

I shot Rafa my best side-eye. "What the hell did you do to my dog?"

"Treadmill. He fucking loved it." Rafael switched to a stupid voice and bent down to Spock. "Didn't you, big boy?

I poured my cream and stirred the coffee then set the mug on the counter. Rafa continued to talk like an idiot to my dog, crunched down in front of him. I walked over, pushed on his shoulder and knocked him to the ground. The green apple fell to the floor and rolled past the sofa.

"I told you. No adorable shit. Go fucking shower. You're gross."

He licked his lips and narrowed his eyes. Oh, no. I lunged for the counter but he was too fast. Rafa grabbed my ankle with one hand then lurched for my waist and tugged me down from the elastic band of my pants. He spun me on my back and I was nose-to-nose with his sweaty, hot face before I could say, "Alakazam."

But instead of kissing me, he rubbed his sweat all over my shirt and pants, Spock barking jealously overhead because he wasn't playing with us. It was foul, disgusting and it tickled the shit out of me.

"You like my stank."

I pushed his shoulders and kicked at his legs but he had me pinned and the giggles poured out of me. "I don't like anything about you! Get off!"

He froze and jerked his head up. "Nothing?"

"Zero," I lied.

"Well, in that case, I have nothing to lose." He lifted my T-shirt and rubbed his wet, nasty head on my bare stomach.

"Oh my God. You are beyond repulsive." I shoved him away again, still not making much impact. "Go away."

Rafa crawled on top of me and pushed my shoulders down. "Kiss me and I'll set you free."

"Will you also shower? Cuz seriously, bro, you're a new kind of foul." Honestly, he wasn't that bad, just sweaty. I'd smelled much worse from my parents' friends who thought lemon juice was deodorant.

Spock barked one last time then grumbled as he lay down.

I flared my nostrils. "One kiss. No tongue."

He laughed. "Marigold Pfeifer, you playin' hard to get? After all we've already done?" The quick peck he gave me was gone too fast and completely out of character for both of us, an overall stupid idea on my part. But he rose and fetched his apple while I propped up on my elbows and frowned at the state of my clothes.

Rafa went to the sink and rinsed the piece of fruit then took another bite. "How long before you're ready?"

"An hour?" Wake up, shower, makeup, organize. Yeah, I needed a bit of prep.

"Fine. I'll be back in fifteen for the laptop and the hard drive. I'll go throw them in the river while you get all goth nerdy."

I pushed to my feet and shook my head. "You're going to throw my laptop in the river?"

"Yeah." He shrugged. "I'll steal you a new one tomorrow."

After another disturbing peck, he was out of the door and I could finally sip my coffee.

Shit. I'd never gotten rid of the computers I'd used to hack previous people or cities. They were in my parents' basement, waiting to be discovered by anyone who bothered to look. Sure, I'd covered my steps with IP addresses in India and deleted all the fake accounts, but I'd never gotten actual new physical machines. Mad props to Rafa for his follow-through.

I made myself a second cup of coffee and was halfway through it when Rafa popped back in. He'd showered, his hair was still a little damp, and the crisp scent of his soap woke me up more than the caffeine pumping in my veins.

"Last chance to get anything off these babies. I'll wipe them clean then chuck them over the bridge." Rafa headed to the other bedroom and I followed him with my gaze.

A lesson about the planet and recycling blabbered between my ears, narrated by my mother's voice. Maybe that was why I'd never thought to ditch my own. It would have raised too many questions. Probably stupid.

I finished my coffee and set the mug in the sink. Rafa was back with my laptop tucked under his arm and the internal hard drive of the other computer in his hand.

I asked, "How many computers have you thrown in the river?"

"Fifty?" He lifted a shoulder and stuck out his bottom lip. "Scooter used to bash them with a hammer. He got his rage out that way."

"What's he got to be mad about?"

Rafa's face went somber. "Plenty."

I brushed by him on my way to my room. "Wow. So detail-oriented. You could write a book. Fascinating." I spread my fingers like jazz hands, twirled my wrists and ended in a double flip of the bird. I wanted some fucking dish about the crew.

In my room, I stripped and tossed my clothes on the bed then headed for the shower. Rafa stalked behind me, chucking the laptop and hard drive next to my pajamas. He propped his hands on his hips and hovered in the doorway of the bathroom.

"Something happened to his girl. She's fucked up."

I turned on the spray of the shower and tested the temperature with my hand. "Again, your ability to lay out the fine points is mesmerizing."

Rafa shook his head slowly and closed his eyes. "She was kidnapped, beaten, raped and about five minutes away from being sold on the black market as a sex slave. She sits at home and eats cereal and stares at the nature channel all day long. I haven't even seen her since it happened. He won't leave her, but she's not the girl he fell in love with."

Holy shit. A ping of stupidity stung in my gut. I'd thought I was playing a game in Covington. They weren't. For as smart as I was, I was incredibly fucking stupid.

I stopped myself from getting in the shower and asked in a soft voice, "How did he get her back?"

Rafa stared over my shoulder then flicked his eyes back to me. "He didn't. And that's the whole point, M. No one comes back from that."

A part of me, the one that was too curious for my own good, wanted to ask if that was why Rafa hate-fucked—no risk of emotional attachment, no risk of losing someone you care about. But I stepped into the open shower and Rafa bowed out behind me.

The exit strategy I'd been thinking about was becoming more and more important. The problem was, I didn't want to go back to my old life.

Chapter Seventeen

Rafa

I hadn't wanted to tell her about Scooter's girl — one, because I thought it might scare her away and two, because I was afraid I would let it slip that we'd killed someone. But there had been some dark shit that had gone down before Marigold had shown up unannounced and been stupid enough to stay, and she deserved to know the difference between violent criminals and cute girls who sat at home and spread computer viruses.

With the laptop under my arm and the hard drive in hand, I punched the button for the elevator. Anton came out of our apartment down the hall and the doors opened as soon as he was next to me.

We entered and he rubbed his hands together. "If you're getting rid of that, it means it was payday."

"Yup. Ninety Gs in the bank. Well, in the virtual account. What do you want me to do with it?"

He crossed his arms and rubbed his chin. "Nothing yet. I gotta have dinner with my mom tomorrow night. Actually, it would be helpful if you came with me. Leo was always a good distraction for her."

"Yeah, sure." Being asked to meet Anton's mother was a weird honor. She was criminal royalty in the city. But being reminded that I wasn't Leo? That had gotten old the week after he'd left.

"What about those game locations?" he asked as the doors opened and we crossed the empty entryway.

The sun beat down on us hard once we got outside into the courtyard. Its heat made me break out in an instant layer of thin sweat.

"Just waiting for the addresses from my cousin. Then I have a special delivery to make." My devious smile matched his own.

Jackson was at the bench and I nodded my hello to him. Anton stopped and lifted a finger. "One more thing. You need to fuck Rainbow Brite at our place. You not being there at night gives the impression that you don't want to be there—like you'd rather be somewhere else, which I'm sure isn't the case." His tight smile was fake, and a bit of a warning.

It was so typically Anton. Pat my head and give me the treat of going to dinner with his mother then scold me for bad behavior with a hidden threat. Not even the money I'd just made for him could keep him from flexing his bossman muscle.

Except I did want to be somewhere else. I just didn't know where it was or how to get there. But instead of objecting and reminding him how valuable I was, I just said, "Copy that," and headed west toward the river.

There were no cops in sight, and instead of climbing the bridge like I normally did, I chucked the laptop off the side of the observation deck and it skipped on the top of the water like a flat stone before it landed and slowly sunk. I threw the hard drive right after it, and as soon as it was out of my hands, something poked me in the ass.

I spun around and a little old lady with her cane was waiting for me with a disapproving look.

"You know that's terrible for the fish."

"You really think there are fish in that river?" I pointed my thumb over my shoulder to the filthy and polluted waters behind me.

"Good point. But it's still littering. Give me a hundred bucks and my Alzheimer's will kick in. I won't remember you breaking the law."

I couldn't help but laugh. Not because I wouldn't pay her, but because she had the balls to ask for the money. A littering fine would have probably been cheaper, but it was a way less fun story to tell.

"Damn, lady. A hundred? Really?"

"Don't hate the player, hate the game." She leaned on her cane with one hand and extended the other.

"What makes you think I have that kind of money?"

"Don't dick with me. You just threw a computer and something else into the river."

"Fair enough." I dug into my pocket and unrolled a hundred-dollar bill. I slapped it in the palm of her hand.

"Pleasure doing business with you." She stuffed the bill into her bra and hobbled off. Marigold was going to love that story.

On the way back to Covington, I stopped for a bottle of water at a deli, and as I was screwing back on the top, my phone vibrated in my pocket. Three addresses popped up in a text from my cousin. *Fucking bingo.* Damn, it was turning out to be a brilliant day.

I called my cousin Diego in Queens and ordered six of his nastiest cages with a delivery date for that night. Jefferson Manor and the patrons they'd stolen from us were in for a filthy surprise.

At the bench, I found Jimmy and I put my arm around him. "You're on duty again tonight. I have a delivery to make. Oh, and you'll have to train without me today."

"Got it. Jerimiah was going to come anyway. He can spot me."

I gave Jerimiah the once-over and hoped for Jimmy's sake that he didn't plan on lifting anything heavy. After a squeeze in his neck, I let him go.

More than an hour had passed since I'd left Marigold, and she was in the kitchen, dressed and ready to go. Damn, she wore nerd goth like a supermodel. Black fishnets, black shorts and a white-collar button-down shirt tucked in.

"Stop looking at me like I'm the candy you deny yourself in the name of keeping your body fit."

I stepped over to her and nudged her backward so that she was trapped between me and the counter. "The only thing sweet about you is the way you smell," I whispered and ran my nose along her jawline. I also took a big whiff of that addicting scent.

M pushed into my chest. "Get off, meathead. And don't act all boyfriend-y in front of my parents. My mom is already suspicious of me living in a place she's never seen."

"As she should be. This is a terrible neighborhood." I stepped away, instantly regretting the distance between us.

"I just need to get Spock's bag."

Plastic crinkled as M folded a big blue bag and shoved it into her backpack. I didn't ask the question burning in my brain, but from Spock's sad eyes and folded ears, he didn't like his bag.

"Come on, big boy." She attached his leash and we were out the door. We took the stairs down and were scorching in the hot sun within minutes. I put my arm around Marigold, claiming her yet again in front of the crew as we passed. But the scrutinizing eyes of Anton were on us. I'd failed to tell him I was taking the day off for a home visit.

He came up to us and I stopped with a smile. "Where you two headed?"

"New job, new computers." I smiled. "By the way, my cousin came through. Tell Jackson to get our bar back downtown. He can set up a game for this weekend."

"Good. You mind if I send Scooter with him? He needs to get out of the house. And since you are more lucrative with this one, I'd hate to waste your time on a dice game."

"Whatever you think is best, boss. I'll see you tonight after I take care of Jefferson."

Anton looked us up and down before stepping to the side and letting us pass. M and I walked in silence to the train station where she stopped and dug out the blue plastic bag. If dogs could frown, Spock was owning it, maybe even giving the evil eye to the oversized sack.

"How often do you lie to him?" Marigold handed me the leash then twisted to open her bag.

Shit. I was busted. Worse, I'd lied *for* her.

"You want him to know where you live?"

She froze. It hadn't been a threat, but it had sounded like one.

"No. So thank you for keeping that nugget for yourself." Marigold crunched down in front of her dog, who refused to look her in the eyes. "Dogs can be in the train as long as they're in a bag. Come on, Spock. In."

"M, seriously. Don't treat my homie like that. I'll pay the damn fine. Besides, why are you — of all people — so keen on obeying the law?"

"I'm trying not to draw attention to us."

That? That was hilarious. "You mean with your unicorn fart hair and resting bitch face?"

"Fuck off." She stood and refolded the bag.

We jogged down the stairs and swiped our cards through the turnstile. The train came, we boarded and no one said a damn word about the giant blue pit bull and his lack of a bag.

But the oddest thing did happen. About halfway through the ride and with Spock at our feet, Marigold wove her fingers into mine. Her hand was a little sweaty and I gave it a quick squeeze, neither one of us making eye contact. I suspected she was just as nervous as I was. It wasn't every day I went to meet the parents of the girl I hate-fucked and sorta liked.

And *there* was a hard truth. I did like Marigold Pfeifer — not just her banging little body. Her warped mind had me mesmerized. How she knew how to be everything I wanted was a fucking mystery. *Shit.* My pulse raced and my knee started bobbing. I didn't hate her at all. *Oh, fucking hell.* I was crushing on her. What was wrong with me? I was holding her hand! In public! I didn't even want to let go. *Who am I?*

"Hey!" Marigold shout-whispered. "What the fuck is wrong with you?"

"Me?" Oh, for fuck's sake, my voice cracked.

"No. The lady with three kids over there." She rolled her eyes. "Yes, you. You're all jittery and shit."

I didn't know what to say, so I just stared at her, my mouth agape. Soon enough, the horror washed over her face as well and her gaze drifted in stupefied dread to our hands. She withdrew hers then stared at her palm like the villainous traitor it was.

The shock and disgust in the look she shot me would have made me laugh, but I had to admit it stung a little. Plus, I'd liked holding her hand. *Fuck*.

"Why did you do that?" she spat.

"Me?"

"Who else am I talking to?" M shook her head and wiped her hand on her stomach. That was slightly over the top. I didn't have cooties. We'd had sex, for fuck's sake.

I shifted in my seat and glared at her. I wasn't going to take the blame for her random act of tenderness. "You did that. You interlaced your fingers into mine."

"No. No, I didn't." Her denial was weak, as if she'd already known the truth and was trying to convince herself she was innocent. *Ha. Hardly*. Her stumble was enough for me to get my swagger back.

I licked my lips and leaned into her ear. "You did. You reached out and took my hand. And you know why?"

Her eyes raced over mine. "Because I've been possessed?"

"Because you like me." So what if I was projecting? She was too destabilized to pick up on it.

"Eww. No, I don't."

I clicked my tongue. "Taking me home to meet Mom and Dad. Letting me sleep in your bed and snuggle… Marigold, do you have a crush on me?"

She scoffed. "You wish. And by the way, you're basically holding me prisoner. The only reason you're here is because you would never let me go alone for fear of me leaving your pathetic ass."

All true. "Stockholm syndrome is real, baby."

"Jesus Christ. Did you do some of the drugs you sell?" She crossed her arms and glared at me, but there was a flicker of realization behind all those fake daggers she was sending my way. Damn it, she was beautiful.

"I'm high on life." I grinned from ear to ear.

"Gross." M mumbled more objections under her breath, but she knew what she'd done. She could deny it six ways till Sunday but the truth was just that.

"So what are we telling your parents, anyway?"

She grimaced. "I told them you were my friend and I was helping you with a job."

"Friends with benefits." I waggled my eyebrows to piss her off. It totally worked.

"You say that to my parents and the next time I use my teeth, I'll bite." She recognized the empty threat as soon as it was out of her mouth. "You'd probably like that."

The rest of the ride, I sat with a smug smile next to her—her side-eye and curse word babbles only making me more pleased with myself. Also, I might have been thinking about the next time that she had made pretty apparent was on the table.

"This is our stop." M stood and Spock stretched.

"And guess what? No doggie-bag police." I scratched Spock behind the ears and followed them through the open train doors and up the blackened cement stairs. To fuck with her even more, I reached for her hand once we were outside. She swatted it away several times like she was murdering a bug that had dared to crawl on her sweet skin.

We walked down a few blocks with delis and odd shops then turned onto a tree-lined residential street. The houses had small, fenced-in yards and concrete driveways. It was about as normal as one could get. Poor M had probably stuck out like a sore thumb. She stopped in front of a simple house with a minivan in the driveway.

"Before you make fun of me for that, it's the neighbors. My parents only believe in public transportation."

That was a huge insight into a lot of things. If her family didn't have a car because of their beliefs, there were probably many other tree-hugging habits that Marigold had rebelled against. It totally explained the junk food. A lightbulb exploded in my head. Her parents were greenies. Being a sci-fi computer nerd was her way to rebel. Bless her twisted heart. It was all an act of severing the emotional umbilical cord from her parents. They were probably the nicest people on the planet.

She opened the gate and unhooked Spock from the leash. He immediately pissed on a bush then rolled around in the grass, spreading his scent.

"He has to tell the neighborhood squirrels and cats that he's back. They taunt him when he's inside. Come on. Let's get this over with."

Chapter Eighteen

Marigold

An electric shiver ran up my spine as I placed my hand on the knob of my parents' front door. I'd never taken a guy home to meet them. Hell, I hadn't had friends over since...since I'd had friends.

I gave Rafael one last fleeting glance. He'd have to do. Better to have him on my side than working against me. My mom could be a lot to take in. *Okay, big-girl pants.*

The frosted glass in the entry way gave a little rattle and Spock nearly took me out as he raced inside.

"Mom! I'm home," I called out and gave a warning glare to Rafa. He smiled softly in return. My stomach turned sour. If he was going to play the sweet and innocent card with those gorgeous eyes, my mom might not be able to be the big bad controlling tyrant that only I saw her to be. Also, I might have to puke.

"There you are." My mother crossed her arms as her eyes raked over Rafa from the threshold to the kitchen. She clocked the ink on his forearms, his wide chest and probably cursed his leather boots. "Who's this?"

Rafa stepped forward and extended his hand. "Rafael Santos, Mrs. Pfeifer. Nice to meet you."

They shook hands and I counted down from three to one in my head.

"Ms. Carlson. I didn't take my husband's name." She smirked.

Yep. That had been entirely predictable.

"My apologies." Rafa offered a tight smile.

"Marigold must have forgotten to mention it." Cue the internal gagging on my part. *Nope.* I hadn't forgotten anything. The omission was equal parts to annoy my mom and show Rafa who she really was.

She sighed. It was dramatic. Her pity party had officially kicked off. "Well, at least she mentioned me. I was beginning to think she'd forgotten that she lives here."

I let the zinger hang out in the air. After years of fighting with her, I'd learned that silence had proven to be the one way to annoy her the most.

"Dad here?" I asked after we were all thoroughly uncomfortable.

"He'll be back for lunch. Let's have a cup of tea and talk about your new job."

My mother's mood brightened, but I could see the claws she was trying to dig into me for information.

It was highly probable that there was nothing abnormal about my mother, that she was just like many other overly concerned parents out there. In fact, I was more and more convinced that the problem was me. I loved her. She was my mom after all. I just didn't like her. It sounded horrible, but it was a hard and ugly truth that had eaten at me for years. We didn't understand each other and were both too stubborn to see the other one's point of view. Eventually, I'd just stopped sharing mine. In her opinion, I was always wrong, always too young to understand or far too reckless.

"I'm going to show something to Rafa on my computer. Call us when lunch is ready." I stepped toward the basement door but was blocked by my mom.

"Excuse me? You've been gone for days doing God knows what with a tattooed pretty boy and you brush me off just like that? I need some answers, especially since the police knocked on the door looking for you."

Holy shit. "What? When?" Damn the shock in my voice. I'd been entirely too quick with my questions.

"Yesterday. I thought we could discuss it today." She let out a little huff laced with exasperation. "But if you want to show your boyfriend your Batcave, be my guest."

Rafa searched the floor before holding his arm. He twitched his lips to the side. *Shit.* I was a liability to everyone. I didn't know much about the Covington Heights crew, but I was sure someone with the police on their tail was an unwelcomed guest.

"Why didn't you call me?" I hated the thread of weakness in my voice. It was the opposite of how I'd wanted Rafa to see me. And I hated the dynamic between me and my mom that had brought it out. We hadn't even been there ten minutes.

"I sent you a text, since that's the only way you communicate with me...which is ridiculous. We're human. We need to interact."

I closed my eyes, but I was sure she could tell I was rolling the crap out of them.

Rafa took the moment to speak up, though his voice was tender and calm. "I'm going to wait outside."

My mother and I huffed in tense anxiety as he slipped out of the door. The moment it clicked shut I yelled, "I bet you were just fucking dying to throw that in my face. Does it make you feel all powerful and controlling that you got to do it in front of my friend?"

"Your friend," she scoffed. "Really, Marigold?"

"What did the police say?"

My mom pursed her lips and flared her nostrils. "Nothing. They were never here. It was a test to see if you were up to something sneaky, which you have confirmed that you are."

Snap. That was a dick move. If I wasn't so pissed about the fact that she'd done it, I could have respected her sneaky tactic. Would Rafa even believe me if I said she was lying? Shame on me for not seeing it coming. Our history was filled with similar examples.

She continued, "I suggest you wheel your bag back home with Spock, get a real job instead of chatting with strangers online and we can forget about whatever it is that you've gotten yourself into."

That made sense...for her anyway. I'd always been afraid to wonder if one day I would need to cut the ties to my parents. After all, I'd been running an illegal hacking business out of their basement for the previous two years. But in that moment, it was crystal clear. Wither away in a life she chose and be miserable or finally break free and try to find some happiness.

I marched to the front door and swung it open. Rafa startled on the step where he was sitting.

"How soon can you have a van here?"

"Why? Did you murder her already?"

"Hey," I snapped, "you're on my side. Get a van or something. I'm moving all my shit to Covington."

"Whoa, whoa, whoa. What happened?" Rafa stood and damn those lines around his eyes for showing his true concern. Damn his furrowed forehead and sympathetic tone, too. I liked him much better when he was accusing me of murder. Gentle Rafael was destabilizing, much like I'd been to him when I'd fucking reached out and held his damn hand when I was nervous on the train. But he was the only ally I had.

Some of the anger I had slipped away and regret climbed into the hole it had left. "She lied. There were no police. She's trying to manipulate me to stay. I'm her daughter. She sees me for what I am. No good." I swallowed and looked away to avoid any pity or judgment he might have. "Don't fucking try to hug me. Just get a van."

He tilted his head ever so slightly and smiled. Fuck if it didn't warm my cold heart. "I do like it when you're bossy."

"Much better." I turned and walked back inside. My mother was crouched down in the small hallway, scratching Spock's chin.

"I hope that was you saying goodbye." The nonchalant, dismissive look on her face enraged me.

"Not yet." Behind my brave face and sneer, my heart was breaking. I didn't want to cut the ties to my family, despite all my attitude and bitterness. It was why I hadn't done it previously. They were all I had. My foolish, misplaced pride was running away with itself. But I realized I could no longer have it both ways.

Whereas my mother had suspected I was up to no good down in the basement alone, and with one look at

Rafa and my telling shock at her mention of the police, I'd proven it. I marched up the stairs to my room and did inventory. I wouldn't need anything from my bed and had already taken my favorite items from my closet. The stuffed animals, posters and childhood journals that my mom had already sifted through meant nothing. My parents' low-waste lifestyle had also applied to my simplistic accessories.

Tears burned in the corner of my eyes and my chest heated. Maybe my parents had been right all along. Worldly possessions meant nothing. I took a deep breath before closing the door and jogging back down the stairs.

As I hit the bottom step, the front door opened and my father's confused gaze washed over me.

"Who's the muscle man on the stoop?" He closed the door behind him.

My mother rolled a shoulder on the doorframe from the kitchen. A glib sneer highlighted the wrinkles around her makeup-clean eyes. "It's a criminal. Your daughter is dating a criminal. Seems like she's keen on becoming one herself."

A faint voice in my heart begged me to argue my case in front of my father, but the logic in my head extinguished the glimmer of hope that had come with the plea. That time would not be different from any of the rest. My mother was in total control and that included her spouse. Their shared values and marital bond were no match for my emotional petition for him to see my side of the story.

Besides, arguing my case would only prove my mother right. Tainted pride was the only thing I had left.

"What she said." I cornered around the banister and clunked down the stairs to the basement. Through the floorboards I could hear my parents bickering as I rustled around for a mini screwdriver at my father's workbench in the corner. The tools clanked and covered up their muffled voices until I found what I needed at the bottom of his wooden chest.

All my old virus programs were worthless. I'd sold so many copies that I would never be able to use them again. Anyway, there was something calming about writing code and cracking firewalls. A new way to break into a small town or medium-sized business's servers and hold them hostage would keep my true identity a big question mark if anyone tried to locate me.

But just in case my mother was feeling vengeful, I unscrewed the back of the tower to my main computer and took out the hard drives. A beige cloth bag hung on a nail and was a home to all the different kinds of tapes my father used.

I emptied the spools on the bench and filled the little tote with the drives, then tucked my laptop under my arm. The only thing left was Spock.

My parents were seated at our kitchen table and their heated debate ended the minute they saw me.

"Marigold..." My father's sad eyes broke my heart, but there was no going back.

I shook my head and miraculously held back tears. Maybe stubborn pride served a purpose after all. My mother watched me like a sly cat. She was waiting for me to realize the error of my ways, to stop being a child. Good thing she wasn't holding her breath.

"Come on, Spock." I tapped my thigh.

My dog stood and stretched, his hesitation just enough time for my mother to hook a finger in his collar.

"According to the city, Spock is my dog. You were a minor when we got him. And your actions today only highlight your immaturity. He stays."

I'd once heard that breathing was natural, automatic. But my mother's vicious words and power play had forced my body into a stiff and shocking breathless state. Over the years, there had been name calling, manipulation and sometimes some truly questionable intentions. But cruelty? That was a new low. She'd gotten Spock for *me*. He'd been a gift, my only true friend since the day we'd found him at an adoption event next to the waterfront. He'd slept every night with me and literally weathered every storm.

I searched her gray eyes. "You can't—"

"I can. I am." Her words were so flat, so empty of emotion, so bored. She could have been filing her nails.

"Honey..." Before my father could finish, my mother shot him a death look.

I didn't need to know any more. She was ready to use my dog—my fucking safety blanket and the only reminder that I had a heart—against me. My cheeks heated as I stared into the eyes of the woman who'd raised me. Her own glare challenged me back, ready for me to surrender. I couldn't bear a final glance to the animal who had gently nudged me out of isolation or to the father who had failed me. She'd finally won. It just didn't look like what she'd imagined.

With a slow nod I turned to leave...for good. A lonely tear stung as it fell down the side of my face. I emptied my backpack of any temptation that might bring me back to their world and didn't dare turn around.

Instead of slamming the door, I closed it with a quiet click.

Rafa's concerned eyes darted over me.

"You can call off the van," I said, defeated. "There's nothing to take."

A long beat passed between us as I silently poured out my broken heart. My bottom lip quivered, betraying my confidence and brash façade, revealing that I wasn't the tough, didn't-give-a-shit girl I'd pretended to be.

"Come on," he said without an ounce of pity or judgment. Rafa drooped a lazy arm over my shoulder and prodded me into forward motion. It was exactly what I needed. We walked at a slow pace down to the waterfront where we sat on a bench and gazed up at the massive bridge before us.

"You want to talk about what happened in there?" His voice was so soft that it cut me like a switchblade.

"No." I sniffed and looked away. The sting of puddling tears was nothing compared to the terror running through my veins. I'd finally done it. I had no one. Fate had taunted me over the years, sometimes reminding me I was an only child, mostly throwing in my face how much I was socially awkward. But underneath its small lessons had always been the cruel prophecy. I would end up alone, misunderstood and rightfully so.

Rafa laid his hand on my thigh, the warmth awkwardly comforting. "Families are fucked up more times than not. If you want to talk about it, I'll listen. I won't even hold it against you. Although, I may make fun of you to piss you off."

Damn his little head tilt and eye twinkle.

I drew my chin back. "You'd use my pain to make me mad for hot sex?"

"Probably." His small shoulder shrug and playful tone was helping. It reminded me that even though he was probably kidding, his brain worked like mine. Maybe I wasn't completely alone.

He continued, "I mean...can you blame me, really? You are—by far—the hottest girl I've done that shit with. Jesus, M. How you crept up on my shit with Angela?" He shivered. It was fake and exaggerated, but he'd said I was hot and was sorta admitting to liking me, so I forgave it.

"Why did you go out with her, anyway? If I'm so much your type? She's pretty much the opposite of me..."

"I told you family is fucked up. I had to do it for my cousin to give me the info I needed against Jefferson Manors."

"How many cousins do you have?"

"Countless. But we all work on a self-serving barter system. It comes from most of us being parentless and trying to get in the good graces of our *avozihna*."

"Your what?"

"My granny. Her house was basically like an orphanage for her grandkids. I think at one point there may have been like eighteen of us living there."

I flicked my eyes to the ground then out onto the water. "Your childhood was basically the opposite of mine."

"And yet, we're the same now."

I couldn't argue with him, and, somehow, I didn't even want to. The wind blew the salty air by us and it shifted our mood. It may have even shifted our dynamics. But one thing was clear. Rafa had seen me. The real me.

I didn't even mind when he draped his arm around me again and tugged me closer to him. With my knees tucked into my chest and my head on his shoulder, we both let down our normally well-guarded walls. We were equally vulnerable, the honest moment both terrifying and freeing.

Rafa rubbed my upper arm. "You know what you need?"

A snarky rebuttal crept to my tongue but stayed there. Instead, I hummed, not quite ready to leave our holy space of truth without masks.

"Rats. You need rats."

I drew away from him and quirked an eyebrow.

"Trust me." He grinned.

"You're mentally warped."

He smiled. "Thank you."

Chapter Nineteen

Rafa

On the way back to Covington, we stopped in tourist central and I nabbed a laptop for M from a crowded coffee shop. The woman's designer bag had been left open by the door and Marigold had taken a great amount of pleasure in creating a diversion by spilling her coffee on the opposite side of the crammed restaurant. She was proving to be a worthy sidekick.

When we got back home, Spock's empty bowls glared at us from the floor — a slicing reminder of what she'd lost in order to become her true self. I decided to let her grieve in her own way and didn't offer to remove them.

She grabbed a can of soda from the fridge, said something about a new code then sat cross-legged on the couch with big headphones over her adorable ears. I probably stared at her too long. After all, there was a new weight on our relationship. The night before we'd made a commitment to the physical, and on the bench not far from her parents', something else had transpired.

The acknowledgment of our delicate and twisted connection had solidified our unlikely bond. While it had be thrilling and invigorating and sorta heartwarming, an alarming trepidation ran through my veins. I was in unchartered territory with a woman. Moreover, I didn't know if I could trust her.

Marigold spun around and rolled her eyes. Yeah, I'd been hovering. She shooed me away with her hand, and when I didn't move, she bugged out her eyes and flipped me off for good measure. Maybe all my gooey thoughts had made it into her consciousness, but she was right. I needed to fuck off. And she deserved a bit of space after a morning where she had cut ties with her family and dog.

It had been too long since I'd shot the shit with Jackson, so I was happy to find him in the gym. Better, he was alone and running on the treadmill. Sweat streaked down his dark, bald head and he huffed each time his giant foot landed on the spinning belt. His pace was faster than normal, which meant that he was running away from something, not warming up.

I let him be and focused my attention on a steady rotation of crunches and tricep pull-downs. Twenty minutes later, with the best kind of burn in my stomach and the back of my arms, I got what I'd waited for. Jackson stopped running and leaned over to catch his breath.

When he looked up, my eyes were already waiting for his. He held the knowing stare a beat, exhaled hard through his mouth, then said, "My sister called."

Jackson's sister calling only meant one thing. There was something bad happening to his family. Good news was a text. Painful honesty required an actual exchange between humans. Jackson had managed a safe distance between his current lifestyle and his previous good-boy-athlete one. Interactions were rare and superficial at best. His sister had moved out of the neighborhood years prior, thanks to a decent job, and their dad lived with her and her young family in a small but comfortable house in Queens.

"My pop's got cancer. They say six months."

Damn. My heart went out to him. He and his pops were top-of-the-line men. It wasn't like my own parents, who'd bred like rabbits and left us on our own. Jackson's dad had wanted more for him, had tried to give him that through sports.

I winced. It was probably a terrible excuse for sympathy. "Sorry, bro. Can I help?"

My best friend slumped his shoulders as he climbed off the treadmill. I met him at the press-up bench and sat next to him. Apparently, it was a day for me, benches and broken people I cared about.

Jackson swiped a white towel from the empty bar and wiped off his face before hanging his head. "I never wanted him to see me like this — like a low-life fucking dealer."

"You're a good dad, Jackson. You're making him proud by raising Junior."

"Nah. It's not enough. I need to get out of here. I can't watch Bridget fucking deteriorate in front of her son anymore. And I can't be the one fucking encouraging her to do it." He rubbed the defined muscles in his neck, sat up with a stiff spine, then shot me a cautious glance. "Leo called me."

What? I would have thought Leo had wiped himself and Fiona off the face of the earth. Why the hell would he reach out to Jackson? A coup? That didn't make sense. Leo and Anton were tight.

Jackson let out a stifled breath. "Apparently he and his brother have started something legit."

I worked my jaw. The only thing I could imagine Leo Ricci doing legit was beating someone's ass to a pulp. He was a lethal weapon with a warped sense of loyalty and a need to fight.

Jackson worked his jaw. "He said he needs people he can trust."

A small pinch of jealousy squeezed my gut. It was two-fold—one that Leo had chosen Jackson over me to trust, and two, the possibility of Jackson cleaning his hands of Covington. If Anton was going to let someone out of the crew freely, the chances of it being Jackson were pretty high. There was a kid in play, after all. And as to Leo? Maybe the only real opportunity without consequences. Leo could take out anyone, Anton included.

But one tends to think selfishly in moments of disappointment. Already being number two in charge wasn't really my thing, but at least I'd had Jackson in my private corner. If he left, then what? What would I do? And what the hell had Leo done to become all legit in a matter of months?

"For what, anyway?" I asked through a narrowed brow.

"Security. He and his brother do high-end, and I mean high, high-end security now."

I let the envy fade away. In truth, I had always hoped Jackson would find a way out of Covington. He'd grown up in the building across the courtyard, and his shitty grades had never been enough to support his decent basketball talent. He'd been a local legend and hero, according to the other guys who had never escaped the concrete walls around the dark part of our city. But after high school and no college scholarship, his all-star status had become a lot less shiny. Leo's offering was the first glimpse of a chance Jackson had to change his life after basketball.

I stood, only to crouch down in front of him in a squat. I frowned, but it was more resolve than sadness. "You should go. You should take Junior and Lisa and get the fuck out of here. There's a line out of the door of desperate younger dealers and crooks who want to take our place."

"What about you?"

I smiled. It was fake. "I'm a criminal. We all know that."

"You're not interested in redemption?"

"Not really. The high of stealing keeps me from chasing the other monsters." I winked, but shit could go sour at any moment. Every member of the crew had a story of a friend who they never thought would be an addict but fatefully was. Not being that person was an intimate and unspoken goal for most of us who'd grown up in the projects. My family and neighborhood were full of examples, people who let the reality of their struggle settle too long in their bones — sweet, well-meaning human beings who wanted to escape one single time from their shitty life, then just 'once again' blurred to 'once a week'. By the time they'd convinced themselves it was recreational, it was already a habit. And habit is the gateway to addiction.

I stood and offered Jackson my hand. We clasped, but before I added any muscle, I asked, "You tell the bossman yet?"

Jackson scrunched his nose and mouth together. "I was hoping you were going to do that for me."

My laugh turned into a coughing fit and I let go of his hand and bent down, trying to catch my breath. I regained my composure. "Nah... If it comes from me, I'm a failure for not keeping you here. It comes from you, he'll understand and probably even give you his blessing."

I pulled him to his feet. He stepped back, crossed his arms and scanned my face. "What's eating you?"

"It's nothing. Probably a preliminary case of the heebie-jeebies. I'm on rat duty tonight."

Jackson shivered. "Better you than me."

"But I'm going to take M. Get her mind off shit. Her mom took her dog."

Shaking his head, Jackson crossed the room to the massive leg press machine. As he adjusted the weight, he said over his shoulder, "That's your date, man? Filling game rooms with rats? I know you get off on drama and shit, but I fail to see the intrigue and romance in that shit."

"She's gonna love it." I hoped.

"Jesus and Mother Mary. If she loves that, Lisa is right. You two have each met your match."

We finished working out. I showered, did a bit of recon for the night and found Anton on our couch watching a boxing match as I was on my way out of the door, my lucky baseball hat in hand.

"Hey, boss." I thumbed over my shoulder to the door. "Just on my way to make a special delivery to those Jefferson Manor fuckers. Don't think the high rollers from downtown are going to be interested in their secret locations tonight."

Anton tipped his beer to me and said, "Nice work, Number Two. By the way, Jimmy is a great earner. Another stellar day for the newbie. If he keeps it up, he may just be third-floor material."

"Earning is everything, right?" The slight sarcasm in my voice didn't go unnoticed.

The bossman turned toward me and narrowed his eerie eyes. "Don't go getting all jealous cuz I like a new guy. We both know the kind of money you bring in is nothing compared to the stupid shit we sell on the streets."

He'd misread the snark and I was grateful. I didn't give a flying fuck about Jimmy coming up in the ranks. Hell, it had been my idea. What had led to my small but still apparent lack of conviction was that I seriously wondered when the last time was that Anton had gone out and earned anything on his own. Sure, he sat down at the bench and flexed his muscle, but none of our regulars actually asked to buy from him directly. And yes, he did all the runs upstate and got the product, but that was the easiest fucking part of it. He had a house up there with a pool and total seclusion. It was like a vacation twice a month from the cesspool that was Covington Heights. *It must be good to be king.*

Anton glanced over me and said, "Have Jackson set up a game for tomorrow night. Can we still use your cousin's back room?"

The knowledge that Jackson would be long gone by tomorrow gave me drip of power that I didn't normally surrender to. "My cousin wants me there. I'll set it up."

"We have dinner with my mom. You're my distraction, remember?"

Jesus, the way he made it sound was as if I was meat being fed to the tiger while the zookeepers cleaned the cage. "I can do both. And I'll take Jimmy. It will be good for them to see a new face with an old one. You know, new branding after they thought we were a bit trigger happy."

Anton mulled over my suggestion. I had to be there with my cousin to assure all was smooth with a new location. And he couldn't go against me taking Jimmy after he'd just sung his praises. But behind his light eyes, I could see him working all the angles. As he nodded his head, it affirmed he'd landed on the most obvious outcomes. I'd never led him down the wrong path before. Why would I start?

I was almost out of the door when he said, "Just a reminder that you sleep here."

"Yeah, yeah. I got it." I closed the door behind me and headed halfway down the hall to Marigold. I tapped in the code and the door popped open. She was exactly where I'd left her, except she'd drank three more sodas. The empty red-and-white cans lined the coffee table, each one slightly bent and deformed.

Her head bopped in little movements and tinny guitar sounds escaped her headphones. I smiled and walked over to her. The background of the laptop's screen was black, but a rainbow glowed with random letters and commands. She was into the thousands with her lines. She'd been busy.

I grabbed her shoulders like the boogie man and she leaped out of her skin.

"Jesus Christ." She cupped the headphones and pulled them off with a gorgeous evil eye.

"You need to change. All black. And some pants. It's rat time."

"That all sounds ominous. I'm on a massive roll here. I should keep going."

No, she shouldn't. She needed real crime, first-hand bad behavior. It would be a Band-Aid to her emotional day—a sort of revenge, except the victims were strangers. I took the laptop off her thighs, closed it, then set it and the headphones on the coffee table next to the abandoned evidence of her caffeine and sugar high.

"Trust me. You're going to like this." The devious grin on my face spread to her own.

"You keep saying 'trust me' like it's going to happen. But you're right. I could use a break. So fine…rat time it is, whatever the hell that means."

She stood and I swatted her adorable ass as it passed by. "Hurry up. The rodents are waiting."

She looked over her shoulder. "You have mental problems."

I shrugged. "You keep saying that like it's going to change something."

Chapter Twenty

Marigold

The cool night air was a welcome change from the normal heat. A fog had settled over the city hiding the moon. Streetlights glowed and a black van idled on the street across the courtyard from Covington.

Rafa took my hand and I clasped back, even though I wasn't entirely comfortable with the significance. But after the day I'd had, the small reassurance of not being alone — even if temporary — was welcomed.

A skinny version of Rafa with the same beautiful eyes hopped out of the driver's side of the van and lit a cigarette. He crossed his feet at the ankles, leaned against the van and took a long drag. His gaze followed us, and when we reached the vehicle, he wiped his lower lip with a tattooed thumb.

Rafa release my hand and man-hugged the guy who I assumed was his cousin…because everyone was his cousin.

"This is M. She's going to ride along. M, this is Diego."

Diego gave me a quick hello nod then looked back at Rafa. "Only you would bring a girl along for this shit." He flicked the rest of the cigarette into the street and it landed in a pothole. "Come on. I haven't fed them since you called. They're ready."

We circled the van and I climbed into the middle of the bench seat. I was the meat of the Brazilian boy sandwich, and yeah, it was a nice distraction. Rafa had showered since I'd last seen him and his fresh scent so close to me was sending tingling naughty thoughts to all the best places in my body.

"Where to first?" His cousin put the van into drive and check the side mirror as he pulled out into traffic.

Rafa dug out his phone from his back pocket, brushing his opposite arm against my chest with the movement. He checked the screen. "Closest one is twenty blocks down and seven over. There's a window in the alley that opens to the shitter. We can dump two cages there."

Oh. When he'd said 'rats', he'd mean rodents.

I turned to him. "You're going to infest someone's place with rats?"

"Big, hungry rats," Diego said with a childish grin.

The devious beauty in Rafa's twinkling eyes somehow made him more everything—more handsome, more dangerous, more wonderfully sick in the head.

"Why?" I asked.

"I want their clients to be happier somewhere else."

"That almost sounds like customer service." I winked at him. Why did I wink at him? I turned back to face forward, a small, warm flush spreading from my neck to my cheeks. Real, icky crime was too much fun. I practically bounced in anticipation.

Diego drove us down a small backstreet and parked per Rafa's instructions. We all exited the cab and Rafa led us to a small frosted and dirty window next to the ground. He crouched down and held out his hand. Diego dug a pen-like tool out of the pocket of his cargo pants and handed it over. A slice and gentle tip of the glass later and Rafa had successfully cut through half of the window without a sound.

His cousin circled the van and opened the back doors. They made a quiet squeak, but it wasn't the metal on metal scraping that got my attention. Within seconds, Diego was around the side of the van carrying a wire cage full of rats. Their tails swung back and forth and their fat, dark gray bodies pressed against the square wires. My stomach clenched and my saliva turned sour. The rats made quiet airy sounds as if they were anticipating the work ahead of them with precise pleasure.

My skin crawled when I locked eyes with a particularly snarly looking one. Yeah, any client was going to be happier any-fucking-where else. Distaste and admiration for the slimy, dark beast mixed in my tight stomach. They were big rats, but on the scale of dog and cat, they were still smaller. How they managed to get a world full of people to despise them was worth a nod of respect.

Rafa's cousin set the cage in front of the window. He'd put work gloves on. It wasn't his first rat rodeo.

"Tilt it down," Rafa instructed with a gentle calm, as if he'd done it a thousand times. Maybe he had. Diego lifted the edge of the cage closest to the van and Rafa unlatched the trap door. The rats tumbled down, only a slight thud confirming their landing. The men repeated with a second crate, and not even five minutes after we'd arrived, we were backing out of the dark street and headed to our next location.

The second place required Rafa to pick two locks, one from the outside storage entrance and the other into a pristine room with a poker table in the middle. I would be lying if I didn't admit that breaking and entering was a new aphrodisiac. Diego opened a few cans of tuna and tossed them in various directions before he and Rafa simultaneously opened cages and backed out of the room as quickly as they could. I'd waited in the doorway under the mental pretense of being a look-out.

Rafa held the empty cage and lifted his eyebrows as he passed by me in the dimly lit hallway. He and Diego loaded the back of the truck, and once again we were on our way. An electricity buzzed between the three of us, our dirty deeds almost done. The filth of it all was enchanting. Plus the margin of profit was probably through the roof. How much would a bunch of sewer rats plus the cousin's labor for two hours cost, anyway?

Budget smart crime. *Brilliant.*

Our final destination was going to be trickier. Downtown had more crowds, more eyes. But Rafa had a plan for that as well. He paid off a doorman as Diego wheeled a trolley with the cages that were covered in a dark blanket through the front fucking door. I stayed on the street, still thinking I had some kind of job that was helping them, noting how smooth it all was.

In some ways, Rafa and his cousins were just like those underground, discreet, underestimated creatures. They were everywhere and only annoying when they came to the surface. It was quite a network, once I thought about it.

"All set." Rafa smacked me on the back and the three of us headed to the double-parked van. We drove to Covington without a second glance behind us. It had been that easy.

"You're a much better sidekick than Jackson," Rafa said, after his cousin left us on the street opposite the courtyard.

Okay, so I was kinda excited to be a criminal sidekick. That was the first thing that ran through my warped brain. "Why's that?"

"He fucking hates rats." Rafa's face fell. "Guess that won't be a problem anymore."

We crossed the street and I asked, "What do you mean?"

After a sigh and a glance to the bench where Jimmy was the one in charge, Rafa said, "Jackson, J.J. and Lisa are leaving Covington. Stay here. I need to make an appearance."

He walked over to the bench and went through the formalities of saying hello to those in his favor and eyeing those he was suspicious of. I hadn't observed much of the crew together but one thing struck me. The guys liked Rafa, wanted to be his friend. They feared Anton.

With a tight grin and his arm hooked around my shoulder, we entered the building. Rafa punched the call button to the elevator.

"I have to stay at my place. So…"

I smirked. "So if I want to hang out with you, that's where it's happening?"

A middle-aged woman with dark hair exited and gave Rafa a careful glance. He pressed into my shoulder blade without returning eye contact to her and we rode up to the third floor in silence.

With every step I took to my new apartment, my new life, the solitude of what I'd chosen hit me. There was no more Spock. And even though my parents and I secretly wondered if we'd hit a wall one day, the finality of it was much heavier than I'd allowed myself to realize until I was faced with spending the night alone.

Because, truth be told, the last time I'd been officially alone had been that storm all those years prior. I stood in front of my door, staring at it while the voices in my head taunted my foolishness, my recklessness. Those hypocritical whispers that some days encouraged aberrations and other days mocked me for being weak and stupid.

The rats had been a welcome distraction, but the cold truth sat in front of me like an iceberg. I was small, I had nothing and I only had myself to blame.

"Ugh, fine." Rafa's sharp voice broke through my mind's wicked chatter. "I *want* you to come over. Jesus, you can be stubborn."

I blinked a few times, hoping the darkness wouldn't follow me down the hall, then turned to him. "I mean, I don't want you to be all lonely without me."

"Whatever."

We shoved and fake-hit each other down to his door, and once inside the empty apartment, I escaped him by plopping down on their lush couch and reaching for the remote.

"I gotta rinse off. Fucking rats." Rafa shivered a little, the first sign that he hadn't had nerves of steel from his vandalizing. "We can figure out food when I'm out of the shower."

"Okay." I waved him off and flipped through the channels.

With the spray of the water in the distance, the solitude of the moment crawled under my skin, not unlike how the rats were probably worming around their new homes. I stood, and before I realized where I was headed, I'd shucked off my boots and thrown them at the foot of Rafa's massive bed.

My clothes followed in a messy trail leading to his bathroom where the door was open a crack. The rolling steam was the perfect cloud to capture any doubts or nerves about what would happen next.

Rafa scrubbed his face behind the fogged glass of the open shower then caught my eye. His gaze trapped me, locking a part of my spirit with his.

"I think I need a rinse, too," I said in a small, confident voice and stepped into the shower.

His naked body shimmered and little streams of water traced the deep lines in his chiseled torso. A need swirled inside me, a call only he could answer. I placed my hand on his chest where he had a detailed and colorful butterfly tattoo — a soft image on a rough body.

Rafa's eyes flittered as he took a breath.

But before I could question our gentleness, before I could realize what I was asking of him, his lips were on mine and I was against the cold tile wall next to the large, round faucet. His hands framed my face as our tongues twisted in desperation. Rafa rubbed against me hard, my back scraping against the sharp joints in the tile.

Frantically, he grabbed my ass and I hopped up, his erection already prodding between my open legs. I wrapped my arms around his neck and we spun. He carried me to the sink, all the while the shower filling the room with more and more steam.

The cold hit the back of my legs but I couldn't stop kissing him. Any time he pulled away, I tugged him closer. I needed him closer — all of him, taking all of me.

Rafa was clever, so without breaking the kiss I so desperately gave, he maneuvered around the bathroom with me clinging to him and managed to find and open a condom. Our lips never parted as he rolled it on and pushed in.

My eyes were sealed tight, not wanting to witness my own vulnerability, afraid of seeing the truth of the moment. His thrusts held no hate, no anger — the connection too overwhelming to complicate with games.

A terrifying knot tied between us. I was sure he felt it as much as I did. I focused on my physical pleasure, the future too volatile to grasp. We moaned into each other, and if I sensed he was going to pull away, I kissed deeper, harder.

But an arc of his stiff spine finally was too much for me to hold on to and he let out a mighty roar as he came. Rafa's body tweaked and shook with after-effects of his release and, still inside me, he rested his forehead into mine.

We caught our breath and he pulled out, leaving me naked and exposed on his countertop. Rafa walked to the toilet, pulled off the condom and flushed it down. Without making eye contact, he returned to the shower and washed.

When he was done, he grabbed a towel, dried then finally looked up at me. "Pretty sure you came in here for a rinse. I'll go order that food."

Still drying body parts with the beige towel, he exited the bathroom and closed the door behind him.

The fog had spread to my brain and I hopped off the counter and showered. I turned off the water and found my own towel next to where he'd grabbed his.

In his bedroom, I rummaged through the drawers and slipped into some boxers and a T-shirt. I wrapped the towel around my head and found Rafa in the living room, sitting where he'd left me a half an hour prior.

He stared into the TV, although the sound was muted. "What just happened?"

I worked my jaw and bit my lip, deciding if the question was rhetorical or not. I could have made a joke. I could have made a million excuses. I could have built another brick on my emotional wall. But for some reason, I tried the truth. "I think we just had normal-ish sex... Do you need to talk about it?"

His nostrils flared. "Nope. Please tell me you don't." He closed his eyes then glared at me.

He was painfully uncomfortable. How could I not tease him? "Why? Because Mr. Hate Fucker actually liked something else?" I taunted.

He frowned. It was fake, deep and adorable. "Say another word and I'll make you hold my hand in public for a month."

I grabbed the throw blanket from the back of the couch and snuggled into it — far, far away from Mr. Uh-Oh, He Likes Normal Shit. I wasn't mad. He was just as confused by the undeniable and scary-as-fuck emotions as I was. It was new, and it was unchartered for both of us. I let him have his space. We all had new realities to adapt to.

Chapter Twenty-One

Rafa

I upped the speed of the treadmill while Anton beat the shit out of the jumbo heavy bag in the corner of the gym. Scooter's morning workouts were sporadic at best since he'd taken a beating from the Bradford fuckers. Plus, his girlfriend Callie needed him around a lot more, so he got a pass from the bossman.

Problem was, now that Jackson was filling boxes down the hall and had broken the news to Anton that he was leaving, that left me. Correction, me and one fucking pissed-off Anton.

And I was in no fucking state of mind to take on his fiery ass. My head was eleven kinds of fucked up from the night before. I'd had sex — regular, passionate, *good* sex. No name calling, no hitting, no *anger*. And it had been...ugh — I hated to even admit it to myself — nice. I cringed and inclined the track below me to make it tougher.

Nice.

I'd taken a girl that I *liked* on a *date* to deliver fat rodents around the city and we'd come back to my place and had boyfriend-girlfriend-type relations. At least my next evening would be spent with Anton and his scary-ass mother. I could avoid Marigold for the day, and if she snuck into my bed that night by some off chance of wanting more of me, then so be it.

A sharp pain pierced my side and I powered off the machine, huffing until my jog became a walk then stopped. I grabbed my water bottle and took a long swig before wiping my brow with the back of my forearm.

Anton continued to wage war against the bag, his combination punches in perfect rhythm with the swing causing them. Yeah, he was mad all right.

I forced out a few exhales with my mouth open, shook off my nerves and went to face him. Anton gave a crushing right hook to the bag and I thanked every star in the galaxy that it hadn't been my face or ribs.

He dropped his fists and said, "I told Shelia she could have Lisa's place and job. She has some kind of roommate. Get the minions to help them."

I nodded. Good for Sheila for finally getting something out of her lopsided fling with Anton. *Kudos.*

"Jimmy worked the bench all night, so I'll go shower and get on it," I said with more enthusiasm for that fucking bench than I'd ever had.

Anton looked to the door then cut his eyes back to me. "He's going to have to move up. Get Scooter's stuff out of his studio. He practically lives with Callie now anyway. Have someone clean it and tell Jimmy to meet us in the mornings now. And don't you start having fantasies about leaving me. Two of my main guys gone in three months after winning a mini war doesn't look good for business. Makes me look like a weak fuck." He shook his head.

I could have rebutted him, but he was right. Taking over Bradford territory only to have the highest guys leave wasn't transmitting the bat signal of strength over the neighborhoods.

I'd just about made it to the door when he asked, "Did Leo call you?"

I turned and gave my head a slow shake. "Nope. He knows I'm a thief. We're untrustworthy by nature." It had meant to be a reassurance but it may have come off as more of a threat. But then again, who wanted to be part of a sinking ship?

I managed to escape without throwing down with Anton, showered and left him some scrambled eggs. Maybe I was kissing his ass a little, or I might have been feeling a bit sorry for him. He and I had always gotten along, but I had been a sad replacement for Leo. Of that, I was constantly aware. Leo had tested him, pushed him and somehow gotten away with it. I was just a soldier who fell in line. I didn't mind a fight, but I didn't seek it out like Leo or Anton. Those two needed to hit things...and people.

Jackson had probably laid it all out for the sake of his kid, and even Anton wasn't that cruel to screw with a child's future. Me? I offered some muscle, a few laughs and a side hustle. While Anton and I had some things in common, mostly we didn't.

For starters, I hated selling drugs. But I would do it for the sake of posterity. I tugged on my favorite baseball hat and was out of the door.

M's hot fucking rasp stopped me dead in my tracks. At the end of the hall, Marigold and Lisa jabbered on about something then both laughed. I shot her an angry glare—*How dare she make me like normal sex?*—then stopped at the elevator and repetitively thumb-punched the down button.

"Oooo…" Lisa's voice was high-pitched and girly. "Trouble in paradise?"

"Nah," Marigold said with a confidence I wasn't sure she should have. "He's got a lot on his mind with you guys leaving. Let him be."

I didn't like her sticking up for me, and I liked her sticking up for me. It was all so fucking confusing. Without looking in their direction, I moved to the stairwell and jogged down the three flights to the beat-up entryway to our building. Jesus, we really did live in a shithole outside of the third floor.

At the bench, the day passed like a blurred blessing. Familiar faces came and went. We took their money and fed them our drugs. It was an endless vicious circle that could lull a person's conscience. Sometimes I would even believe the lie that our customers were sick and I was just selling them their medication. Then one of them would smile and their broken teeth and bloodshot eyes would remind me just how fucked up I was.

Stealing was different. Objects were involved, not people. And I didn't rob the poor. Rich, insured tourists or socialites were my targets of choice. Their backstories were far less depressing. Just call me Rafa-hood, except the poor I gave to was me.

Around seven, Scooter made an appearance at the bench and said he was going to watch it for the night. Apparently, Callie's sister had come over and he couldn't take it. He also seemed a bit pissed about moving from his studio. Maybe he was trying to get back into Anton's good graces, and the only way to do that was money or violence.

I hurried back to the apartment, washed the junkie stank off my body and dressed in a button-down black shirt. I'd noticed that on the rare occasions that Anton met his mother, he was less hood-rat and more downtown socialite.

Once I was clean of my dealer persona, I headed to the living room where Anton was on his phone, pacing between the couch and the kitchen.

"Yeah. Fine." His words were clipped and insincere. "But you said I would only see you again if I didn't hold up my end of the deal. I did. Now you dip your greedy fingers back into my fucking crew — the same crew I *let* you be a part of."

As he listened to who I was sure was Leo on the other end, he stopped pacing and dramatically dropped his head back. Then he laughed. It was hard to know if it was fake or just flat-out maniacal.

"Jesus Christ, now I've really heard everything. Fuck you. But okay, I'll fucking bite. You take Jackson, but the minute I need you *and* him, you fucking come running."

Good for the bossman for negotiating something. Chances were that Leo had gone soft if he was in the real world making legit money. Besides, from what Jackson had said, he was still with Fiona. She would be pissed if Leo got back involved with her old neighborhood.

Jackson was my best friend, but I hated the position he'd left us in. Plus, I had to spend the night with the cranky fuck Anton and his scary-ass mother. I reminded myself to keep my mouth shut and try not to piss off the bossman more than he already was. I nodded to Anton and followed him down to a Covington SUV.

We drove to the East Side and parked on a tree-lined side street. Sophia Myer's brownstone glowed with warm lights from the bay windows of the first two floors. The cleanliness of it all struck me. There were no stains on the pavement, no cracks in the road. In fact, there weren't even people.

"Did you grow up here?" I asked as we climbed the steps.

"Nah, man. We started downtown. It wasn't until my ma took over everything that my family made real bank. It still makes me laugh to see her dripping in jewels. When my dad was in charge, he spent the money as soon as he earned it. My mother's ambition changed everything. Don't be surprised if you see some politicians here."

Anton opened the door and clapped me on the back. "Don't forget your table manners. And good fucking luck, Goldie." He offered a rare smile, maybe realizing he would need a friend for the evening. Or maybe the fear of losing another upper member of his crew had made him kinder.

Light classical music and chatter drifted from down the hall, past the grand staircase on our right. Anton let out a quick breath and led us to the gathering.

The drawing room held a cast of characters unlike any I'd ever mingled with in my life. Anton's mother sat in an antique chair, her legs crossed at the ankle and her black heels shining. She wore a black dress that fit her frail frame to perfection. The long V neck was filled with ropes of pearls varying in length. Her light hair was combed back and curled at the end just above the nape of her long neck. It was hard to imagine such a small creature was so powerful—that was, until her eyes flashed in calculated judgment. Then the electrifying potential behind them cracked like a lightning bolt.

A shiver ran down my spine as she scrutinized me, then her son. She gave a curt smile to the older man she'd been talking to and rose. Anton cleared his throat as she crossed the room. Her crisp perfume was both spicy and fresh, a scent I could only imagine her wearing. She'd probably invented it.

"Anton, thank you for being on time." Her tone was both was warm and ice-cold.

He leaned in and kissed her cheek. "Mother. You remember Rafael."

"I do. In fact, I'm delighted to see you." No lie, her words scared the shit out of me. I didn't want her to remember a damn thing about me.

She held her clasped hands just above her waist and I shoved mine into my back pockets.

"Have a drink, be nice to the guests and we'll talk after dinner." After a tightening of her eyes, she left us.

I followed Anton to the bar where we both ordered a beer then turned to survey the room. Most of the crowd were older and all were in either designer dresses or suits.

I took a sip and asked, "Will we have to sit at the kids table?"

"Oh no. We will be front and center. Hope you can make small talk."

He had to be shitting me. What the fuck was I going to say to those people?

A butler rang a bell and led us to the formal dining room. I honestly thought I was dreaming. Sure enough, Anton sat next to his mother at the head of the table and I was directly to his left. The woman on the other side of me looked like she'd had her share of facelifts. Her skin was abnormally shiny and tight.

"I won in the seating chart tonight." She put her hand on my wrist and squeezed. My balls retreated to my stomach. "So thick." She batted her false eyelashes then whispered into my ear. "You know what they say about a man's wrist…"

Oh. My. God. My eyes widened and I stared over to Anton, who chuckled then coughed. He shrugged and extended his hand as he was introduced to the balding man sitting opposite. I took a second glance. *Jesus.* It was the mayor.

"And this is my right hand, Samantha." The mayor gestured to the beautiful woman at his side and I wondered what 'right hand' meant. Anton nodded to her and she offered a tight smile then started talking to the person on her right. Bossman's gaze lingered over her just a second longer. She wasn't anything we were used to in Covington.

The woman to my left looped her arm around mine and tugged me close. "My name is Araminta, but everyone calls me Minty."

That couldn't be true. Who the fuck has a nickname that described toothpaste? But I was in another world, so what the hell did I know?

"Nice to meet you," I lied and shifted closer to Anton.

By the grace of the good Lord, she had to detach herself from me to be served the soup. I ate as slow as I possibly could, hoping that Minty would keep her long claws off me. I focused on the mayor and noticed how at ease Anton was with all the powerful people.

At a break in the main conversation, I leaned over to Anton. Out of the side of my mouth I said, "I'm being sexual harassed and assaulted."

He snickered. "She's harmless. Well, pretty much anyway. I think she actually grabbed Leo by the balls once." Anton smiled. "Let her have her fun. She'll be drunk by the end of the meal and pass out in a corner. My mother sat you there on purpose. She's fucking with you. Sorry, bro."

Uh…no. Minty was not going to have her fun with me. Minty needed to behave like a dignified older woman. Her hand crept up my thigh, the bangles around her wrist letting off a slight jingle.

Minty continued her conversation with her other neighbor and I flattened my back into my chair.

"Enjoying yourself, Rafael?" Anton's mother's small smirk and mindful gaze required a positive answer.

"Everything is…" I searched for a word as Minty's fingers squeezed my quadricep. "Unbelievable."

Anton carried on local sports talk with the mayor and his mother's haunting eyes finally focused on the younger blonde woman across from me. But the normally strict face transformed into a soft, gentle, attentive one. It was a bit of a marvel and I would have like to have known why, but I had bigger problems.

Minty's hand was creeping between my legs.

"Boss," I said under my breath and thankfully he heard, "I will make you twenty thousand dollars tomorrow if you let me get up from this table right now."

"Forty."

"Deal." I grabbed the cloth napkin from my lap and tossed it over the back of my chair. "Excuse me." I nodded to Anton's mother and hightailed it out of the dining room. Once out, I found a waiter who pointed me in the direction of a bathroom under the stairs and I locked the door behind me.

I came out ten minutes later, and to my relief, Anton's prediction had been correct. My dear Minty had over-indulged and was being gently guided to the room where we'd started with drinks. I caught a hiccup as I passed by and went to finish the uncomfortable dinner in peace.

After the meal, we were summoned to the study, where Anton was told in no uncertain terms to lie low until the mayor was officially the governor. The pretty blonde from the table lingered in the corner and a silent scolding unfolded from Sophia when her son had appraised all the fine assets. *Uh, oh.* Mama's boy couldn't get a new toy.

All that made the cranky Anton from the morning evolve into a bearish bossman, and he stewed and swore under his breath as he stomped to the car. The pattern of 'everyone piss off Anton and leave Rafa to deal with it' was getting fucking old.

Nonetheless, I had an idea.

I gave Anton the broad strokes as he drove me downtown to my cousin's bar, where I met Jimmy to restart a successful poker game. Three of our old clients had shown up and the business of managing the cards took my mind off all the other bullshit. Plus, those warm, fuzzy feels for Marigold had a much-needed break.

Chapter Twenty-Two

Marigold

I'd worked all day on building three new fake people on social media. As a surprise to Rafa, I'd hacked all the surveillance cameras around the locations where we'd left the rats. He would be able to see the reactions of his rivals himself.

But I was alone. Lisa, Jackson and J.J. had packed their shit and been gone before the end of the day. She'd said none of the furniture was theirs. It all belonged to the crew. So other than their clothes and a few boxes of toys, they hadn't left with much. I could relate.

I swung back and forth in my chair and stared at my phone. I wasn't tired, not really hungry, but I could have used a little conversation after spending the day with no one. If I still would have had Spock, I could have curled up with him or even gone for a walk. The crew was forbidden from talking to me. Maybe I would need to pay someone to do it. Like a therapist. Or a waitress...

I stood and tucked my phone into my pocket and found some cash in the drawer where Rafa kept random things. I put on an extra layer of makeup and headed out of the door. At the end of the hallway, two pretty blondes were entering Lisa and Jackson's old place. Damn, that was fast.

They glanced at me after my door shut.

"Hi," I called out, sounding way more chipper than I was. "I'm M."

"Good for you." The taller one sized me up, rolled her eyes and said, "Come on," to her friend.

Okay. So the new neighbors didn't like me. Well, they could fuck off and see how much they liked shitty Internet. I moved to the elevator and punched the down button several times.

Outside, the guy they called Scooter was at the bench, and it looked like business was slow. One of the younger crew stopped me and asked where I was going.

"Just to the diner for a slice of pie. Simmer down." I pushed by him and crossed the street, a brisk wind at my back.

The diner was empty and I sat in the same booth I had my first day in Covington. A minute later, an older woman with bright red hair came over and handed me a menu.

"Is there any of Jessie's cherry pie?" I asked.

The woman's eyes darted around my face. "Sorry, honey. Jessie passed away last week. Heart attack. No more pies."

The glass door opened and closed with a howl from the wind and gave me a little start. "Just a cup of herbal tea, then." I frowned and handed her back the menu. The lights buzzed overhead and the waitress's sneakers squeaked as she walked over to the coffee station behind the counter.

An orange flyer whipped around in the street, did a double loop in mid-air before landing on the windshield of a beat-up car. A prickly shiver ran up my spine and I was colder than I'd been in months. The ping of raindrops started slow, before a giant whoosh brought them down in cords. A tightness squeezed my throat. *Fucking storms.*

The waitress slid my cup and saucer in front of me on the Formica table. "Looks like you made it just in time."

In time for what? I wanted to ask but offered a simple smile instead. The door swung open and a homeless man I recognized from the train station pushed through with his dog.

The waitress huffed and propped her hands on her hips. "Hal, you know you have to buy something."

"Come on. For the dog." Beneath his weathered skin, his warm, brown eyes smiled. I wondered how someone with no home, no money and a stench that was already making its way to my side of the diner could maintain such a gentle regard.

"I'll buy. Whatever he wants and whatever you can rummage for his dog."

She rolled her eyes at me but marched over to Hal. "It's your lucky day. You found a sucker."

I opened the paper packet with the tea bag inside and dipped it into the steaming water. The sugar called my name from the end of the table but I left it there. It was odd that I was trying to sooth my lonely soul the same way my mother would have, especially since I'd rejected her on so many occasions.

If I were honest, I missed home—missed my dog, my dad more than my mom, and maybe even the healthy meal she would have prepared. But that bridge was burned. Time and distance might mend it, although I wasn't sure. It was possible I was too much like her for us to ever co-exist in harmony.

I took a cautious sip and my phone vibrated in my back pocket. The sight of Rafa's name brought a little warmth back to my spine, or it could have just been the tea.

I heard you're at the diner. It's pouring. I'm on my way back. Do you want me to come and get you?

My first instinct was to say no, to tell him to shut up and leave me alone. I could walk across a street and find my way through the courtyard. I even thought of the numerous insults to throw out just to prove how brave I could be. But something stopped me from writing my normally witty and sarcastic comments.

I had rolled the dice of fate by coming to Covington Heights. The day before I'd forsaken my family. I had no dog. Lisa, who I'd imagined to be my new bestie, had left in a heartbeat at a chance for a new life with Jackson and J.J. The girls down the hall didn't seem to want to come over for a drink and some bad reality TV. My online friends were just that…online.

I'd made Rafael realize he was vulnerable the night before and I owed him the same courtesy. I didn't want to do it. I really, really did not want to let down my guard. But I hated storms and that gorgeous thief had offered to come and get me. Damn him for being sweet.

I would really appreciate that.

God, the words had stung my pride as I'd typed them. I placed the phone face-down next to my tea so I wouldn't have to read them again. The waitress served Hal a hot coffee and a plate of eggs and bacon. He was a man after my own heart.

I finished my tea and paid for myself, Hal and his dog. The rain continued to beat down outside and the wind whistled through the bottom of the door to the diner. A streetlight flickered. I played a stupid game on my phone until the scraping of metal from the entrance and a cold gush of air stole my attention.

Golden, beautiful eyes smiled at me. Rafa was drenched and he headed in my direction without as much as a glance to the other people in the diner. A drop of water slid down his nose and landed on the table in front of me. Funny how smart I thought I was the first time I'd seen him in the diner.

He held out his hand. "Ready? They say it's going to rain until tomorrow, so either we brave it now or we spend the night here."

We. He'd said 'we', like *we* were in it together. He gestured for me to take his hand. It meant so little and so much at the same time.

I looked up at him. "You're not still weirded out about last night?"

"Yeah, yeah I am." He raised his eyebrows and shook his head. "But I had an old lady try to feel my junk and the stuffiest dinner of my life then had a player go all in after two rounds of cards and walk away with everyone's money within an hour of starting the game. Us being nice to each other is the most normal thing to happen to me in the last twenty-four hours. Also, you like me. You're all shy smiley and eye batty. So I'm a little reassured that it's not one-sided. Come on. I need a shower and a drink. Plus, there's a new project I need to talk to you about."

I interlaced my fingers into his and stood. "Did you know Jessie died?"

"Who's Jessie?"

I pulled back. "The waitress. She made the pies here."

"I don't eat pie." Rafa scanned the diner then turned to me with narrowed eyes. "Did you buy Hal's dinner?"

"Maybe…" I crinkled my nose and cringed a little.

"Sucker."

As we approached the door, Rafa squeezed my hand. I didn't want to face the storm, but I wasn't alone. He'd come to get me. He had my back. Besides, I was probably overreacting. It was across the street then a straight shot through the courtyard. If we ran, we could be upstairs and out of the rain in minutes.

The wind taunted me with a high-pitch howl. I swallowed over the lump in my throat. Theory was a hell of a lot easier than practice.

"M, there are no cars on the street. No pedestrians, either."

I furrowed my brow and shifted my eyes to the street then back to him. "Can we stop and get my fuzzy pants on our way to your place?"

He laughed then stopped suddenly. "Wait! Are you asking if you can spend the night with me again?"

I placed my free hand on his chest and stepped closer. It was the most petrifying step of my life. It wasn't just that I didn't want to be alone. It was that I wanted to be with him. And by the twinkle in his lovely eyes, he'd figured that out.

His soft smile reassured me even more. "On the count of three, just run."

"Why are you being so nice to me?" *Better question, why am I being so nice to him?*

Rafa leaned down and kissed my cheek. "Because you're my girlfriend, weirdo."

"I'm not—"

He threw open the door and yanked me along with him. "Three!"

The cold rain pelted my face, probably flattening all my hair into a multicolored mess. Rafa's long strides were hard to keep up with, but in no time—and with our hands still interlocked—we were across the street. A gust of wind whipped and sent me into a little wobble, but Rafa's strong arm kept me steady.

My senses were overloaded and my brain buzzed. There was too much information to process at one time. I was his girlfriend…in a storm…holding his damn hand. We passed the empty bench in a flash and were in the building faster than I thought possible.

I threw my arms around his neck and jumped up, forcing him to hold me. We were both drenched and the heat between us warmed me up.

"Thank you." I kissed up his neck as he spun and called the elevator.

"Don't make me into a hero, M. Remember who we are."

I pulled back enough to look him in the eyes. "That's the thing. We know exactly who we are."

His chest rose and he held his breath before letting it all out. "This is fucking scary."

"No shit."

Chapter Twenty-Three

Rafa

When the first drop of rain had hit the windshield on the way back from the game from hell, I'd known. I'd known I'd go to Marigold wherever she was and I'd make sure she was okay. The only thing that struck me as odd was how easily she'd agreed.

I'd spent the day being freaked out, avoiding and being a general pussy all around. But as I'd sat and listened to Sophia Myer's big-picture plan with the fucking mayor of the city next to her, I'd realized two things.

One, Anton's mom was fucking the mayor.

Two, I could help.

And three, I couldn't stop thinking about M. She'd consumed me in a way that I hadn't understood but was terrified to lose. That was when I knew I had a choice. I could continue to freak out or I could fucking man up and prove to her that I was worthy of her beautifully wicked heart and mind.

And kissing her in the elevator on the way to my place was a whole new kind of experience, because — heaven help us — we were a couple. It was a fun kiss, M giggled, we were soaking wet from the storm and I only let her down when we got in front of her door. At the end of the hall, opposite Anton's and my place, boxes sat outside of Jimmy's new apartment. He'd moved up fast, but what choice did Anton have? It was like reloading a gun. The bullets were all the same. What mattered was that they were in the cylinder.

"Get whatever you need. I'm gonna go talk to Jimmy." I smacked M on the ass and she laughed again, the storm the farthest thing from her thoughts, just as I'd intended.

I walked down the hall and man-hugged the newest member of the upper crew. "Hey, man. You getting settled in?"

"Yeah. Beats the shit out of my old place. Thanks for the good word."

I hadn't said anything impressive about Jimmy to the bossman. His earnings had spoken enough.

I smirked. "Don't get too excited. Tomorrow morning will be your first Anton ass whoopin'. See you at nine." A friendly gesture would have been to help him with some of the boxes on the outside of his door, but we weren't friends.

As I turned to watch M walk down the hall with a pink fuzzy blanket around her shoulders, he said, "Just so you know, Angela gave me her number."

"Who?" I looked back to him.

"The girl you were on a date with. She said she knows your cousin. She might — you know — come over."

That Angela. I briefly wondered if she was playing a game to try to make me jealous. Jimmy wasn't exactly a wall of muscles. But what did I care? I had the perfect mischievous match walking right at me.

"Good luck with that, bro." I tapped his chest and went to open my door.

"Hey, Jimmy." M glanced at the new neighbor then back to me with wonderfully naughty eyes. No mystery at what was on the books for us.

I punched in the code and the door popped open to…a major cock block.

Anton sat on the couch with a beer, clicked off the game he'd been watching and said, "Good…you're both here. Did you fill her in yet?"

"Not yet." I frowned. The entire day had been like ice on my libido. "I need a shower."

"Jesus. Do I have to do everything?" Anton shook his head and I seriously wondered about the last time he'd done anything besides go fetch the drugs that we sold for him. He tapped the couch, signaling for M to join him. "Goldie, grab some beers. M, you will not believe how utterly perfect this job is for you. It's like you came into my life at the exact moment I needed you…"

What the ever-loving hell? *She* came into his life? I'd fucking found her. Besides, what we were going to do wasn't fucking brain surgery. But there went Marigold like a proud puppy who'd finally been called by her master and was getting rubbed on the head for giving him her damn paw.

I allowed myself one snarl as I opened the fridge and grabbed the beers, then wiped it off my face when I sat at the end of the couch, trying not to leave a massive wet spot with my soaked ass.

Anton started, "So my mom is in love with Mayor Chesney—which is fucked up and a whole lot of things. Speaking of which, did your boy tell you about Minty?" He chuckled and M whipped her head around.

"Who's Minty?"

I grimaced. "A child molester. I don't want to talk about it."

M gave me a curious eye but turned back to Anton, who said, "He's being dramatic. Anyway, Mayor Chesney is running for governor."

"Wait." M shook her head. "Isn't he like super tough on crime? And we're like — no offense — criminals?"

"Have you ever met a politician?" Anton asked.

"No..."

Anton took a swig of his beer. "They're more criminal than we are. They take bribes left and right and will do anything to stay in power or gain more. Case in point...Chesney."

I'd had enough of my girlfriend looking into Anton's baby blues. "We're going to be his online shadow. Make all the dirty stories about him — and the rumors about Anton's mom — go away while we brew up lies about his opponent." I tipped my beer in their direction and drank.

"Great." M smiled but it was directed to the bossman. "When do we start?"

"Tomorrow. What do you need?"

She shrugged. I didn't think Anton or his mother or the mayor understood how simple it would be for M. "Some pre-paid credit cards. This is going to be so much fun."

Anton smiled. If his mother was happy, so was he. "Right. So drop everything else and just work on this. Rafa, you have another game tomorrow night. Let's hope this one lasts a little longer."

If flipping him off would have been an option, I'd have done it. Not only had he delayed some much-needed consummation, but he'd also wooed M then put me in my place.

"Have I ever let you down?" I asked, keeping my cool.

The bossman stood and pulled out his phone then glanced over to me. "No. You haven't. That's why you're number two and not three."

Who would be number three anyway? Scooter, with his broken spirit and girlfriend? Jimmy, who could barely bench press his own weight?

"I'm headed down to Sheila's to meet her roommate." Anton cracked his neck and finished his beer. Poor Sheila... She was about to find out that 'meet your roommate' meant fuck her friend while she either watched or joined.

"Is that the blonde down the hall?" M asked.

"Yeah, why?" he asked as he cornered around the couch.

"Not a fan." M was already testing her newfound power, but I wasn't sure Anton would step between a cat fight. Then again, M was his new favorite employee.

"She's harmless. Probably jealous that you got to the third floor before she did. I'll talk to her."

He'll do what now?

My temples started throbbing. It was possible I was nauseated. The second the door closed, M hopped into my lap and I spilled a bit of beer on my pants.

"Oh my God. I'm like a real member of the crew now!" Her pretty eyes twinkled and I couldn't fault her for being excited. She had her own project from him. I remembered what it was like to be in his good graces. Anton had charisma. People were drawn to his implicit power. "I hope he bangs Sheila's roomie into next week."

"Speaking of banging. We need to get naked immediately." I pushed her off and stood. "Come on."

Marigold chatted about targeting ads online, digging up dirt and all the lies she could invent about

Chesney's opponent. It was as if deviant lightbulbs were going off at record speed around her head. Her buzzing energy was cute, adorable even. I added my approval when she would pause to make sure I was listening. But I was really just waiting for her to stop so I could test the sex waters again. I needed to know if I really was okay with having normal sex with her. If the switch had officially been flipped.

We showered, wrapped ourselves in towels and brushed our teeth. It was entirely too normal. M moved to the bed where she sat on the end.

"I almost forgot," she said, then bit her bottom lip. "I walked through the storm."

"You did." I dropped to my knees and opened her legs. "You did. Such a brave girl." It was a little jab, just for fun.

"Fuck off. You know that was a big deal for me. That's why you came to get me."

I peppered gentle kisses up her inner thigh and could already sense the warmth from between her legs. I hummed. I liked being gentle.

"You called me your girlfriend."

"Did you want to be somebody else's girlfriend?"

She shook her head slowly, her eyes barely a slit. It was sultry, honest and exactly what I'd thought. I slid my hands over her knees, the soft skin of her thighs like smooth silk. She spread wider and leaned back on her elbows which forced the towel to open. Her nipples pebbled on her small breasts and she arched her spine then dropped her head back.

"You know you're beautiful, right?"

"Come here." M crooked her index finger and I obeyed. The friction of our bodies drew my towel off and my erection pressed into the warmth beckoning it.

We kissed and somehow it made me want her more. The need for our connection to be complete, to validate my emotions, boiled inside my core and whirled inside my head. The woman I'd fantasized about, who I wasn't sure would meet all the warped expectations I'd had, was below me, making my dreams a reality. The intensity of her eyes terrified me, but I couldn't stop any more than she could.

"Condom," she said after a long blink.

I reached for the box in the drawer and opened the square, metallic package. M nabbed it out of my hand and tore at it. "I'm going to do this, then you're going to be as slow as possible. I want this to last."

The cool sheath gave me an unwelcome chill, but once I pressed into her, I understood exactly what she'd meant. I interlaced my fingers into hers and we locked eyes. The room disappeared around us and unhurried sensuality was instantly addictive. I stifled all my desires to rush, to push, to thrust, because our sleepy pace was so much more.

It was, indeed, the consummation I'd craved, and also a validation of who we'd become. We'd changed. The only thing unsure was if it was for the better. I couldn't wrap my head around if I was *making love,* but it was the farthest thing I'd ever done from hate-fucking.

The swirling pleasure inside me pulsed, sending warm vibrations throughout my body and settling in my heart. I cried out, confused, and yet perfectly attune with the desire we shared.

I kissed her again, deep and needy, then pressed my forehead into hers.

She grinned, tapped my cheek and rolled to her side then propped her head up with her hand. "Was that weird for you? Did I ask you to do something out of your comfort zone?"

I flipped to my back and shot her a side-eye. "Do we *have* to talk about it?"

"It's either this or Minty. What kind of name is that anyway? That's more of a toothpaste description."

If there had been an ounce of uncertainty before or during sex, it was washed away with the proof that our brains floated into the same direction.

"Yes. That was...unusual for me. But I liked it. A lot."

"Don't get me wrong." She grinned. "I like the fucking, too. I just needed to make sure that it was more for me than lust."

The darkness of the room and the previous hour had made me bold. "And is it?"

M swirled her fingers over my stomach and bit her lip. "I'm pretty sure it is."

Chapter Twenty-Four

Marigold

I was a sneaky bitch. I knew it, but I couldn't believe the crew didn't. Or maybe they'd chosen to forget. Anton wanted me to drop all the other work to set up some bots and pay for some disinformation? Fine. That took me less than an hour.

In fact, under the online disguise of a supporter of Chesney's opponent, I'd hacked their server at campaign headquarters and was downloading all the files before lunch. So I considered it totally normal to continue to hold small towns for ransom. I just didn't have to share anymore.

"Hey." Rafa walked into our little office with a brand-new laptop in its shiny box. He tapped it. "Courtesy of Chesney."

"Does he know you're going to throw it in the river in two weeks?"

Rafa walked over and kissed me on the cheek. Jesus, we were domestic all the sudden. But I liked it, which was probably worse than the act itself.

"Or," he said with a sparkle in his light eyes, "we keep it as a get-out-of-jail-free card, in case we ever need to remind them who did their dirty work."

"See...?" I pointed to him. "This is why I stopped hating you and let you be my boyfriend."

He mumbled something about 'letting' and sat down at the opposite table. Rafa unpacked the computer and fired it up.

"How was your workout?" Was that small talk? Were we doing *that* now?

"M" — he grinned from ear to ear — "Jimmy got his ass *kicked*. Oh my God. You would have loved it. I almost felt bad for him."

That didn't seem like something to be happy about. "I thought you liked Jimmy."

He looked up and shook his head. "Jimmy is a means to an end. He can sell all the drugs he wants. I'm much happier being a delinquent online."

"Wait! You don't like working the bench?"

"I fucking hate working the bench. Jackson and Leo did, too." He exaggerated a shiver. "Same people all the fucking time. I honestly don't understand where they get the money to feed their addictions. It's fucking depressing."

It sounded like it. "But then why do you do it?"

"I don't have a choice. Make money and Anton is happy. Live the life."

I swiveled in my chair and Rafael continued to work on his new laptop. It was all a bit bleak what he'd laid out there. I wasn't sure I would be able to stomach living around drug addicts for as long as he had.

Already the ones I'd crossed in the courtyard or hallways of the building made me depressed. And what about J.J.'s mom? She couldn't manage to stay clean for her kid, and now he wasn't even around. What kind of dark hole had she fallen down? And the crew only encouraged it.

"Why don't you leave if you don't like it?" I asked.

"And do what? Bartend? Work construction? No thanks."

True, his skill set was particularly good for crime. The straight and narrow was indeed narrow. "What about what Jackson is doing?"

"Not for me. I love to steal. Leo knows I wouldn't last a week with a rich fuck before I lifted something."

Probably true, as well. But one thing had been eating at me since Anton had told me about his mother and the mayor. Was she really going to let her son run a gang if she was the wife of the most powerful politician in the state? I didn't think so. She'd use him now and put him on a leash later. I was sure of it. And what did that mean for Rafael? That he would be the head of Covington? It didn't sound like that was very appealing to him. But he was loyal and that might just be a problem.

I checked the download bar on my computer then got up and walked around the desk. I threaded a leg between Rafa's inked arms and his thighs, making a perfect little perch of his lap and bringing us nose to nose. It occurred to me that I didn't like sharing him with anyone—not Angela, not Anton. What could I say? I was selfish and acted on impulse more than I should have.

"I have a present for you." I raked my fingers through his hair and clasped my hands behind his neck.

"We're going to go back to being mad at some point, right? I don't know how much more of well-behaved Marigold I can take." He sighed and he was right. I was dying to piss him off. To piss anyone off.

"Do you want your surprise or not?" I whispered in his ear then kissed just below his soft lobe. He smelled like fresh soap and original sin.

"Give it to me."

I dug my phone out of my back pocket and opened the three cropped videos I'd edited earlier in the morning—each location of the rats and two goons from Jefferson Manor's finding out their games would be canceled. I spun around so I was facing the same way as Rafa and held the phone in front of us.

"Don't think they were thrilled about the rodent problem." I clicked on the first video—which was by far the funniest—two men screaming like little schoolgirls after they entered the basement where Rafa and Diego had dropped the rats. They must have suspected foul play—I guessed one would in the criminal world—because once they were over the shock and disgust of rat shit and infestation, twenty minutes later a new set of men was at the second location. That time they were visibly angry, and by the third video, they'd understood what they would walk into.

Rafa snickered then asked, "You remembered the locations and hacked the security cameras?"

"Yeah. The closed-circuit stuff is pretty easy to bust into once you find the server. No one really has cyber security for security. I mean, who cares about an alley downtown besides the police? Even they don't really care."

Rafa spun me around and kissed me. "One, you just got hotter. And two, do you think you could get into Jefferson Manors? I've been trying to get eyes on them for months."

I grinned. "I do love a challenge."

"That's why I let you be my girlfriend." He smiled, and damn it if he wasn't fucking gorgeous. And mine? That would take some getting used to.

But I rolled my eyes. I still needed some banter between us to ground us. Otherwise, the weight of deciding to rush into a relationship would be entirely too overwhelming. Lisa's words rang through my ears. Maybe I *had* met my match.

"I have to work a poker game tonight. Will you wait for me at my place?"

An odd thought popped into my head. Maybe Rafael didn't like to be alone either. Maybe that was part of his loyalty to Anton. And maybe if I wanted whatever it was that we were doing to be more than a fling, that I would need to take him, force him away. Show Anton for what he really was — selfish.

"Will your roommate be home?" I asked with a coy tone, hoping to once again draw the contrast that Rafa works and Anton does dick squat.

"Yep. You can talk to him all about his soon-to-be stepdad's bid for office. Or maybe he'll ask you to join him and Sheila and her roommate. That seems like your cup of tea."

I pretended to be shocked. "I could hate-fuck Sheila. You're a genius."

Rafa clicked his tongue. "There's a problem though. I'm pretty sure you made some kind of rule about only us until there's no more us."

"Damn it. Just you. Blerk." I made a disgusted face.

"Blerk? Seriously?" He lifted his thick eyebrows then tapped my ass. "Come on. I need to eat and you probably need a thousand grams of sugar."

We had lunch at a taco place not far away, and on our way back when we passed the bench. Rafael let out an audible, quick exhale. J.J.'s mom was trying to negotiate something with Jimmy. Rafa's posture stiffened and he shook his head a couple of times as we headed to the entrance of the building.

I interlaced my fingers into his, a gesture I was getting entirely too fond of, and rubbed up his strong arm.

"You know, you don't have to do this forever."

He laughed and kissed the back of my hand as we waited for the elevator. "There are two ways this ends for me, M. Jail or death. Take your pick." His voice had an eerie truth to it. Perhaps the scene outside had put a damper on his mood.

I stepped in front of him. His pretty eyes glimmered with a sadness I'd never seen. "Do you really believe that?"

"Don't you?"

"No. I'm going to move to Mexico, live in a hut and drink cocktails with little umbrellas in them."

I was sure he would give me a smart-ass comment or tease me for my silly dream, but he stayed silent as we rode up to the third floor. When we got to my door, he stopped.

"I need to check on our place for tonight and make sure Jefferson hasn't found it and retaliated."

"Right. Can you get me a few external hard drives? I'll have some info for Chesney by tomorrow."

Rafa tucked his chin. "Already?"

On my tip-toes, I pecked his soft lips. "It's kinda what I do. I'll be waiting for you in your bed, dreaming of ways to make you mad at me."

"You could hate-fuck Sheila and video it. That would piss me off." It was a relief to find his playful side again.

I rolled my eyes and turned to enter the apartment, but Rafa didn't let go of my hand.

"Don't move to Mexico too soon, okay?"

The meaning was not lost. He was asking for a chance, and I knew one thing. I would give it to him. But there was also a real possibility that our reality would catch up with us.

That night, I probed Anton for random details about the future as casually as I could. He told me his mother had instructed him to lie low and keep business as usual. But I read through the lines. Anton was going to jump ship. He gave exactly zero fucks about his crew — men he'd claimed were his friends. He certainly didn't care about Sheila or her roommate.

As I waited for Rafa into the wee hours of the night, the future weighed heavy on my mind.

Chapter Twenty-Five

Rafa

I pecked Marigold on the cheek and rolled out of bed. Over the course of the weeks she'd been sleeping on my left, one thing had become abundantly clear. She was a shitty morning person. I pulled on my shorts and a T-shirt and found Anton at the island in our kitchen, sipping a chocolate protein shake, which meant he'd already worked out.

We nodded our hellos and I scratched my head. I needed a haircut.

"Jimmy's getting thicker but it's slowing him down," Anton said, then set the coated glass in the sink. "I like sparring with him, though. He lets me hit him in the face."

The bossman had an uncanny way of making a compliment to one person an insult to another.

"You've hit me in the face plenty of times." I pointed to a fading bruise under my eye. "I seem to remember you complaining that my bone hurt your knuckles."

"Scooter's waiting for you. Don't you dare go easy on him. You've gone soft now that you're in...whatever it is you two call yourselves."

Another dig. No mention of me being the best fucking earner he had. No credit for basically torching any chance his new stepdad's opponent had to win the election. Without me, Mr. Anton Myers would be a hell of a lot poorer. Marigold had been telling me for months that Anton didn't appreciate me.

But I let it slide because, where the fuck else was I going to go?

I sent my cousin Juliana a text to see if she could cut my hair, and she wrote back some excuse about not having room. It was a lie. We were money-hungry hustlers. She always had twenty minutes to make a buck.

"I gotta go to some fucking bullshit family thing later. Keep the peace and make me money." Anton cracked his neck on the way to his room. When had I done anything but?

As I was opening the door to the gym, Angela snuck out of Jimmy's apartment. It hadn't taken him long to upgrade from Bridget to her. She kept her eyes to the ground and darted to the elevator.

"Hey, what's going on with my cousin?" I called to her after she'd walked by.

Angela jabbed the call button several times.

"Hey." I stalked toward her. "I asked you a question."

"Fuck off, Rafa."

"Excuse me? Are you forgetting where you are?" I crossed my arms. Jesus, now I had to take shit from her, too?

She rolled her eyes and readjusted her bag on her shoulder. "We all get off on something, big boy. Your cousin? It's getting her ass beat. From the look of her face, she's in fucking heaven."

The doors opened and Angela's resting bitch face stared at me until they closed. I dropped my head back. Juliana was going to end up dead one of these days.

In the gym, I let Scooter have it. I sucker-punched him every chance I got. Anton had been right. I had gone soft. It didn't matter how much money I brought in. The appearance of danger was what he was really after.

Scooter held up an arm and stepped back. "What the hell has gotten into you?" He huffed. "You jealous of Jimmy?"

Jimmy had an aura. It was true. He was ready to cross lines that I wasn't. You could see it in his eyes. Whatever the past had done to him, he was the most jaded fuck I'd ever met. I was a lot of things, but the evil that lived inside Jimmy seeped out of him like a black cloud. The minute he'd moved up to the third floor, it had blossomed, and Anton had taken note.

"I'm not jealous of that prick." I grabbed a towel and tossed it over to Scooter.

"Yeah, well, I am. He out earns me every fucking time he plants his bald ass on the bench. You think the bossman doesn't remind me of that? I miss Leo. It was like he kept him in check. And what the fuck am I supposed to do? Callie won't even come out of the apartment now. I couldn't move if I wanted to."

I eyed Scooter. He wasn't the only one who'd been considering an exit plan, but I sure as fuck didn't want to let anyone know I had. "What are you saying? Exactly?" I let the threat in my quiet voice hang between us and jutted my chin in his direction.

"Fuck off. You know I'm Covington for life."

Death or jail, as I'd told M. "Just be careful."

I went back to my place, and Juliana's fucked-up taste in men was gnawing at me like a dog on a bone. When I got out of the shower, M was stretching on the bed.

She rubbed her eyes. "Hey, fucker."

I grunted. I was in no mood for more insults.

"You cranky? That's odd for you." She wrapped herself in the blanket. Her hair stuck out in all directions, reminding me that mine was as much of a mess.

"I need a haircut." I yanked on my black jeans and threaded my arms through a black tank.

"Okay…" She squinted and shook her head a little.

"Anton is basically sucking Jimmy's filthy dick, Scooter is thinking about leaving and I need a fucking haircut."

She stared at me until I couldn't take it anymore.

"What?" I barked.

"Don't take your shit out on me. You're mad that you don't get enough credit. You're afraid to leave Covington because you don't know where to go or whether or not Anton will hunt you down, even though two guys have left and nothing has happened. I don't know what the fuck the haircut thing is, but that's not my fault either."

I shot her a dirty look. She was right about it all. I just didn't want my nose rubbed in it. Also, I was mad at her because I had all kinds of feelings I didn't know how to explain or verbalize, and I was pretty sure she did too. And since she was my least and biggest problem, I grabbed my boots and stormed out of the bedroom.

M didn't follow me, and that pissed me off even more. In my cloud of unreasonable anger, the only thing I thought I could do something about was my hair.

A new guy I didn't even know — probably appointed by Jimmy — was working the bench, and he nodded to me out of respect — maybe the most I'd gotten the entire morning. I drove to Juliana's salon, parked on the street and slammed my door shut — my four-alarm tantrum still brewing at a boil.

The chatter from the filled chairs ceased when I walked in. I stalked to the back of the salon where Angela and Juliana sat at the small table behind the beaded curtain. Juliana had a swollen eye, a split lip and a bandage peeked out of her long sleeve. No matter how many times I'd seen her beat up, it never got easier.

Angela shook her head at me. "You know this is your fault, right?"

"No," Juliana said and her hair framed her face as she looked down. "I was stupid. I betrayed Stevie. I deserved it."

"He's double your size, Jules."

Juliana laughed but it was fake, desperate. She stopped and placed her hand on her ribs before turning her gaze to me. "I just wish you would have told me you'd used Diego. I said something about my cousin and rats and, well…"

There was nothing to say. The damage was done. I kissed her head and apologized softly then left.

I sat in the car for a long ass time…maybe two hours. I'd had enough—enough of not being tough, enough of being trapped, enough of the fucking peace I was in charge of keeping.

When I got back to Covington, I didn't go home. Instead I went to the M's place and found her at the computer in what was what we joked as 'our office'. She pulled off a pair of headphones.

"You still have that look in your eye and you didn't get a haircut." She placed the headphones on the table in front of her.

"I need the feed on Jefferson. Pull it up." I toggled my finger at her laptop.

"Why?"

I ground my teeth. "Can you do one fucking thing without questioning it?"

M narrowed her eyes and her nostrils flared. My beast had awoken her own—probably a mistake—but there was no going back. I'd made up my mind about what I was going to do about my cousin's broken face.

"I thought I was pretty clear earlier. I'm not the cause of your problems. Don't be a bitch because you can't shit or get off the pot." Her breath went shallow and she stood up.

Oh, I hadn't just awoken her beast. I'd prodded it…with a branding iron. Another day, one when my head would have been screwed on in its normally happy place, I would have gone in for the kiss. Making out with her when she was pissed was hot. But a desperate switch had flipped inside me. My desire to impress Anton and myself overruled my otherwise-still-horrible judgment.

"You are the cause of my problems. Anton told me this morning I'd gone soft since you came along. And you know what? He's fucking right." The diarrhea of my mouth wouldn't stop. I was out of my body, looking down, knowing I would regret every word, but I lacked any ounce of self-control to stop. "You fill my head with bullshit about not getting my props, then when I want to do something — fucking finally take some action — you stand in my way. Your pussy isn't that fucking sweet, M."

She sat back in her chair and lifted her eyebrows. "You fucking coward." Her penetrating stare burned through me. She shifted her jaw a few times then looked away. In an unexpectedly soft voice she said, "If it's easier to blame me than to say what's really going on, fine. But at least have the balls to be honest about that much."

After a sigh, she wheeled up the desk and clicked a few times to find the Jefferson Manor feed she'd successfully hacked into months ago. In that time, we hadn't really used it for anything, not wanting to tip our hand. Their bullshit recording on loop was still what the city saw and only Anton, Jimmy, M and I were aware of the real one. It had been another thing that pissed me off when Anton had overshared with his new favorite.

The frustration of the day lightened a little with M's resolve. She was on my side. I couldn't lose sight of that. I welcomed her calm, appreciated her loyalty. She was keeping me from my worst instincts. I pulled out the chair from my desk and focused on the four black-and-white squares of live feed.

The screen in front of us showed nothing out of the norm. Drug deals went down in plain sight, people loitered or went about their business.

But after only fifteen minutes of watching, Stevie's smug face caught my eye. Even through the grainy feed I could tell that Juliana had hit him in the head with something. I suspected a frying pan. The women in my family were known for using items in the kitchen as weapons.

"That fucker is going down." I pointed to him.

"Raf…" M's pretty eyes couldn't stop me. The pull between us couldn't stop me. I didn't know how to do the right thing. It was why we were perfect for each other. She didn't either.

"He beat the shit out of my cousin. It was my fault. I used her for the info then forgot to give her the details."

M rolled her head on the back of her chair. "So what? You're going to drive over there and pick a fight in front of his whole crew? Alone?"

Okay… When she put it like that, it was a stupid plan.

I frowned. "You got a better idea?"

"Not yet. But waiting until he's alone is a much better option. Or at the very least, take Jimmy."

"I hate Jimmy."

She smiled and fuck if it didn't warm the coldness my heart had been trying to keep all day. "We all hate Jimmy. He's a slimy fucker."

"Your buddy Angela doesn't seem to mind."

M pretend to puke a little in her mouth. "I don't trust either one of those idiots. Hey—" Her eyes lit up. "You still pissed? It kinda made me horny."

A massive wall of revelation smacked me in the chest. I was falling in love with Marigold.

Chapter Twenty-Six

Marigold

Wrangling Rafa's worst intentions had worked once, but he watched the video feed of Jefferson Manors every chance he got. It would only be a matter of time before he struck out and sought his revenge.

In the meantime, I didn't like bumping into Angela on our mutual morning walks of shame. It had been all too convenient how she'd stopped obsessing about Rafa and moved on to Jimmy. I tried not to care, but there she was *every* morning with the lowest of the crew after she'd wanted Rafa first. So, in my paranoia, I did what I did best. I hacked her phone.

Rafael still had her number in his contacts and the dumb bitch left her location setting on, it was so easy that I was bored. While Rafa obsessed about the guy Stevie, I yawned my way through Angela walking from work to Jimmy's and vice versa.

Her presence pestered me. There had to be more to her motivation than just flaunting her ass in Rafa's face. He didn't care. Plus, Jimmy was okay-looking but she was out of his league. She was a stunner. It didn't add up.

So I dug deeper. Social media was the perfect way to slide into people's lives. It had worked when I held more and more small towns hostage and it worked for Angela. I just had to do it when Rafa wasn't around. I didn't want him thinking I was an obsessive stalker.

I met Anton in the kitchen while Rafa got dressed for their daily workout. He drank his coffee black and mine was more of a milkshake with caffeine. It wasn't as if Anton and I had become friends, but the project for his new stepfather had brought us closer. He liked it when I made up ridiculous rumors and planted them all over the Internet. I relished in him underestimating me. It worked in my favor.

Sometimes I wondered if Anton had registered that we were rivals for Rafa, but his ego was so enormous that he didn't take the threat seriously. That was okay. I did. I had a goal, and it included the man I was pretty sure I loved, a beach and a shitload of money.

I finished my coffee and my pitiful small talk with Anton and opened the door to be hit with Angela and Jimmy swapping spit across the hall. I stared at them, searching for a tell. Their relationship had to be fake. I was certain.

Angela broke away and snarled at me. "Take a picture. It lasts longer."

"You should consider bottling that as a diet plan. I think I've lost my appetite for eternity."

Rafa slinked an arm around my waist and whispered, "Play nice," in my ear. I scowled at the sight in front of me then ignored Angela's middle finger as I walked down the hall to my place.

But that beautiful witch had been right about one thing. Pictures did last longer. I searched all her online photos and one massive thing stuck out. *Zero Jimmy.* There were recent videos of her and her friends dancing in clubs, a few pictures of client's hair she was particularly proud of and some family gatherings, but Jimmy's face was noticeably absent. And considering they'd been dating for almost the same time as Rafa and me, it was suspicious.

I had no online presence on social media and neither did Rafa. We were smarter than to trust the world wide web with our secrets.

The little tracer flashed on my screen, Angela was on the move, but that was information I'd already known. I scanned through her recent pictures again. There had to be something. She wasn't *that* smart.

Nothing. Not a single clue. Maybe I was imagining something that wasn't there.

"Hey." Rafa stood in the doorway, freshly showered. How long had I been pillaging through Angela's social media accounts? I hit 'Command W' a few times to close the incriminating windows on my screen.

He continued, "We're going to the shooting range. Jimmy's idea." A little eyeroll followed. "Oh and I changed all the codes to the doors. The list is on the counter if you need to get into our place before I get back."

Rafael should have known better than to trust me with that. The evidence that he was softening because of me just kept piling up.

He was almost out of the door when I thought of something.

"Hey."

"Yeah?" He turned around with his bushy eyebrows up.

"Remember how we were talking about how much of an advantage it is to be underestimated?"

He chuckled. "Yeah, that was a mistake you kept making when we first met. Why?"

"Well, it worked for you. It was a good tactic."

He crossed his arms and studied me with a tilted head. "You got something you need to share?"

About all that money I was making on the side? Nope. Not yet. But about Jimmy and my suspicions? Probably too soon without proof.

"I just…" I pressed my lips together, still not sure what to say.

"Spit it out." His voice was flat.

I owed him some truth. "I don't trust Jimmy."

He rolled his eyes. "You don't trust Angela."

"That too."

He checked his phone and slid it back in his pocket. "I gotta motor. You have any other psychic premonitions you need to share?"

I grinned. "I predict hot sex later."

"Will you tell me you hate me, for old time's sake?"

"Always." I waved goodbye and waited until I heard the door click shut before I popped up, showered in record speed and beelined to an electronics shop.

A listening device was taped to the backboard of Jimmy's bed and connected to my phone within two hours. God, I just hoped he and Angela didn't do their talking while they fucked.

That night, Rafa had to work the bench, apparently to make up for a bet he'd lost at the gun range. He was cranky, but it let me listen to Angela and Jimmy in real time.

"It almost seemed like you enjoyed that kiss this morning." Jimmy's didn't waste any time proving to me that they were a sham. But why?

"Do that again and your boss will cut your balls off."

Anton would do what?

Jimmy laughed. "I doubt that. Anyone who sends his girlfriend to sleep in another man's bed doesn't think much about his girlfriend."

I sat my phone down next to my laptop and scoured Angela's social media again. *Who the fuck is her real boyfriend?*

Angela scoffed and a crackling noise came through my phone. She must have gotten into the bed. "You don't know much about his girlfriend or him. He likes to watch me get fucked, then he beats the shit out of the idiot who did it. If you're lucky one day, it might be you. Now go be a good little soldier and sleep on your couch."

"You can report back that Rafa is hopeless with a gun but Anton is almost as good as I am. Almost." Jimmy's confidence had always been what the crew had liked about him, but it was a fault in my eyes. He was a traitor and the only thing that made sense was that he was working for Jefferson.

"Do me a favor. Make a move already. I'm sick of seeing Rafa's smug face."

"Suck my dick and I'll pull the trigger tomorrow." Jimmy's slithery tone gave me the chills.

"Anybody else's dick and I might be tempted."

They really hated each other. No wonder we only saw them saying goodbye in the morning. The show of the relationship was the only thing that mattered.

A door shut and I quit the listening application on my phone. I clicked through Angela's photos one more time, still coming up with nothing. I was going to have to get my information the old-fashioned way — gossip.

I powered everything down and went down the hall to Anton and Rafa's place. I wasn't even tempted to tell Anton he had a rebel in the ranks. Information was power. I just needed to confirm who, then I would have to work fast to get Rafa and myself out of Covington.

Rafa came in late and took a shower. When he climbed into bed, I laid my head on his chest. It was still damp and a little cool.

"I fucking hate working the bench. Bridget is so fucking strung out. It's fucking hard to look at."

"Then don't do it anymore."

He let out a long moan. "And do what, M? I can't live if I don't steal. I'm just as much addicted to crime as those people out there are to drugs."

I interlaced my fingers into his. He couldn't see past the concrete buildings that was Covington Heights. But he didn't have to. I would do all the work.

"Remember when you hated holding my hand?" He tucked his chin and turned to me.

"I was a fool." I kissed up his chest and moved to straddle him. His lovely eyes scanned over my body. The moment was there. One of us could have showed the courage to confess to what we both knew was true.

And I probably should have told him about Jimmy and Angela, but I couldn't risk him proving his loyalty to Anton and ending up dead. Dead or jail... That was what he always said.

I ground my hips into his crotch, his erection starting to come to life.

"You're many things, Marigold Pfeifer, but a fool isn't one of them." Rafa flipped us and stared down at me. The words were on the tip of my tongue but I needed to save them for when it really mattered.

He slipped his hand into my pajama shorts. "How do you want it?"

"Rough." I crinkled my nose. "I hate you. Remember?"

The sex was a tool. By being physical, we avoided the emotional. And fucking hard and fast and animalistic allowed us to forget how much we needed the tender moments between us. The grunts and gasps blanketed over the true feelings we'd caught. It was a show we put on for each other, a safe place to exist in lies.

But as much as we tried to hide from the connection, it always wiggled back. We could spend thirty minutes slapping our flesh together but inevitably we would finish and someone would forget to keep pretending. I would take care of the condom or he would get me a glass of water. The honesty was in the details.

I crawled out of bed early, determined not to run into Angela for fear that I may say something stupid. A small town on the West Coast had paid their ransom overnight. It was the third of the week. I really needed to change computers but didn't want to explain to Rafa why.

From the tracking application, Angela's little dot didn't go to work. It went downtown instead, and I took the opportunity to head to Juliana's salon. It was relatively quiet, just a middle-aged woman getting her hair straightened.

I waved from the reception and Juliana came over, her light eyes matching Rafa's.

"Hi, I don't have an appointment, but Rafa said you could squeeze me in."

"How do you know my cousin?" She rubbed her lips together, spreading the gloss that was already shining.

"I'm fucking him."

"Huh." She tilted her head. "That actually makes perfect sense. Have a seat. I'm free after this one."

Juliana washed my hair, and it wasn't until I was back in front of a mirror that I started digging for little nuggets.

"I think I know one of your friends, too."

"Oh, yeah?" She combed a lock of my hair and snipped the ends.

"Yeah. Angela...although she doesn't like me very much. I stormed in on her date with Rafa."

Juliana laughed. "Yeah, that was funny. She was all about him for weeks then nothing. She must have realized she wasn't his type. I tried to warn her. Now I think she's given up on love altogether."

"That's sad." *But interesting.*

"Yeah, she used to date my boyfriend's older brother. Then he dropped her for no apparent reason. I think that fucked with her self-esteem. Criminals are unreliable pricks. But you probably already know that if you're dating my cousin." She smiled and clipped. "Who does your color?"

We chatted a bit more and I left her a nice tip when I paid. After all, she'd given me all the information I needed. Angela was a plant from Jefferson Manors, Jimmy was a fake and I needed to make my move.

Chapter Twenty-Seven

Rafa

I was a chicken, a complete coward who had no idea how to express my *feelings*. Even admitting that I had them made me cringe. That was why I had promised myself not to say anything until she did. Also, I was horrified of rejection. Marigold could very easily just have been in it—whatever *it* was—for the thrill. Criminals didn't exactly skip down stone paths and find happily ever afters. We had baggage.

Plus, she'd gone quiet. The mornings when I was at the gym with the crew, she snuck off to the office and worked on shit she was hiding from me. I was pretty sure she was still holding towns hostage for money, and I couldn't say that I blamed her. Besides, Anton's family project didn't occupy that much of her day.

All that suspicious behavior had me wondering if she wasn't just biding time before she was going to leave. Marigold Pfeifer had her eye on a prize, and it didn't seem to be in Covington Heights. That didn't make the risk of professing ewwy gooey love for her any easier either.

But if she picked up and left, there would be hell to pay—not because she knew too much, but because it would be Anton losing yet another upper member of the crew.

We didn't have initiation parties or shit like that, but once third-floor status was acquired, it was official that you were an important person to him.

So I had to put my pussy sentimental self aside and figure out what was going on in her gorgeous head. Because one, I fucking *wanted* her to stay. And two, I *needed* her to stay.

Marigold sat behind her desk, the excuse she called coffee in a cup next to her little notebook. She'd showered and was all dolled up in a sailor gothic dress, as if she had big plans for later. Not that I would know… I'd been working the private games since we'd taken them back from Jefferson. Their revenge was brewing. It hung in the air and added to my list of shit that was eating at me.

Her gaze met mine and she offered a simple smile. Discreetly, she clicked out of everything on her screen as I walked over. I'd never been a fan of confrontation without fists. It was why I delivered rats in the dark and stole shit behind people's backs. But there was too much riding on the line and I couldn't hit her.

"We need to talk." I grabbed the chair opposite her where I usually sat and wheeled it around the desks. I sat down and cradled my head in my hands.

"Can I ask you a question first?" she asked in a sweet voice.

She could ask me a thousand questions first. I peeked up at her.

"What would you do if you found out someone in the crew was betraying you guys?"

Shit. She *was* running a side hustle. Maybe she could just give Anton a slice of her pie and the whole thing would go away. Right, because that had worked so well when Leo had seduced a girl meant for the bossman then stolen Jackson away. And she was my responsibility. Covington was the only home I had, and I didn't want to sleep on one of my cousin's couches. Diego had rats in his basement, for fuck's sake.

I exhaled through my mouth. "I'd have to do what was right for the crew."

Marigold scooted closer to me and rubbed her soft knuckles on my cheek. The warmth in her eyes was confusing. "Would you ever do what's right for *you*?"

"I don't even know what that is." Right, wrong, good, bad — it had all muddled in my brain over the years. Some days I wondered if I even had a conscience.

Marigold closed her eyes and let out a little huff. "I have a confession."

At least she was coming clean. At least we still had some trust and honesty. I scrubbed my face and sat up straight.

She chewed her lip then said, "I'm not just running the disinformation ads and hacking into Chesney's opponent's email."

It was good. She was confessing easier than I thought. "It's probably Anton's fault for not thinking you could do both." I shook my head and she smiled.

"You knew." She didn't seem to be picking up on my disappointment — or maybe she just didn't care.

"I suspected. I just thought..." What? That she would tell me all her secrets because we shared a bed? Obviously my feelings had blurred my judgment. Anton was right. She'd made me soft, weak. Now I had fixing her situation on my plate.

M scrunched her face. "I have a little problem, though."

I hated that I wanted to help her, even after she'd gone behind my back. I was loyal to a fault—to her, to Anton, to the fucking concrete walls that surrounded our neighborhood.

She would ask and I would give. At least it would buy me some time to figure out how to negotiate something with Anton.

"I kinda need a new laptop. This one might be compromised."

"What do you mean?" My tone shifted to fucking serious laced with pissed off.

"Calm down. I said *might* be. But I need you to get me a new one."

I stood up abruptly and the chair rolled halfway across the room. "Why don't you go buy one with all the money you've been stealing?" There was a hint of hurt in my voice. God, had that been what was really making me mad? Not that she'd gone behind my back, but that she'd left me out of her scheme? That I didn't mean enough to her so that she would have shared her big plans? I was a fool.

"I'm sorry you're mad." She was entirely too poised. Why wasn't she reacting to my anger? If that laptop was compromised in any way that lead back to Covington, she wouldn't go down, we would. The crew were known dealers, crooks and convicts. M could bat her eyelashes at a judge and walk away with a slap on the wrist. Fuck, she could narc on all of us and skip town with the money. Double fuck, maybe she'd planned it like that all along.

"But you're not sorry you did it. Are you?" I scoffed. How could I have thought that I was in love with her?

"No." She held my stare, taking in all the rage I was sending. She didn't even seem to mind.

I stormed over to her desk and yanked off the laptop. "Let's go. I'm not letting you out of my sight."

She was docile and it spooked me. Her quiet, calm energy seeped under my skin and taunted me. It snickered that she'd used me, crept into the crew and made me vulnerable all the while stockpiling money on the side. That was the other thing. She was fucking greedy. Had she even spent a dime since she'd came to Covington?

Jesus, she was calculated.

The little smile she offered once I threw the laptop into the river wasn't reassuring. In fact, it made me fume even more as we rode the train down to tourist central.

I didn't even want to take her traitor hand for fear of looking like more of a sucker than I'd already been. We exited in Midtown, and every step we took erased the emotions I'd been so convinced I'd had for her. I wished she'd been cold or a bitch, her Little-Miss-Polite act was fucking annoying.

There had been some kind of demonstration that morning and the cops were still lingering to patrol the fading crowd. But the more people the better, as far as I was concerned. I just couldn't lose her among them. I didn't know what I was going to do, but pay for her sins wasn't an option.

A middle-aged father bent down and shrugged off his backpack to tie his little boy's shoelaces. As he explained ever so patiently to his son how to do it for himself, I nabbed the bag and shoved M deeper into the group of tourists in front of us.

She came to an abrupt halt exactly when I needed her to walk a tiny bit faster and spun around to face me. Tears puddled in the corners of her made-up eyes. She blinked and one escaped down her lovely cheek. My heart pounded. What was she doing? She knew the drill. Before I could object, she swallowed and said, "I'm only doing this because I am madly, deeply, profoundly in love with you. It's the only way you will be safe. *Police! Someone!*"

The pedestrians around us stopped and M stepped backward and held up an accusing finger at me.

"He just stole this bag from that guy over there!"

I froze. I wasn't even sure I was breathing. Her betrayal cut me like a knife and her confession had my head spinning. She was a liar, a conniving beautiful faker. She'd deliberately brought me out of Covington where I had no allies and was going to get me arrested.

"That's my bag!" a masculine voice called out from behind me as a cop yanked it out of my hands.

I didn't even fight back as I was thrown to the ground and my face smashed against the pavement. The last I saw of Marigold, tears streaked down her cheeks and she mouthed that she loved me, then spun around and was lost in a sea of people who were no longer interested in the scene since the police were handcuffing me behind my back.

Chapter Twenty-Eight

Marigold

I wiped away my tears and let out a shaky breath. It had been a risk. The hate and disgust in Rafael's voice and eyes had nearly rattled my courage. But getting him out of Covington Heights was the only way I was going to save his life.

That morning, when I'd listened to the recording of Angela and Jimmy, where she'd given him the order that at the next game it would be time to show his true allegiance, I'd known I would have to act fast. And based on the answers to the questions I'd asked, if I told Rafa that Jimmy was a plant from Jefferson, he would barge over and pick a fight with a guy who was some kind of gun expert. Then, if Rafa got shot or didn't win whatever fight, Jimmy and Angela wouldn't have thought twice about erasing me from the planet. Unfortunately, Anton would have to fend for himself. I couldn't save everybody.

I jogged down the stairs at the train station and checked the departure board. A non-stop to the airport was leaving in ten minutes and I went over to the kiosk to buy a ticket with one of the pre-paid credit cards I'd never actually used when buying crappy ads all over the Internet for Chesney.

As the train chugged away from the city—my city, the place I'd called home—my confidence that Rafael would understand my motives tapered and my guilt for leaving Anton unprepared festered. But if I called him, he might get his golden boy before confronting Jimmy, and Rafael would still be in danger. He'd also know I'd fucked him over—and that could be bad for the man I loved as well.

I pulled my phone out of my bag. I would need to lose it before I got on the plane, so if I was going to make a move, it had to be within the next hour. I tapped my black fingernail on the screen for a full five minutes. I was a lot of things—a thief, a hacker and generally a cranky bitch, but I wasn't a killer.

Shit. I scrolled through my contacts and slid over Lisa's name.

"Hey! Perfect timing," she answered with too much cheer. "J.J. is asleep and Jackson is at work. Let the gossip begin." Hearing her voice was reassuring but it also made me realize I might be the last time I had such a luxury.

My throat tightened and my neck burned.

"Hi." I managed to squeak out the little word then sniffled.

"Oh shit. What happened? Did you two break up?"

"Not exactly." Maybe we had, I just didn't know it yet. After swallowing through the lump in my throat, I continued, "I did a bad thing...but for a good reason."

Lisa let out a small laugh. "That's Covington Heights in a nutshell, sweetie. What happened?"

I would tell her everything, but I needed one simple assurance. "Promise me you won't let Jackson bail him out of jail tonight. That's all I ask."

"Whoa." She dragged out the word. "Did he hit you?" Her tone flipped from glib to concerned. I was going to miss my friend.

"No he wouldn't…well, he would…but…" I shook my head. "No. But I need your word. Promise me."

"M, I can't control Jackson. Rafa is his best friend."

"Please, Lisa. Rafael's life depends on it."

"How do you know that?"

I was happy to get to some facts. The emotional roller coaster of the day was draining. "Do you remember that smarmy prick Jimmy?"

"The one who came from Bradford and was banging Bridget?"

"Bingo. Well, turns out he's from Jefferson now. They're going to take out Anton tonight. And if Rafa knows, he'll run straight to the game and try to protect his crew."

There was a long pause before Lisa finally said, "Where does that leave Anton?"

"He's not my problem." It was cold and brutally unfair. I was essentially throwing a fast ball down the middle to Lisa, and she would have to deal with how to hit it out of the park. But honestly — and I knew it was bad — if Anton were out of the picture, Rafa would be more likely to come to me. His loyalty to Covington was astounding.

Lisa let out a big sigh. "Jesus, M."

"I know. I'm sorry. Just keep him safe."

"Do you want me to call you back after I talk to Jackson? Because he would never forgive me if I kept this from him. Anton may be a grade-A asshole, but he put food on our table. He gave me a job and kept me away from drugs. I can't just not do anything."

That was what I was counting on, a little help from my friends. Problem was, Anton wasn't going to be my friend if he found out I'd thrown him to the wolves and maybe taken just a little of the money he thought he was entitled to. I really had horribly out-of-control compulsions.

I owed Lisa a final bit of honesty. She was a good person who I'd shoved into an impossible circumstance. My selfish tendencies knew no limits. "I'm leaving. Covington isn't for me."

"What about Rafa?" An offended shock ran through her voice.

"He'll either come for me or he won't. At least he'll be alive."

Lisa huffed and the static made me pull my phone away from my ear for a second.

"I'm sorry." A feeble apology was all I had to offer. "I'll miss you." I didn't wait for her goodbye before I swiped to end the call. My mother had been right to keep me under wraps, away from society. I was more than a menace. I was a toxic time bomb. Rafael would be best to stay away.

The train slowed as we reached the airport, and I sent a text to the person I was supposed to meet for my passport. As soon as I had it in hand, I would drop my phone in the nearest trash can and be on my way. I'd instructed the service to send Rafa's documents to Juliana's salon. I would have preferred Diego, but I didn't have time to fish around for his address. Hell, I'd only figured out the details of my dodgy plan that morning. It was far from perfect — surely — but it would have to do.

I exited the train station and made my way through the busy airport to the drop-off curb of the departures for a major airline. Outside, the wind whipped and I searched for a green SUV. A drop of rain landed on my cheek and all my muscles twitched before tensing. What if a storm would keep my grounded? Worse, what if I had to fly — for the first time — in a storm?

The screeching of brakes tore through my eardrums and exhaust fumes engulfed me with their heat and stench. I broke out in a sweat and brought my hands to my ears as I crouched down. My stomach clenched in a tight, small fist. What had I been thinking? I couldn't fly alone.

I rocked back and forth on my heels in a little ball, still pressing my palms into my ears. I'd put Rafa in jail, sabotaging the one precious thing in my life. I'd known about a threat to the crew who had taken me in and given me a home, and I'd done nothing. I'd shattered any friendships I'd had. For what? For money, that was why. Because I was a thief, a rotten to the core, cannot-be-trusted soulless bitch.

A dark-haired dude with bright tattoo sleeves on his arms leaned down and smirked at me. His blue button-down shirt reminded me of something. I just couldn't think straight enough to remember.

"I got your envelope in the car. Don't like doing business out in the open." His words were a foggy awakening.

Right. I needed my documents, but I was in the middle of a massive panic attack. I waved him off and he laughed.

"This was not how I'd thought I would find the powerful Majel213." The stranger pushed to his knees as something rattled into my brain. What screen name had I used for the passport?

Blotches of heat pulsed on my arms and chest, and I tried to regain control of my breathing.

"Come on." He tilted his head, his smile also sounding a distant alarm. "I have some water in the car. You can regroup for a minute."

I stood on shaky legs. Another dog whistle of warning faintly blew in my head. But I was causing a scene and I didn't need the unwanted attention. I closed my eyes for three long breaths and nodded. If I didn't get his precious commodity, I didn't get out of the country.

With every step I took, I reassured myself. The guy had checked out with all the online sneaks I knew. His document replication had been sworn on by my most trusted contacts. And for the price I'd paid, I couldn't let it slip away. No, I needed to get my shit together, get my fake ID and get the fuck on a plane.

He held the back door of the SUV open and I slid in along its tan leather bench. He sat next to me and closed the door. I didn't greet the driver and was grateful for the tattooed counterfeiter as he unscrewed a bottle of water and handed it to me.

"Gotta loop around, the cops are pulling up," the driver said.

I understood. We didn't need more of a spotlight on us. "Yeah, sure." I sipped the cool water and let it stifle the three-alarm fire that had spread over my body. It was so effective, as we pulled away from the curb, that I drank half the bottle, not caring if I looked desperate. Besides, I was pretty sure we'd already surpassed that.

Cold air from the vent soothed my skin from the outside and the colorful signs of the various terminals flashed by.

"Oh. Hey," I said, finally with a bit of composure. "I think you missed the turn-off."

The driver didn't reply. Instead, he accelerated and merged onto the highway.

"What the — ?" I narrowed my eyes and the identity of what I now understood as my captors came into crystal clear focus. I'd seen the guy next to me a thousand times but never close up. He was the one always standing next to Juliana's boyfriend when Rafa obsessed about the footage in Jefferson Manors.

"Fuck…"

He grinned and reached for the water bottle. "Ding. You won't be needing any more of this. You've had plenty."

My head spun and a warmth blanketed my muscles, completely relaxing them. I fought to keep my eyes open, but the lids were like iron curtains.

"Gotta admit," the guy said. "I am dying to see if your carpet matches the drapes."

My heart stopped and lodged itself into my throat.

The driver chuckled. "Rainbow pussy. I've heard it all now."

I managed to keep my eyes open long enough to know I was headed back to exactly where I didn't want to be.

Chapter Twenty-Nine

Rafa

The guard poked her finger between my shoulder blades as she led me down the empty corridor. When we got to the end, the lighting hummed overhead and the metal gate buzzed then clanked open in front of me. It had been a surprise when she'd called my name from the community holding cell. I'd only been locked up four, maybe five hours, and I'd refused my phone call because I couldn't think straight.

Once the gate had shut, the short guard stepped around me and motioned for my handcuffed wrists. With a click and a jangle, I was free.

"Sorry about your face." She sounded like a bored cartoon character. I suspected she was far, far from sorry, but it was a small price to pay for my freedom. I signed for my personal belongings, threaded my belt back through the loops and re-laced my boots. I had no idea who I would find on the other side of the door.

And I hated that a part of me wanted it to be Marigold. I still couldn't make heads or tails of it.

I hadn't spent time wondering who would pay my bail. I'd spent time wondering why the fuck M would sell me out like that. Why—if she claimed she loved me—would she have me fucking arrested? I'd even wondered if she'd concocted some plan to make me hot and horny. And as fucked up as that sounded, it actually made the most sense.

Except the fact that she was a callous, lying bitch who I should have never trusted. She'd fucking hacked me, found me, manipulated me, toyed with me and was probably laughing at me from wherever she was. God, I was a fucking headcase.

I cracked my neck and shoved my phone in my back pocket. Out the door I went but stopped in my tracks when my massive best friend's frown hit me. *How the fuck?*

Jackson leaned against a bike rack in a dark suit, his arms crossed. I shook my head and trotted down the stairs of the police station. I'd never seen him out of black jeans or workout gear. His energy pulsated maturity, class and wisdom. He was almost a stranger.

Jackson exhaled a whoosh. "Well, you certainly picked a firecracker."

We did a man-hug and a chest tap and I rolled my eyes. "Pretty sure I'm finished with that one. Fucking arrested, Jax. In the middle of the day. For a computer she asked me to steal." I made a little trumpet sound with my mouth. There was a lie in my disgust. My best friend had probably heard it as loudly as I had.

Jackson smirked and waved me toward a massive SUV with tinted windows.

I followed, still complaining, probably whining like the little bitch she'd turned me into. "You know the fucking kicker? She had the balls to say she loved me. Un-fucking-believable."

The lights of the truck flashed, and I cornered around the hood to the passenger side and jumped in.

Jackson powered the ignition and I turned to him with narrowed eyes.

"How did you know I was in there?"

He checked his mirrors and pulled out of the parking spot then glanced over to me, thoroughly unamused. "Your fucking whack-a-doo called mine."

There was a black cord to charge phones and I dug mine out and plugged it in. It had sounded a lot like Jackson had just said M had called Lisa to bail me out of jail.

"Why would she get me arrested then ask you to come get me? All that just to skip town? She could have done that no matter what."

The bemused grin on his face disappeared, replaced by disgust. "Because we have bigger problems. That fucker Jimmy is a mole."

I sat back, my spine like a cold, iron rod. Jimmy as a mole was bad, real fucking bad. But Jackson had said, 'we', so that was... Better? Was he back in the crew somehow?

As we drove across town, Jackson explained to me what Lisa had told him about her phone call with Marigold. And if the story were true, she had wanted to save my life. While that may have lightened the blow, she hadn't had the confidence in me or the crew to work our shit out. And, she'd kept her online dealings from me. Not fucking cool either. But get me arrested to save me? Worst fucking instincts in history.

On a tree-lined street that was quintessential upper middle class, Jackson found a parking spot and he led me to a brownstone. He typed in a code and the door clicked open.

"Do you live here?" I asked. *Holy Shit*. How much was Leo paying him? The lifestyle of the straight and narrow had never looked so appetizing.

"Nanna's house," he said with a warning, whatever the fuck that meant.

I found out soon enough as I walked down the entryway and to a living room that looked like it hadn't been modernized in decades. It must have been a Covington Heights crew reunion. Leo Ricci, our former number two in charge, also in a classy-as-fuck suit, paced behind a small, antique couch with his phone at his ear. Anton glanced at me from a side chair, his cold eyes revealing nothing, and Scooter walked in from the opposite doorway, carrying a coffee pot and cups.

So Leo and Jackson were back. Was I relieved or terrified?

Jackson must have sensed my confusion and he leaned back and whispered, "M called Lisa. Lisa called me. I called Leo. Leo called Anton and he and Scoot got the fuck out of there. If there is one mole, there may be many."

Anton sat in silence until Leo had finished his hushed call. "So, the way I see it, Raf sends Jimmy a text saying he'll meet him at the game. Scooter and I will go with you and be waiting when he shows up. We beat the shit out of him and drop him on the border. If anyone else in the crew is working both sides, it will be a two-fold lesson. One, they will suffer the same fate. Two, it didn't work."

I rolled my shoulders back and a bit of the tension I'd been carrying since Marigold had screamed her betrayal in the middle of a crowd left me. If we had Jackson *and* Leo back, we'd just got a hell of a lot more dangerous. I'd always suspected there was a bond between Leo and Anton. If his friend were in trouble, he would have his back. Leo might have even felt as if he owed Anton, after how he'd left.

"Okay." Leo circled around the couch with a twisted frown. "What if Jimmy isn't alone? What if Jimmy has some Jefferson pricks waiting somewhere in the wings?"

I didn't need to check in with Scooter or Jackson. We were witnessing something rare — questioning of the bossman's judgment. Anton and Leo stared at each other for a solid minute. They had a communication channel that none of us had ever figured out. So far, it had served them well.

Anton rubbed his neck then admitted, "He's really good with a gun. Fast. Accurate."

"Okay. Jackson and I will find a place to hide. They aren't expecting us."

"But what aren't *we* expecting from *them*?" I asked and all eyes turned to me then blinked away as the possibilities filled our heads.

My own thoughts went to Jimmy. M had mentioned several times that she didn't trust him. Maybe that had been her way of warning me. But if she'd bugged his apartment like she'd told Lisa, she should have told me that. It was possible I'd been too wrapped up in wanting Jimmy to succeed that I'd failed to notice his shortcomings. After the absence of Leo and Jackson, Anton, Scooter and I had all been hungry for someone to step up. Jefferson knew it and they were probably double pissed since we'd taken back the games. Yeah, their revenge would be raw.

The doorbell rang and gave me a shock. I'd been in fights. I'd even been in vicious brawls. But I'd never walked into a gun fight. The only thing that gave me a little bit of relief was that I had faked my shooting skills in front of Jimmy. When we'd gone to the range together, M's advice about being under-estimated had rung louder than the shots we'd taken at the paper targets. I'd faked being bad and couldn't understand why when I had. But standing there, the reason hit me. It had been my instincts. I hadn't trusted that slimy fuck any more than M had.

Scooter came back from the door carrying plastic bags of food—'fight fuel' as Leo called it. I ate, somehow I ate, despite my dry mouth and tight throat. Every swallow was a stab reminding me that I was the reason we were in the fucking mess to begin with.

Leo wiped his mouth with a thin paper napkin. "Every possible scenario. Think this through. We only come out of there alive if we've got the advantage. That means mental, too. However they walk in there, they are expecting to have the upper hand or a surprise factor."

"Goldie"—Anton nodded at me—"if they bring your cousin, you're going to have to make a hard decision. I'm not making that for you."

Jackson studied me from across the table, the mental voodoo the bossman and Leo had between them wasn't working with us. But just in case Jackson had learned some Jedi mind tricks in the months he'd been with Leo and had broken into my brain, I changed the topic to him.

I lifted my fork and waved it up and down. "You look leaner."

Jackson took the bait. "Aww. You miss my big muscles, Goldie?"

Truth was, I missed the chemistry the five of us had as a group. Leo had never respected Anton's authority, but our dynamic had shifted when he'd left. For starters, no one had heard from him until he'd reached out to Jackson. Then...no fight, no contest. Jackson got to walk out of Covington and into Leo's legit new word, zero fucking questions asked.

But sitting there, surrounded by the men I trusted with my life, the power and confidence between us soared. We were stronger together. With Leo and Jackson back, Jefferson didn't stand a chance.

There was no question of physical. Jimmy would come with a gun. We would have to be smarter. Our calculations would need to sum up the situation in a fraction of a second. Consequential decisions would need to be made without remorse. It was go-time.

I played through all the moments when I'd caught my sparring partners off guard. They all shared the same common denominator. I'd only gotten the advantage when I'd done the unexpected.

Chapter Thirty

Marigold

My brain had turned to mud or mush or something equally dark and swampy. The odds were unfair. If I didn't have my wits about me, I had nothing. Not only was the asshole next to me at a physical advantage, I could no longer rely on any intelligence I may have had.

Well played, Jefferson Manors.

We were back in the city. The honking, jackhammering and pollution was a loud and suffocating reminder that I had not flown away on a jet plane to Mexico or an equally sunny destination. My rash judgment had been faulty. If I hadn't been drugged, I would have remembered to panic, to realize that I was in the hands of Covington Heights' biggest enemy. I might have even been scared. But the buzz at the base of my brain seemed to be blocking emotions and intellect.

I was conscious enough to understand that the missing raindrops from the windshield meant we'd gone into a parking garage, and the two men from Jefferson Manors got out of the car. The horn beeped once, I suspected locking me in. I didn't have the strength to test the handle. Hell, I didn't have the strength to fully open my eyes.

Realizing I was alone—and perhaps in a bit of a holding pattern—I let go. I allowed the numb in my head carry me all the way into oblivion. I fell down a dark, deep hole and everything went black.

It was impossible to tell how much time had passed, but the beep of the horn startled me awake. The door opposite me opened and the cool air shot up my thighs. I adjusted myself as best as I could, tugging my dress lower and righting my posture. Any saliva I'd had was gone and my throat was like sandpaper. An ache in my temples throbbed and tensed.

The slam of the driver's door woke me even more, the sound slapping me like an angry bitch.

"Yeah, you've been a very good girl," the guy next to me purred into his phone. "I'm not even gonna share you tonight, baby. Fuck, you're such a queen. I may never share you again. Stay home. This should be over in an hour." He hung up as the SUV started, then handed me an energy drink. "Here. You're going to need this. No tricks. Scout's honor." His evil grin said something else, but damn it if I wasn't thirsty as hell.

I sheepishly took the thin can but just stared at it. Why would I trust that fucker? He'd already lied and drugged me.

He adjusted a bit in his seat an pulled out a gun from the back of his pants. "Or don't drink it and die here." He waved the gun in a small circle.

My chest clinched around my heart and I wasn't sure it was beating. I'd seen a gun or two…but pointed at me? That was an incredibly sobering first.

Chills raced up my spine and I longed for the dark place from which I'd just awoken. He nudged the gun in my direction and I popped open the can. Sugar had never been so poisonous. Its venom coated my tongue and glazed my throat, spoiling any pleasure I'd ever had for overly sweet beverages.

"All of it. I need you alert." His scrutinizing eyes were like dark holes leading to hell. Whatever he 'needed' me for was only buying time. He was going to kill me after he'd gotten what he'd wanted — maybe my money, maybe my body. It didn't matter. My clock was ticking and I was as good as dead.

The realization washed over me and my mother's voice echoed in my head. I'd done it to myself. I'd gone hunting for danger, I deserved what I was getting. I didn't understand how to be dangerous in real life. I was a coward who hid behind a screen, tormenting strangers who never meant anything because they were random people or towns on the Internet. My reckoning had come, and as a tear rolled down my cheek, I wondered how my path had led me so fucking astray.

We pulled into an alley downtown and my capturer said, "Showtime," with a devious grin. "Do what you're told and maybe I'll keep you around. I hear my girl is dying to scratch your eyes out. Could be fun to watch."

The caffeine and sugar had me on high alert and it sounded a lot like if I just went along with whatever his plan was, he wouldn't kill me. *Yet.* I exited the car, because what the hell else was I going to do? My only weapon was to think my way through. Screams and pleas weren't going to get me anywhere with Jefferson Manors, of that I was sure.

The driver pulled out a handgun from the back of his pants and Jimmy stood at a door with a wicked smirk across his loathsome face.

"Ahh... M." He took out his own gun—a gun he would use expertly. *Fuck*. As his eyes raked the length of me, a thousand spiders scattered over my skin. I prayed to any higher source that would listen for Rafael to still be tucked away in a jail cell. That, even though my planned had failed—miserably—the man I loved would not be harmed. *Today*.

Shit. If it went down badly for Covington, Rafa would be at the top of their list. I was such a fool, such a stupid, careless idiot. Why had I taken measures into my own hands? I was not like them.

"Mind if we keep this one alive?" Jimmy asked the guy next to me. "I'd like to see what all the fuss is about."

"I'd say you deserve that."

A perverted and altogether-hideous smile spread across Jimmy's face. Death suddenly seemed like a very viable option.

Jimmy opened the door and walked down a dark hallway. The driver shoved me in front of him. We stopped as the guys from Jefferson Manors all nodded to each other. Jimmy wrapped his knuckles on an unmarked door.

From the other side, the unmistakable voice of the man I loved answered. "It's open, bro."

No.

My heart raced. Why wasn't he in jail where I'd put him to keep him safe? *Fucking Lisa*. Worse—way fucking worse—why hadn't she told them that it was a set-up? Nothing made sense. But I didn't want to show my cards. I wasn't sure what Jefferson knew or didn't know, so I swallowed down all the emotion trying to stew up from my stomach.

Jimmy grinned and entered, followed by the guy I'd foolishly thought was going to give me a fake passport…then me, then the driver.

Rafa's amber eyes clocked me and flashed something before jetting across the room where Anton and Scooter sat, guns pointed directly at the men from Jefferson and…me.

"Ah, you're not as fucking stupid as we thought," the head of Jefferson said, cocking his handgun and aiming it at Rafa. "Problem is, you spend all your time fighting. We go to target practice. Who's got the shot, Jimmy?"

"Just Anton. The other two are harmless." Jimmy sounded bored. Too fucking confident.

I tried like hell to get Rafa's attention, but he wouldn't look at me. His eyes were on Jimmy. Anton stared at the leader and Scooter at the driver. I was the only one clocking the entire room.

Jimmy jutted his chin in Rafa's direction. "What's a matter? Not even going to put up a fight for your girl?"

"Not my girl."

If I hadn't been surrounded by so many guns, I would have been sure a dagger had impaled my heart. I wasn't his? He didn't understand. Everything I'd done was for him. For *us*.

"No," I pleaded. "I messed up." Tears streamed down my cheeks and my knees buckled. "Please." Jesus Christ, someone was going to die. Maybe we all would. "I have money. I can pay—"

The driver took his eyes off Scooter and said to me, "Shut the fuck up."

Rafa finally looked at me and the hate he sent nearly knocked me over. "You know that thing you said earlier?" The snarl on his face was a side of him I'd never imagined possible.

I started to shake. He had it all wrong. I whimpered. Speaking was beyond me.

He said one more word and it was as cold as ice. "Same."

Then everything went slow. Rafa raised his gun and pointed it directly at me. His index finger squeezed and a bullet crossed the room. There was a brief fraction of a second where I didn't believe he'd shot me. But when heat and pain blasted in my thigh and crimson blood seeped out above my knee, I could no longer deny the reality in front of me.

I cried out as I fell to the floor. Hyper speed replaced the lethargic moment as gunshots echoed over my head in every direction. I clamped my eyes shut and prayed for Rafa's safety.

None of it mattered — not the pain, not the bodies dropping around me. What I'd had with Rafael hadn't been strong enough to pull him away from his crew. I'd wanted a dream life and forced my fantasy without consulting its key player. I deserved his scorn. I sobbed into the filthy floor, hoping to die.

Chapter Thirty-One

Rafa

As the bullets scattered across the room, I ducked behind the bar. Leo and Anton would kill them. I had no doubt in their abilities. It was impossible to breathe and I gasped for air.

I'd shot her. And I'd actually hit her exactly where I'd wanted. As soon as we'd locked eyes, I'd known. Jefferson thought they were going to play with my emotions. *Nope.* Anton had been right. I'd had a hard decision, but at the same time, it had come to me in a flash. If I didn't shoot her, they would. Maybe not then, but eventually. Jefferson wouldn't have expected me to do that and it had put them into reaction mode.

The shots ceased and I inched back up to survey the scene.

"Fuck!" Leo screamed as he dropped his gun. "Bring some towels! Jackson, get the car. Now!"

Jimmy, the unknown guy from Jefferson and their leader lay dead on the floor. Between them, Marigold rocked back and forth, holding her leg and crying.

Sorry, M. It was the only way.

But way fucking worse and requiring immediate attention was Anton. He'd been shot in the chest and was lying next to a dumbfounded Scooter.

I rummaged around the bar and found some towels as Leo ripped open Anton's blood-drenched shirt. M's sobs haunted my ears but she would live.

"Look at me." Leo tapped the bossman's cheek. "Anton."

I rushed over with the towels, passing Jackson, who hurdled dead bodies on his way out the door. Scooter followed Jackson, his frozen moment of shock having passed.

The strength and power had been sucked out of Anton's limp body. He was unrecognizable. Leo grabbed the towels from my hand and pressed them into Anton's chest. A deep red stain quickly grew on the white linen. He shot me a glance and said, "That was smart. Shooting her. They didn't expect it. Good thinking." Then to Anton and much softer, "It missed your heart. Probably nicked a lung. Slow breaths. Stay with me."

Anton blinked. He was still alive.

The calm in Leo's voice gave me the courage to finally really look at Marigold. I'd shot her. I'd fucking shot her. Did that make us even? I went behind the bar and found another towel then knelt in front of her.

Her black makeup streaked her cheeks and she rocked back and forth over her bleeding leg. "I'm sorry. I'm so sorry, Raf. I messed up."

"I know." I removed her red hands and pressed the towel into her thigh. "For someone so smart, you're incredibly stupid."

"Car's here!" Scooter came from the doorway and Jackson quickly followed.

"Press here." I placed M's hands where mine had been and went to help carry Anton.

M's lower lip quivered and I hated leaving her like that, but she was in far better shape than the man I owed my life to. Anton had taken me in when I had just been a runt. He'd built me up to be the man I was. The four of us held our bossman by the limbs as he strained for breath. A trail of blood followed us out into the dark hallway and stained the gritty pavement of the alley.

The color had vanished from Anton's skin and he stared straight up at the dark sky. We slid him into the backseat, a long blotch of crimson spreading on the tan leather. Leo hopped in after and continued triage with pressure and the now-soaked towels.

Jackson got behind the wheel and Scooter ran around to the passenger side. Before I was about to close the door, Leo threw me a phone and I caught it chest level. "Call his mom. Tell her we're going to the private hospital downtown and tell her where you are, so she can deal with Jefferson. Code is all eights. Contact is 'Satan'."

I slammed the door and they peeled off.

The blood on my hands smeared the glass screen as I quickly found 'Satan' in Anton's phone.

"Hello, darling." Anton's mother's voice shot a chill through my entire body.

I cleared my throat. "Ms. Myers. It's Rafael. There's been…an incident."

There was a pause that would haunt me for the rest of my life.

"Is he dead?"

"No, ma'am. They're headed to the hospital downtown."

"Who's 'they'?" She asked the strangest questions. And how was her voice so fucking calm? It was eerie.

"Anton, Leo, Jackson and Scooter," I said as I made my way down the hall, thankful the gunshots had scattered the public instead of drawing them near.

"Do you require assistance for a scene?" Again, what the hell kind of question was that?

"I do."

"Drop a pin." She hung up.

Marigold was still on the floor, pressing her hands into her wound. The bleeding was under control and she peered up at me with deep blue eyes.

"You fucking shot me."

"Yep."

The phone I was holding vibrated. I glanced at the screen.

ETA seven minutes.

"I know you hate me, but do you think you could, like, take me to a fucking hospital or something?" She sniffed then let out a pained exhale.

"I'm pretty pissed at you." I squatted in front of her.

Her mouth gaped before she said, "You fucking shot me. I'd say that makes up for spending, what, two fucking hours in jail? I had a plan. You should have stuck to it."

"No offense, but your plan sucked."

Marigold winced as I took over the pressure on the gunshot…*my* gunshot.

"You're going to be fine. Just hold on."

Her voice went quiet. "You're not going to leave me?"

"No."

"K." M leaned back on her elbows and whispered, "He fucking shot me. I plan a brilliant getaway and a life on the beach and he shoots me."

Exactly six minutes later, the door opened.

Anton's mother's crew was older, a little wrinkled, but just as lean as us. And damn, they were efficient. They'd even come in with body bags. One of them talked in a whispered voice, giving calm, matter-of-fact orders to the others. He came over to us and dug out plastic gloves from the side pocket of his black coat.

"Show me," he said, gesturing to the wound with his index finger.

I took off the pressure and gave him a look.

After a little head tilt, he shrugged. "Pretty clean. Still, she should see a doctor." He turned to M. "Can you walk?"

"I can barely breathe."

The man shot me an annoyed glance. Her wound was probably a splinter compared to the shit he'd seen over the years. But still, it was her first shooting. We had to cut her a little slack.

"I'll carry her."

"So chivalrous." She glared at me and I smiled. If she had her spunk, she wasn't freaking out. I was still mad about what she'd done and we needed to have a major talk, but those whirly feelings in my chest came back the minute she was in my arms.

I carried her out to a black SUV with tinted windows and climbed in the back after her.

The man tapped the door and stared at Marigold. "You live in a crappy neighborhood. Shit luck that stray bullet hit you."

She nodded then closed her eyes. It was a quiet ride uptown to the private doctor. We had so much to say but the timing wasn't right. Plus, I'd just shot a woman I was pretty sure I still loved after she'd spied on my crew without telling me, continued her scam of holding town's hostage and had gotten me arrested. I had some internal wrestling I had to get done before I could lay all my shit out in the open.

In a dimly lit office, the doctor shot her up with a muscle relaxant and numbed around her leg while he searched for bullet fragments. He did an X-ray, which confirmed the bone hadn't been shattered. Overall, I was pretty damn proud of my shot.

Except Jimmy had been faster than Leo.

M's eyes fluttered and she turned to me. "I'm sorry." She reached out her hand from the examination table where she was lying on her back.

I stared at that hand. How ironic that she wanted me to hold it. Three months prior, when we'd held hands for the first time on the way to her parents', it had been half accident, half silent confession. If I interlaced my fingers with hers in that moment, it would be no accident and I wasn't sure I was ready to make my confession.

"Please," she whispered. Her broken voice reached down deep into my soul. "You're all I have."

That seemed unfair of her and it touched on a button she'd been pressing the entire day. Was she calculated? Despite everything, I still needed time to sort through all that had happened—not just that day, but since she'd come into my life. And that was why I had to push her away. I would have loved to forget all the voices in my head sounding alarms, hold her in my arms and comfort her, but my heart and future were on the line. I couldn't just make impulsive decisions anymore.

"You don't have me, M. Not after today." Maybe I was being cruel after everything she'd been through, but I needed her to see the damage she'd done.

She withdrew her hand and her lips quivered before resolve settled over her blood- and makeup-stained face. "Well, you have me, Rafael. No one on this planet will ever understand and accept me like you do. And I know you're mad and worried about Anton, and I know I fucked up, but you said it. *'Same.'* I heard you."

She glared at me, daring me to deny it, which I couldn't. I just didn't know how we were going to dig out of the heaping hole of hell she'd gotten us into.

Chapter Thirty-Two

Marigold

Anton's mother wouldn't let anyone go back to Covington, so once my leg was bandaged, Rafa and I were driven to an apartment on the East Side, facing the river. The doctor had given me crutches and I hobbled onto an elevator in an underground parking garage where we'd been dropped off.

Rafael had spent the ride talking to Jackson, and from what I'd gathered, Anton was in surgery. The most attention he'd given me was a glance and a 'she's fine' into his phone. I didn't know how I'd expected him to react. Maybe that was the problem—I hadn't even thought about it—but the angry brooding hadn't occurred to me. At a time when I needed someone, his cold shoulder was a bitter slap in my face. The only solace was that he hadn't abandoned me. That counted for something. I just didn't know what.

On the seventh floor, we entered a studio apartment. Rafa tossed the keys on the small counter and they landed with a clank. He rummaged through a dresser by the bed and found a change of clothes.

"I need a shower." He went to the bathroom and slammed the door.

I, too, was in desperate need of a scrub, but most importantly, I wanted to get out of my bloody dress and shoes. I made my way over to the couch and sat down, leaning the crutches against the coffee table. The feeling was starting to come back to my leg and with it, a throbbing pain deep inside my muscle. Each movement woke up the sting and sent a wave of fatigue throughout my entire body.

It was late, only the streetlights glimmered below, and the magnitude of the day finally settled on my shoulders and in my chest. I'd been the root cause of my agony, there was no doubt, and as I finally allowed the bloody memory of downtown to play in my head, I realized Rafael had shot me to save me — a harsh irony.

Had things gone different, Jimmy would be raping me at that very moment and Angela would indeed be scratching my eyes out. There was no way I could take that street-smart beauty. Rafael had known that when I'd caused a scene on their date. All that time, he'd been protecting me. I'd wanted to extend the same courtesy, to prove to him I deserved him, but I was pathetically hopeless and no match for the instincts it took to survive as a hardened criminal. My plan hadn't just failed. It had imploded. I'd been so focused on saving what mattered most to me that I hadn't bothered to consider what *he* wanted.

I managed to untie and yank off my boot from my healthy leg but reaching the other one was impossible without screaming in pain. I tried to wiggle out of my dress but I pulled a muscle in my neck and stopped with it halfway off. I couldn't even succeed in undressing myself.

Rafa's light chuckle came from the opposite side of the room. "Need some help there?"

"Do you have a gun?" My joke was muffled below my dress. I wasn't sure how to play our mood, but humor had always been our safest territory, and yes, I did require an extra set of hands to get me out of my clothes. He may not have wanted to help me shower, but getting me naked had never bothered him.

Thankfully, he didn't make me say please or beg. Instead, he delicately lifted up my hurt leg and untied the boot. Rafa dropped it to the floor with a thud then said, "This will be easier if you stand up. Give me your hands."

When we'd first started—whatever the hell it was we'd started as—the paradox in Rafael had always given me pause. On the one hand he was a nice guy and on the other a drug-peddling criminal and giddy thief. Its contradictory reappearance struck me again. He was good, despite himself.

He guided me to standing and I put all my weight on my healthy leg. I steadied myself on his shoulders, my blood-stained hands a sharp contrast to the clean white V-neck he'd found in the dresser.

As his fingers fumbled with the last button of my dress, he dared a glance up. His eyes were the most naturally beautiful thing I'd ever seen. A deep golden yellow below dark lashes, they flickered with the light that was in his delicate soul.

The energy he'd been trying so desperately to keep at bay could not be denied in the quiet, solemn moment. While he may have tried to avoid it, ignore it, I bathed in its warmth. That connection we shared was still there, even if its glow had been diminished. Rafael threaded his fingers under the neckline of my dress and eased it off my shoulders. It fell into a puddle on the floor as he closed his eyes.

"I need a shower, too." I hoped I wasn't pushing my luck and prayed that soft side of him would come back to me.

"Yeah, you do." His forehead grazed my stomach as he reached around and unclasped my bra. The straps slid down my dirty arms and I removed one hand at a time from his chest to let it drop between us.

"I can't do it alone." My voice was as tender as I could make it. The confession was for more than just the shower. It was for life. I wanted him. I needed him. He was my oxygen and the strongest craving I'd ever had.

"No. You can't." He wasn't giving in, but he wasn't giving up. There was disappointment and regret in his quiet tone, but also a hint of the tiny thread still connecting us. Rafa led me to the shower and held me steady as I washed away the dirt and blood of the day. I sensed he needed silence, so I nodded or shook my head with his logistical questions. We managed to keep the bandage on my leg dry and remove the rusted stains from my body without facing harder decisions. I couldn't help but hope the act of doing something so mundane together might take us one step closer to healing.

He turned off the faucet for the shower and I stood there, naked and dripping, and as vulnerable as he would ever see me. The sight did not go unnoticed, and he had to look away. Rafa reached for a fluffy towel, patted me down, then scooped me up and carried me to the bed.

Being that close to him, that fucking intimate without knowing exactly where we stood, was shattering. He was there, but he was so far away and I didn't know if his playfully sweet spirit would ever glimmer in front of me again. I studied him for any sign, any opening, but found nothing.

I'd grossly underestimated his loyalty to Covington. I wanted to shake him, to scream, to cry, to plead, fucking beg him to come back from the shell into which he'd retreated. But it might have been me who'd forced him to go inside. I honestly didn't know.

Rafa handed me a T-shirt like his own, then went and turned off all the lights. On his way back to the bed, he grabbed two throw pillows from the couch and propped them under my leg. His kindness was killing me faster than his retreat.

"You good?" His question was for my leg, but I couldn't resist honesty.

"No." I swallowed over the lump that didn't want to remove itself from my throat. "You?"

"No." His tone was flat. He wasn't ready to let me in. But he climbed into bed next to me and lay down.

"I am sorry, Rafael. I honestly thought I was saving you. I know it doesn't make any of it better. If you can't forgive me, I hope you can at least understand." I could have reached out and touched him, but his tense posture, his broody grimace and his blocked energy warned me not to, had me cautious of further rejection.

My mind spun. Curiosity had always been my greatest attribute and weakness. It was what led me to want to write code then tempted me to hack. It had put me on the train to Covington and kept me there for the previous months.

My need to discover, learn and know was a passion that pulsed through me with every heartbeat. Occasionally, it served me well.

I reached out for his arm and stopped before infecting him with a touch he no longer desired. But that damn inquisitive mouth couldn't be muted. "Do you hate me?"

"Always." It was another placeholder. He wasn't ready. He might never be. And after my colossal fuck up, I owed him the respect to stop pushing. I folded my hands on my stomach and closed my eyes. At least he was still with me. That fact comforted me enough to find some much-needed rest.

But when I woke up, he was gone, and I finally allowed myself to heave the regretful sobs that had been lurking behind my brave persona from the night before.

Chapter Thirty-Three

Rafa

Jackson pulled up in a different SUV than the day before and I hopped in. The red in his eyes meant he'd slept as little as I had. But his small smirk was like home.

"You shot your girlfriend."

"Fuck off. She's not my girlfriend." I slammed the passenger door.

He crossed his arms and rolled his warm, brown eyes. "You know why I love Lisa?"

I was pretty sure he was going to tell me, so I raised my eyebrows to signal that his lecture could begin but also let him know I didn't want it.

"She knew exactly who I was and what I did. She accepted me and J.J. without batting a blonde eyelash. I may want to change, I may hope for a better life by working with Frank and Leo, but where I come from? I can't change that, and it requires a lot of fucking work to hide it."

"Sounds like a fairytale." I sneered. His point was obvious. It was also what had kept me up half the night. So she'd fucked up. There was no guarantee I wouldn't one day. There was no guarantee I wouldn't *that* day. I might have been a pretty boy muscle head, but I was no fucking catch. For fuck's sake, Marigold's mother had sized me up with one fucking glance.

And yet that day, Marigold had walked away with me.

I rubbed my eyes.

"There's more. She had a side hustle. A *big* side hustle."

"And?" Jackson tucked his chin and opened his arms. "How many times you skim a little off the top or tell Anton you stole a grand but it was really two?"

"Not a lot." But I had. Jackson fucking knew it. I'd confessed to him on more than one occasion. And even as I spoke the feeble defense, it crumbled.

"So," he said in a far too bored and annoyed tone, "you're pissed she didn't tell you, which is downright adorable, Goldie." He shook his head. "Your love spat ends in you shooting her. I should have guessed it."

"I'm not having a love spat, Jax. She had me fucking arrested. She was spying on Jimmy, hacking her fucking brains out and not telling me, and she was going to fly away to fucking fuck knows where."

He laughed. That motherfucker laughed. Hard. "And so you fucking shot her." He wiped a tear from his eye.

"Fuck off."

His chuckle tapered off and his tone switched to somber. "Look... Anton's mom won't let him step foot

Uptown again. Unless you want to take over — which I know you don't. You hate dealing as much as I do — Covington is over for us. Scooter sent Callie's sister to get her and they're moving away. The crew is done."

I stared at him for a beat then forward at the van in front of us. That had been the other thing that had kept me up all night. My future. Jackson had confirmed what I'd feared. Without Anton, there was no more 'us'.

"But you said he's stable, right? Gonna pull through." The hope in my voice was pointless, even if Anton had been nicked by a bullet, his overprotective mother wasn't going to let him keep playing gang leader anymore. We were done.

"He's going to live, just under his mother's roof for eternity."

"Sounds like hell."

Jackson frowned. "Tell me about it. That woman is scary as fuck."

"She was 'Satan' in his phone." I grinned for the first time in twenty-four hours. The honesty I could have with Jackson was like no other. I hadn't realized how much I'd needed and missed it since he'd left.

I sighed. "So what do I do now?"

"Stop shooting your girlfriend." His sarcastic side-eye could fuck off.

"So when Lisa pisses you off, you just forgive her? Just like that?"

He closed an eye. "Lisa doesn't piss me off. I piss her off then she goes all fucking silent, I realize I'm a jack-ass, then I beg for forgiveness. I'm not risking J.J.'s or my overall happiness with my pride."

"And she forgives you?"

"That's how love works, bro. Now get out of this car and stop making me talk about feelings and shit. Ms.

Myers says you can have the apartment until M is a hundred percent. Then you're on your own."

Just like that, I was cut loose. Working for Leo and his brother was out of the question. My sticky fingers would never be able to resist the diamonds and gold they protected. They knew it and so did I. I was what I was and somehow, M loved me for it. And fucking hell, I loved her.

I reached for the handle and stopped before pulling. "I shot my girlfriend."

"Go say sorry like a good boy and send me a postcard from wherever the hell she was planning on stealing you away to."

I nodded and climbed out of the car then watched him drive away. I walked down to the deli and bought a bacon and egg sandwich and a coffee the way M liked it. In the elevator ride up, I gathered my courage. Forgiving Marigold meant severing a loyalty to Anton, but as it turned out, I didn't need that bond anymore. In truth, it had been more disposable than I'd ever imagined.

I opened the door to find Marigold red-eyed and hopping on her good leg to the bathroom. She froze, and I realized she'd been crying.

"I was sure you'd left." The shock in her voice stung—not because I'd hurt her, but because I was a coward to have ever thought of skittering away to a life without her. I closed the door and set the drink and grease-stained paper bag on the coffee table.

"Let me help you." I grabbed her crutches and handed them to her. She disappeared in the bathroom and I sat on the couch.

"Do you bring all the girls you shoot breakfast the next day?" She made her way over to the couch and sat next to me with a tentative smile.

"You're the only person I've ever shot." I handed her the bag and shrugged.

"Lucky me."

She was playing it safe to test the water, but we needed to jump in. No more dipping in toes to check the temperature.

"I am pissed that you spied on Jimmy and didn't tell me. I am pissed that you kept stealing without me. I am pissed that you made a plan without consulting me. And I am really fucking pissed you had me arrested." My volume rose with every word. I hadn't realized how liberating it was to scream at her.

She finished chewing and said, "All completely justified. I am the smartest and stupidest person I know."

"No shit. And FYI, I shot you to keep you alive. Leo told us to imagine every fucking scenario before we went downtown. Guess who I never thought would walk in that door? You. I was sure you were sipping margaritas on a beach, flipping me the bird in a bikini. But noooo.... You get yourself abducted by Jefferson. Do you know what they would have done to you?"

She kept eating and I didn't wait for her response. The release of my worries could not be contained.

"Since the minute you walked into Covington, I have worried about your safety. You have no fucking street smarts. Zero." I made a circle with my hand so she could understand how little I was talking about. "Why the ever-living fuck would you keep the fact that Jimmy was working with Jefferson a secret?"

She picked a piece of crispy bacon out of her sandwich. "I was afraid that if I told you, you would try to kill him on the spot. That that would put Covington before your own safety."

That was probably true, but my rant could not be stopped. I needed to get out my rage. "Having me arrested? That was your plan? So utterly stupid, M."

"Not as stupid as me sending your passport to Juliana. Pretty sure that was what tipped off Jefferson." Too calm... There was too much calm in her voice.

I dropped my head back then turned to stare at her. Maybe my eye daggers would help her realize how careless she'd been. Instead, she popped the last bite of her sandwich into her lovely little mouth.

"It was the only address I had."

I closed my eyes. "You are not allowed out of the house."

"What does that mean?" Her tone had flipped to serious.

The struggle of loving her was my own. Maybe if I'd shown her sooner, admitted my stupid *feelings*, she wouldn't have needed to plan shit behind my back. And while I was officially no longer part of a crew, I did still have her. But the biggest realization over the previous twenty-four hours had been how fucking much I hated the idea of losing her. I'd wanted—needed—her in my life since the moment I'd laid eyes on her. Hell, maybe even before.

I let out a breath. *Deep end, Goldie.* "It means you have to say you're sorry one more time. Then I will forgive you and we move on."

She twisted her lips. "Okay. But only if you say you're sorry for shooting me."

I sat up. "I'm not sorry for shooting you."

Her scrunched frown made her look like I'd asked her to eat a vegetable, but it fell from her face as quickly as she'd concocted it. Her pretty eyes fluttered, and in a small voice, she said, "I'm sorry."

"I forgive you." *Holy shit, I do. Fucking Jackson was right.*

She smiled. "Same."

I opened my mouth to object. I hadn't apologized for anything. Then it hit me what she was really saying.

"Same."

I loved her, too.

Epilogue

Six months later
Marigold

The in and out of the tide had replaced the honks and sirens of the city. I'd convinced Rafa to sell our used laptops instead of throwing them in the ocean and wondered if my mother might be proud.

After some serious mental arm wrestling, my boyfriend had also persuaded me to give a portion of my fortune to Anton as a forgiveness package. I hated letting go of the money but I needed the man I loved in my life more than a bigger house on the beach. We still hacked, but we lived below the radar. No more online tutorials from me, and we only used a malware program once before deleting all traces of it.

It was a simple life, a quiet life. Oddly, it suited us. I'd shaven off my colorful locks and wore my hair in a dark pixie cut that Rafa trimmed whenever it got too long. His own hair was barely a centimeter all over. We were both tanned, relaxed and content. No one from Covington Heights would have even recognized us.

The screen door rattled and I leaned around my computer at the small kitchen table to see who it was. But instead of the local who delivered the fruits and vegetables that Rafa managed to get me to eat—life in seclusion required compromises— a gray puppy nosed its way inside.

My heart fluttered and I grinned from ear to ear. There was no coincidence that it looked identical to Spock. I went over and knelt down, my long flowy skirt puddling around my feet. When I offered the back of my hand, the puppy licked it.

I picked it up, did a quick check to see it was a girl and kissed her soft head. The puppy smell immediately intoxicated me and I fell in love with her in one heartbeat.

"You like?" The amber eyes that kept me grounded and in check stared at me from behind the screen.

"Where did you manage to find a blue pit bull in the middle of nowhere?" I tucked my new dog under my arm and met Rafael on the front porch. The puppy licked my chin before I sat her down in the shade. She sniffed around with her tail wagging and we sat on the steps.

"She wasn't easy to get, but the guy we buy eggs from has a cousin." Rafa winked at me and I nuzzled into his arm.

"We're going to call her T'Pau, right?" I asked but was pretty sure our *Star Trek* logic wouldn't allow for anything else.

"On one condition."

The puppy chased a bug and tried to trap it with her paws without success. Her ears flopped and I couldn't wait for her to fall asleep and snuggle up between us.

"What's that?" My gaze stayed on the dog, and a warm breeze passed over my skin.

"She has to be our flower girl."

I whipped around. "Rafael Santos, I thought we said no mushy shit."

He pulled me into his lap. "Yeah. But you love me, and I love you. No one will ever understand or accept me like you do. And no one will ever tolerate you like I do. So you have no choice, really."

I smiled. He was right. The complete honesty we had between us bonded us, and I wouldn't have it any other way.

"I'd be honored to be your wife. But you know, it won't be legal." I blinked a few times. We'd traveled on illegal visas with fake passports and on separate flights with different connections. One could never be too safe.

"M, nothing we do is legal. Why would we start now?"

An excellent point. "I love you."

"Same."

Want to see more from this author?
Here's a taster for you to enjoy!

Luca's Lessons
Deana Birch & Amelia Foster

Excerpt

A silver foil wrapper tumbled down the stone walkway along the Limmat River, and Luca stepped to the side, his arms crossed. A giggling young couple with too many piercings for his personal preference hurried by, unaware of the menacing, forgotten paper. In his dark suit, crisp white shirt and matching silk navy tie, he waited.

The improperly disposed-of litter flopped one more time, trapped itself at the edge of the stone wall and, away from the light breeze, rested. Satisfied by his small conquest—surely it was his will that had brought its journey to an end—Luca smirked. He walked over, picked it up and secured its fate in a wire bin. A pestering thought of germs poked at his side, but he brushed his hands together at a job well done and continued on his path to the private bank.

While the inconvenience had been a distraction, it had been welcomed. Early and eager were two qualities he admired, but not in himself. He reached for the door of the gray, historic building at exactly seven minutes past his scheduled appointment. *Perfetto.*

After a brief check through security, including a confirmation of his identity, he climbed the two flights of stairs to the private bank of Steinmetz and Favre.

The heavy wooden doors of the suite opened to sleek metal-and-cream marble that created a stark contrast to the building's dated exterior. But the interior did not surprise Luca. He'd already seen the clean, powerful reception in the magazine article about the youngest woman entrepreneur in the history of private banking.

And it was no mistake he'd sought out Claire Favre. Young, driven and on-the-rise was exactly the kind of mind he wanted handling his soon-to-be-acquired secret business. The piece about her and her partner in the weekly publication inserted into the Sunday paper had done more than pique his interest. Fortunately, Luca's reputation and family history had provided enough of a motivation that he'd obtained an appointment without too much delay.

He gave his name to the young, just-above-cheap-suited man behind the massive desk and took a seat in the black leather club chair. Magazines in four different languages were fanned on the iron table next to him. He aligned the one on top to sync with the others and the rhythmed echo of high heels ricocheting off the hallowed walls made him look up.

Madonna mia.

The picture had done her no justice. Claire Favre's sharp hip bones pointed behind the fabric of her tight black skirt and they swayed in a hypnotizing motion as she drew nearer. The formfitting blazer matched the skirt, and a pink silk blouse formed a deep V below. Different from the photo, where her blonde locks had been loose and casual as she'd smiled, her hair was now pulled back into a low, tight bun and her lips remained firmly locked together.

Luca stood, happy his height put him at an advantage, and buttoned his jacket at the waist. The momentary shock of her in-person beauty sank into his gut. It had no business in his throat or chest.

"Herr Bernardi." She extended her small, manicured hand but barely smiled.

"English, please." Luca ignored the slight jump in his heart rate as they touched.

"As you wish." Her light shrug remained formal.

Surely a coincidence.

He narrowed his eyes.

Ms. Favre's smile grew tighter and she spun around. "My office is just down the hall."

Luca followed the banker and stared at the back of her exposed neck. He would not check out her ass, not in a professional setting where the woman deserved respect. He would not.

He did. He most certainly did. And damn it all to hell and back if his palm didn't twitch with desire.

When the penance of being a gentleman and walking behind a woman to whom he owed respect — not ogling — had finished, he squared his shoulders at the threshold of her office and renewed his purpose — business.

Ms. Favre ushered him to a cubed leather chair opposite her desk and he reached for the button of his jacket while she floated to the other side of the impressive oak plank.

A quick glance of her surroundings revealed nothing — no framed photos of her and the late husband the article had referred to or children it had not hinted at. Truly nothing. This woman was clean, uncomplicated and professional — everything Luca desired in a banker…and perhaps other things.

"Please," she said and motioned to the seat behind him. With a quick brush on the back of her skirt — *is hand jealousy a thing?* — she gracefully sat. "Tell me what brings you here, Mr. Bernardi."

Where to begin? The long and challenging path of fully respecting and refining one's own needs? The obvious motivation of a man-made success? Best to start with the not-so-shocking. One never knows.

In the warmest, most casual tone he could muster he said, "I am in negotiations to buy a business. A private club, actually. And I was hoping to keep said investment separate from my others."

Her blue-gray gaze pierced him and she drew her light, thin eyebrows together. "You have a business you'd like to hide, and you want to use my bank to do so?"

"No." Convincing her was going to take some massaging, especially since the bulk of his wealth would not be coming along for the ride. "I have a business I'd like to keep to myself, but I'd like you to handle investing and growing the worth of the account."

Claire crossed her fingers on the desk and circled a thumb slowly into the opposite palm.

"Is it an illegal business?" she asked.

"No, but it is private, much like your bank." Luca flattened his lips and fought a smile. The woman calmed herself with touch. He admired and recognized the gesture. In a cold room full of stark decorations, her softness slammed into him.

He blinked. Business. And the need to hide his new project.

"And what is this soon-to-be-acquired opportunity?" She creased her pink lips.

There was the catch. The hitch. The hard-sell.

He stared into her eyes. "A private club."

She stilled her hands and cocked an eyebrow. "A misogynistic group of racist old men smoking cigars and plotting world domination?"

Interesting choice of words.

"No." This time he allowed the smile to shine. Her spunk and terseness must have helped her along the way.

But what way? According to the magazine article, she was barely thirty years old, and her private schooling, with winters in Gstaad and springs outside of Geneva, had assured her enough wealthy contacts for life. Her path and its perks had been easy — a silver spoon and a glass slipper.

"Are women welcome in your club, Mr. Bernardi?"

Her chest rose then fell slowly.

"Very much so." He dipped his chin.

She'd mentioned it twice now. Maybe empowering women was her motive.

Luca continued, "I welcome all to my club, Ms. Favre. The members and I pride ourselves on acceptance."

This brought a slight tilt to her head and what Luca hoped was a glimmer in her hazy eyes.

"All? That doesn't sound too private."

Her objection was welcomed with fervor, the familiar heat Luca longed for in a challenge. That, and her 'As you wish' comment from reception, braided into a perfect rope of feisty and submissive — not that the powerful woman before him would ever admit to wanting to surrender herself to the will of another.

But, contrary to what were probably her beliefs, she had all the signs. Her manners were impeccable. Her attention to detail…perfection. And that softness… The gentle side of her that Luca would bet his portfolio she didn't think people saw — but he did. He knew exactly the kind of woman who sat in front of him.

"I assure you that the membership fee secures the privacy," he said with a quick nod.

"And what is the membership fee? If I may ask?"

You may. Such lovely manners.

"Fifty thousand euros initially, plus another fifty thousand a year. On top of that, there are certain benefits that members may or may not choose to acquire. But, essentially, ten million would be my earnings in the first year."

She smiled curtly. The minimum balance to open most private banks in Switzerland was usually around a million francs. With a promise of more, maybe the risk of taking on what appeared to be a seedy client would dissolve.

"What exactly transpires at your club, Mr. Bernardi?" Her business etiquette remained flawless.

Well, that would depend entirely on which room one would peep into. But there was no reason to beat around the bush.

"Exploration of one's boundaries, Ms. Favre." Luca met her stare with heavy eyes.

"Sex. You plan to run a high society sex club." Her tone was flat, almost bored.

How could she hold his gaze? He was certain she was more a bottom than a top.

"I'm interested in continuing the initial goal of the founder, who provides a safe environment for all genders to escape without worries or hassles. It has been a tradition for years that every member sign a confidentiality agreement. It covers everything done and witnessed behind the closed, or sometimes open" — he tilted his head — "doors of the club."

Claire Favre appeared to remain unfazed. Is she?

She looked past Luca and he studied the pale, sweet skin exposed from her neck to her chest. From the lack of freckles and spots, it hadn't seen much sun over the summer. He knew its shade well, the perfect cream that would flush pink with proper stimulation.

Luca lifted his gaze. He would not be caught dreaming about bunching up her skirt and examining the most sensitive areas of her body. *Business*, he reminded himself.

"Might I ask why you thought I would be the right banker for your secret investment?"

Luca was still very much denying the answer himself. The woman had intrigued more than his financial affairs when he'd seen her in the photo.

"Empowerment, Ms. Favre. We're in the same business. You want to empower — "

She raised a hand and scoffed. He'd finally rattled her.

"I fail to see how tying up women and spanking them with riding crops is empowering." Her expression must have been attempting to scold him.

Hilarious.

Ah, the misconceptions. The fantasized, glorified, utter wrongness in the perception of the lifestyle… Luca had hoped a woman of Claire's status would have been better read than what popular opinion had painted as the BDSM culture. But alas, stereotypes were indeed festering wounds.

Luca curled his index finger around his mouth and tucked the opposite hand under his elbow.

She sat behind her desk, eyes slightly narrowed and waiting, oh so patiently with her hint of challenge, for his response. The blend was intoxicating.

Before the stirrings of his under-thoughts could bubble to the surface, he said, "I'd like to prove you wrong. The best way to do that I think would be to show you."

Her eyelids fluttered and the rosy flush he'd been trying to deny he craved crept up her neck. Claire swallowed hard.

Sorry, Ms. Favre. Flexing my mental muscle is an unbreakable yet delicious habit.

"Excuse me?" she managed.

Luca cleared his throat. "There are, perhaps, images you have about what goes on in a private setting such as my future club — images that, while they may scratch at the surface of truth, do only that…scratch."

Her skin returned to its cream natural state and Luca grieved the departure of the pink.

He continued, "Why don't you visit? Take a tour. I'm sure you'll find that it's just as much a legitimate business as the pesticides that kill millions of bees every year. Hopefully, more. I assure you that no one gets hurt unless they want to." Another man might have winked, but Luca only shifted his jaw instead.

She stiffened her posture. "You want me to come to a club and watch people get spanked and have sex?"

He grinned. "You seem rather fixated on the spanking part."

She rolled her eyes.

That would never do.

"I'm not fixated on anything. I'm just wondering… If your business is so much on the up and up, why would you want to hide it in my bank, because it doesn't seem like any of your other sources of income are shifting into my vaults with it? And secondly, why then, would I take a risk on you, a stranger to me, for a venture that you would like to brush under the rug?"

Luca crossed his foot over the opposite knee and adjusted in his chair.

"To answer your questions..." He twisted the platinum watch below his starched cuff. "For starters, perhaps I am interested in having some privacy on this matter and wish to not mix it with the accounts that have been in my family for decades. I am well aware of the labels that accompany my lifestyle. I still have a sweet, aging grandmother, and I have no intention of killing her with rumors of my sex life."

Claire's hands folded once again, but this time she rolled her shoulders back and shivered.

"And secondly, I read about you. I know you are a perfect balance of risk-taker and security. Much like anyone, I'd like to see my money grow. As I have no friends who are clients of yours, I feel the risk is mutual."

She sat back and tapped her delicate thumbs together three times.

Stalemate.

Her gaze ran the length of Luca and when it met his, she gave a slight purse of her mouth. "When?"

He wet his lips.

"Friday or Saturday night. You'll need to sign a non-disclosure agreement and you won't be able to visit the higher floors. But you will get a sense that the members are as normal as you and me." He paused at the brief fantasy of her in his private suite. "And you will see the respect and consent of a tight community."

Her eyes raked over him again. A good sign? He couldn't tell.

"I'll think about it."

She rose, as did he, and he followed her to the door.

"I'll see myself out." Luca nodded. There was no way he could follow that ass down the hall after he'd discovered how her skin could blush with just a few words.

"As you wish," she said.

Despite the brakes halting in his mind, Luca exited her office.

How had she known? How could she have possibly known the symphony of music those words were to his ears?

Home of Erotic Romance

Sign up for our newsletter and find out about all our romance book releases, eBook sales and promotions, sneak peeks and FREE romance books!

About the Author

Deana Birch was named after her father's first love, who just so happened not to be her mother. Born and raised in the Midwest, she made stops in Los Angeles and New York before settling in Europe, where she lives with her own blue-eyed Happily Ever After. Her days are spent teaching yoga, playing tennis, ruining her children's French homework, cleaning up dog vomit, writing her next book or reading someone else's.

Deana loves to hear from readers. You can find her contact information, website details and author profile page at https://www.totallybound.com